ONE *Hot* HOLIDAY

New York Times & *USA Today* Bestselling Author

CYNTHIA EDEN

Published by Hocus Pocus Publishing, Inc.

Copy-editing by: J. R. T. Editing

CHAPTER ONE

The gorgeous blonde in the tight jeans, sexy boots, and long, brown coat was about to get her sweet ass run over by a group of elves.

She hauled a suitcase behind her, dragging the massive beast on its clunking wheels as she tried to cross the road. She didn't seem aware of the approaching elves, even though they were ringing their bells like maniacs and singing Christmas carols at the top of their very healthy lungs. The elves careened down the street on their decorated bikes. Bikes covered in merry green and red ribbons, some even sporting twinkling holiday lights. Seriously, it should have been hard to miss them.

The blonde missed them.

She plodded along, her head down, her curly hair sliding over her face, and Sheriff Spencer

Lane knew that he had to act. After all, his job was to serve and protect.

The elves sang out, *"Have a holly, jolly Christmas—"*

Just as Spencer made his move. He lunged into the street, raced toward the woman, and locked an arm around her waist. She screamed when he touched her, and he was pretty sure a delicate fist drove at him, but he grabbed her *and* her luggage, and he rushed out of the line of fire right before the elves came barreling by on their bikes...one after the other after the other...

"Let me go!"

He immediately did. The elves kept flying past them. And singing. Their voices would haunt his dreams. No, not dreams. Nightmares. Definitely his nightmares.

"Listen, buddy, what in the hell are you—" She stopped. Her gaze was locked on his chest. Or rather, on the shiny star that was clipped to his breast pocket. She stared at the star and a tremble shook her body.

"Sorry, ma'am," Spencer told her, keeping his voice mild. "But you were about to get mowed down by the elves, and with them singing so..." *Badly, so very badly. God, would some singing lessons kill them?* "Ah, loudly, I didn't think you'd hear a warning." He inclined his head toward her, but she didn't see the movement. She was still too busy staring at his star. So he lifted a hand and brushed it over the star. A casual flick of his fingers to get her attention. "Just wanted to make sure you didn't get hurt."

As if the movement of his hand had broken some kind of spell, her gaze snapped up to his. She blinked, then her lips—luscious, red lips—parted.

But she didn't speak. She just stared.

Huh. Okay. Well, he decided to do some staring, too. And, damn, but Spencer liked the view he had. *Sexy. Beautiful.* Her face was a delicate oval. Her nose was a cute friggin' button. Her lips—Jesus, no way he'd be forgetting that sensual mouth anytime soon—were full and bow-shaped. Big, hoop earrings hung from her cute little lobes, and a red scarf slid down her body. A body that he'd already noticed was in very fine form.

He cleared his throat. *Get your shit together, man.* "Are you...visiting?" Spencer finally asked. *Be visiting. Be visiting and be single.*

She licked her lower lip.

Fuck me. He cleared his throat and tried to ignore the growing hard-on he had for her. The sheriff was supposed to be professional, dammit. He did not start drooling every time he saw a pretty woman. "Ah, do you need any assistance?"

She backed up. Not just one step—but like five fast steps. The elves were still racing behind her—most of the town was dressed for the practice run of the holiday parade—so he had to grab his mystery lady again before she got hit.

His hands closed around her shoulders, and he pulled her back against him. "Be careful." His voice had lowered. "I don't want you hurt."

Her scent wrapped around him. She smelled like raspberries and cream. Sweet. Delectable.

"You're...a cop."

Oh, yeah, there was a *whole* lot of tension in her voice.

Spencer let her go. He tried a smile for her. It was his...*I'm harmless. Don't be scared of me* smile. It usually worked. "I'm the sheriff here." He nodded. "Sheriff Spencer Lane, at your service." He gave a little incline of his head—

Fear.

He knew it when he saw it, and fear was suddenly stamped on her pretty face. Spencer didn't like that, not one bit. Tension snaked through his body. "What's wrong?"

At his question, the fear vanished. A smooth mask slipped over her face. "Why, nothing. Just a little jarred by the..." She looked over her shoulder and waved vaguely with one hand. "Elves?"

He wasn't going to buy her act. Too late, he'd already seen her fear. Now he was focused, and his instincts were screaming at him. He wasn't just some small-town cop. He'd been a SEAL, he'd been a private government operative, and he'd even been a bodyguard for the rich and famous during a very short stint in his life. He'd seen shit that would traumatize most folks. Hell, wasn't that the reason he'd retired back home to his sleepy little town of Point Hope, Alabama? To get away from the madness for a while?

"Why are there elves on bicycles?" She tucked a curling lock of hair behind one ear. "Is that a normal thing here?"

Normal? Ha. Like that beast existed in this town. "There's not a whole lot of normal in Point Hope. That's a point of pride for us."

Her eyes widened. Night had blossomed in the town, but there was plenty of light. Another Point Hope tradition—holiday lights were everywhere. Like...*everywhere.* Big, sweeping trees lined the streets and storefronts, and every single tree was decked out with small, white lights. The soft glow allowed Spencer to see that her eyes were the darkest, deepest shade of green imaginable.

Unforgettable.

"Normal is boring," he added, his voice gruff. "Life is much more fun when you're coloring outside of the lines."

"I..." She looked away.

Something tells me there isn't a single boring thing about you. "Didn't catch your name," he told her, trying to sound polite.

Her gaze jumped back to him. "I'm...Haley. Haley, ah, Quick."

There was the faintest hesitation there. A hesitation that had his instincts blaring. Had the woman just given him a fake name? *So not boring.* He offered his hand to her. "Welcome to Point Hope, Mrs. Quick."

"Oh, I'm not married."

Excellent to know. He smiled.

Her fingers reached for his. Her touch was tentative, and her skin was insanely soft. His fingers curled around hers. Warmth surged through his whole body, a quick, electric jolt. She gave a little gasp and immediately yanked her hand back.

So she'd felt the spark of attraction, too. Another excellent-to-know point.

"You didn't tell me why elves are on bicycles."

He liked her voice. It was warm and rich, and every now and then, he caught the faint wisp of an accent. New York. *Upper* New York.

"They're prepping for the annual holiday parade. We had a few incidents last year." When you were wearing a full elf costume, peddling a decorated beast of a bike, ringing bells, singing, *and* throwing candy to kids who came out to watch your parade...well, not everyone was coordinated enough to pull off that mega combo. The results had been very unfortunate and not pretty. Elf bike pile-ups weren't ever fun. "So we're taking precautions and doing a run-through this year for safety." They'd ditched the candy treats portion of the event so the elves could keep their hands on the bikes.

"Right. Safety." She looked at the ground. Spied her suitcase and made a grab for it. "Thanks for the save. I was lost in my own head and didn't even hear them coming." She gave a quick wave. "Nice to meet you, Sheriff Lane."

She turned away. He should have let her go. It would have been gentlemanly not to say—

"Liar."

Haley stiffened. "Excuse me?" Her head swung toward him.

He put his hands on his hips. "I called you a liar."

Her mouth opened. Closed. Then... "That's rude."

His own lips twitched. "True. But you didn't think it was nice to meet me."

"I—how do you know that?"

At least she wasn't lying again.

Spencer closed the distance between them. Maybe his nostrils flared so he could pull in her sweet scent. The woman truly smelled incredible. Good enough to eat. "Because as soon as you saw this..." He tapped the star on his chest. "You tensed up. You became afraid."

He waited for another lie. He'd always been good at spotting liars.

And good at spotting trouble.

While Haley Quick was as sexy as the best sin he'd ever seen, he also knew that the woman was trouble. From the top of her blonde head to the bottom of those sexy boots.

When she didn't speak, he prompted, "Want to tell me why you were afraid?"

"I was afraid because I was almost run down by about thirty elves on bicycles."

His head cocked. "That the story you're going with?"

"That's what happened. I was grabbed by a stranger—"

Spencer winced. "I was trying to save you."

"And nearly run down. That kind of situation would stress anyone." Her gaze held his. A challenge if he'd ever seen one.

Did she have any idea how very much he loved a challenge? Spencer nodded. "Fair enough. But, just so you know, you don't need to be afraid of me. I'm one of the good guys."

She laughed. "That's adorable." Haley shook her head. "But there is no such thing as a good guy." She turned on her heel. Dragged the clunking suitcase toward the crosswalk. "Good-bye, Sheriff Lane."

Bam. *That* was how you dismissed a man. He watched her walk away with her chin up, her suitcase rolling, and her shoulders thrown back.

Haley Quick. *I am sure I will be seeing you again.*

He turned away and—

An elf on a wobbly bike barreled right into him.

"Sonofabitch," Spencer growled as they both went down.

***

Haley stopped in front of a massive, wrought-iron gate. She sucked in a deep breath and decided that she was grateful for the fact that, just two weeks before Christmas, the temperature was a warm seventy degrees. She'd walked from the main "downtown" area of Point Hope in order to get to this destination. Walked along a sidewalk lined with an assortment of flowers. Beautiful, blooming flowers...in December. Every street corner had been lit with a glowing lantern and a merry wreath. The night had been quiet, just punctuated by the random sound of insects.

This place...it was so very far from her home. New York wasn't ever quiet. There were always people talking. Cars buzzing by. Sirens screaming in the night. There was always activity and excitement, and that energy had fed her soul.

She'd loved New York. Adored her life there as a gallery manager. She loved the shows. The pulse of the city. The art. The parties. And then...

Then it had all been taken away from her. In a blink, she'd lost everything she'd worked so hard to achieve.

Don't think about it. Not right now. You're almost safe. She just had to get past the gate and get to the room she'd rented. When she'd been planning her escape, she'd found this tiny place online. A rental that she could afford, in a place as far and as different from New York as possible. The perfect place to hide.

He won't ever think to look for me here. He would think that she needed big cities. Fancy hotel rooms. *He won't find me.*

"Ahem."

Haley spun around.

The sheriff was behind her. The ridiculously sexy sheriff who'd *maybe* saved her from an accident in town. There were flickering gas lights on either side of the wrought-iron gate, and those lights let her see him—well, not perfectly—but well enough to recognize the absolute trouble that he was.

"Are you following me?" Haley demanded as she put a hand over her racing heart.

"Nope. In fact, I was here first."

Her gaze shot around. "Where's your car?"

"Where's yours?"

Her hand fell. "I don't have one. I walked here from town."

"And you were...dropped off in town?"

She did not like the suspicion in his tone. *Or the fact that he's been following me.* She totally didn't buy that he'd been there first. "I was dropped off, yes. Just a few clicks on my phone and I had a driver who brought me to my destination." Only she hadn't wanted him to take her *completely* to her final destination. Just in case she was tracked. Just in case someone eventually paid off the driver to get her location.

So she'd been dropped off downtown. After her run-in with the elves and the sheriff, she'd walked to...

Here.

The sheriff crossed his arms over his chest.

A very wide and muscled chest. This wasn't some hick sheriff—and, confession, she'd rather imagined that a town like Point Hope would have a hick sheriff. Someone who spoke with a super heavy drawl and enjoyed drinking sweet tea on a wide porch. Spencer Lane didn't have a heavy drawl. Instead, he kind of sounded like Matthew McConaughey. And he looked *jacked*. Like he worked out every single day and enjoyed the hell out of his workouts. He was probably around six two, with linebacker shoulders, thick black hair, and he had dark eyes that had seemed to see right through her.

Liar.

He'd pegged her correctly. She was a liar. And she'd continue to be one because she was worried about the little matter of her survival.

"There a reason you're loitering out here, ma'am?" he asked.

Loitering? Her spine snapped straight up. "Listen, stalker sheriff…"

Did he laugh? She wasn't laughing.

"I happen to be renting a space at this address. I wasn't loitering. I was preparing to go inside."

"Ah…" A sharp nod. "That's right. The owner does rent out the guest cottage, but to my knowledge, that cottage is scheduled to be occupied by a Luke Shaw."

Oh, no. If he knew who was renting the cottage…

"I mean, that *is* the name I was given when I was contacted through the rental site," he continued smoothly. "I was told that Luke Shaw would be paying in cash for the property when he arrived. I know most folks require a credit card to secure a rental, but, hey, it's the holidays, so I decided to be generous."

This couldn't be happening. Could. Not. "You own the property." The *sheriff* owned the property. Her safe haven—was his?

"Indeed, I do." He smiled as he dropped his arms and strode forward. "I thought it was suspicious that Luke Shaw wanted to pay in cash, but then I figured, I'm the sheriff. If someone is trying to pull something shady, I can handle it."

Her mouth had gone dry. Totally desert dry.

"Are you trying to pull something shady, Haley?" His voice was low. Husky. In another world, she probably would have found it sexy.

Who was she kidding? His voice *was* sexy. Toe-curlingly-so. But he'd asked her a question and she had to—

Think. Give him an excuse. Because she had nowhere to go. If the sheriff turned her away, what was she going to do? "It's not always safe for a woman traveling alone to announce that fact." She swallowed. "I preferred to keep my identity private until I arrived, at which point, obviously, you'd realize I'm a woman."

He nodded. "And Luke Shaw is…"

"A combination of two of my favorite movie character names."

His head cocked.

"Luke Hobbs. Deckard Shaw."

A warm laugh broke from him. "So you like things fast."

He'd obviously caught the movie reference. "And furious," Haley added, as the sound of his laugh seemed to wrap around her.

"A woman after my own heart. I like things fast, too." His laughter faded. "You know, this is the second time you've lied to me."

A fist seemed to squeeze her heart. "I told you, a woman traveling alone—"

"Haley, come on. Let's be real. You want to pay in cash. You booked the cottage under an assumed name. Obviously, you're hiding."

The night was too still. He was too close. And she was about to panic.

His body tensed. "I have to ask, are you involved in anything illegal?"

"You think I'm a criminal?" Haley gave a hard shake of her head. "I'm not. I don't—look, I haven't broken *any* laws."

"But you *are* hiding."

Absolutely. "Listen, Sheriff—"

"Why don't you try calling me Spencer? I mean, after all...we're neighbors."

Not just neighbors. He was her *landlord*. She stared straight at him and said, "Spencer, I'm vacationing. A holiday vacation. Is that such a foreign thing?"

He leaned in close, so close his crisp, masculine scent teased her, and he put an arm out to—

To type in a security code on the gate's keypad. There was a little click and a mechanical whir of sound before the gate opened.

Her breath eased out in a low rush.

Spencer didn't back away. "Most folks take Christmas vacations in the mountains. They want snow. They want ski trips. Guess you were in the mood for something else?"

She swallowed. "Guess I was." He was so big, and those shoulders were actually quite a thing of beauty. If you happened to find super broad shoulders to be—

He stepped back. "Want me to carry the luggage for you?"

Immediately, she clutched her handle even tighter. "I got it."

A nod. "You're not very trusting, are you? I mean, you just found out your landlord is the sheriff. Shouldn't that make you feel more at ease? After all, I'm not some crazed killer or criminal."

Yeah, that would be my ex.

"Haley?"

"I get it. You're the good guy." That was what he'd told her before. But she stood by her previous words. *There is no such thing as a good guy.*

"You don't believe me."

"Let's just say I've heard the line a time or twenty. And just because you have a badge, it doesn't make you good."

"You're right. It doesn't. A badge doesn't make anyone good or bad. We make ourselves that way." Spencer slipped by her. "I'll show you to the guest cottage."

She kept her death grip on her luggage and banged and clunked her way after him.

Spencer glanced back at her. "I was out front because I knew my...new tenant would be arriving tonight. If I'd known you were the tenant, I could've given you a ride from town."

"I liked the walk," she answered quickly. "I didn't need a ride." Her gaze darted around the area. Holy crap. The main house was *huge*. White, with giant, white columns. Two stories. A sweeping porch on the first level and a balcony on the second level. The place was lit up by carefully arranged lights, and she swore it looked like a mansion you'd see in *Southern Living* or something. When she'd booked the rental, she'd been thinking it would be a room. *Room.* But hadn't he called the rental a guest cottage?

The place was insane. And...expensive. It looked super, super expensive.

He turned to fully face her and gave a soft laugh. "Family home."

"What?"

"You were wondering how in the hell a sheriff could afford this place. It's a family home. That's how I got it. When my grandfather died, it came to me. I've been working on restoring it. It's been a slow but steady process. I'm not quite done with the main house yet. Most of the rooms are finished, but a few of the others…" Another laugh. A warm laugh that seemed to slide under her skin. "Let's say they are in transition."

Okay. Transition was a nice word. Her own life was in *transition.*

He started walking again, leading the way as Spencer told her, "The cottage is good to go, though. I actually fixed that up first. I was living there until last week when I decided, hey, why not open it up to guests? I put a few pics online, and you were the first person to contact me."

She'd been lucky. Very, very lucky because this place was perfect…for hiding.

"Eventually, the plan is to turn the main house into a bed and breakfast. But before I can do that, I'll have to get a manager on to help me."

He was looking to hire someone? "Um, when would you want that manager?"

Spencer stopped and swung around to face her. "Why? You interested in the job?"

Maybe.

"Because I thought you were vacationing."

Haley forced a shrug. "You never know what can happen. Maybe I'll like the town and decide to stay."

His gaze drifted slowly over her face. "No, you never know what may happen." He turned away. Pointed to the left. "The cottage has a great view of the bay. You come out tomorrow evening, and you'll see a sunset that you'll never forget."

They strolled down a small path, one nestled under enormous oak trees, and she caught her first view of the cottage. One story. Small, but glowing with lights. Big shutters. Enormous windows. It looked like something out of a storybook. It was unbelievable.

Wonderful.

She had to blink away tears. *It's the exhaustion, that's all. I've been running on fear and fumes. I'm just tired.*

Spencer marched up the steps and unlocked the door. "You have your own kitchen and bathroom. There's a small den and a bedroom. It's stocked with towels and food, but if you need to do any laundry, you can come to the main house." He swung open the door. "After you."

She pulled her suitcase up the steps. Haley eased past him and hurried into the cottage. As soon as she crossed the threshold, some of the tension leaked from her body.

Safe.

That was how she felt in that warm cottage. Black and white photos of the bay and of the small town were carefully arranged on the crisp, white walls. There was a massive, white couch, one that had a comfy-looking blue throw on the arm. A big bookcase. A TV arranged in the middle of the wall. The hardwood floor shone beneath her feet. The kitchen waited to the left. A galley-style kitchen with white cabinets and a gleaming, marble countertop.

"Put the countertop in myself," he explained as he shut the door and followed her inside. "You watch a few home improvement shows, and what can I say? You get the urge to try things yourself."

She spun toward him. "It's amazing!"

His brows climbed.

She'd been way too excited. She should settle down. "I really like it. Thank you."

He pointed to the left. "Bathroom and bedroom are that way. Bedroom has French doors that open to a small patio area. You head straight from the patio and you'll find stairs that take you down to the bay. By the way, I *don't* recommend going for any late-night swims."

"Don't worry about that." She didn't mention that she couldn't swim. Haley cleared her throat. "The place is perfect, but, ah, is there a security system?"

His dark eyes narrowed. "The sheriff is right next door. You can consider me your personal security system."

That was nice and all but..."I'd really rather have an alarm."

His lips curved as his eyes gleamed. "We don't exactly have a lot of crime here in Point Hope."

"You can never be too careful. Sometimes, you think you're perfectly safe, then you find out that you were dead wrong." *You find out that someone you trusted actually wants to hurt you, and you have to run.*

Vanish.

Start your whole life over.

Haley let go of her suitcase. "There are dead bolts on the front door. That's good."

His square jaw hardened. "What are you afraid of?"

My past coming back to swallow me whole. "It pays to be careful."

"True." Spencer nodded. He stepped closer to her, and she tipped back her head to stare up at him. The man was ridiculously attractive. He looked like he should have been on a magazine cover or making blockbuster movies. Muscled and sexy, he was the last man she'd expected to have as a landlord. *Sheriff Sexy.*

He leaned toward her. "If anything scares you, I'm right next door. My cell number is already written down next to the phone in the kitchen. If you need me, I'll be here in a flash."

She didn't know him. She certainly didn't trust him. But at his words, a little more of her tension slipped away. "I have my payment for you. Just give me a second." She turned away and bent as she fumbled with her suitcase.

"How long have you been traveling?"

"Too long." She'd gotten tired of looking over her shoulder. Tired of always being afraid. So she'd packed up. She'd left. No forwarding address. No clues given to her whereabouts. She'd taken all of her cash, and she'd vanished.

Haley found the envelope that she'd prepared, and she slid it from her suitcase. She rose and extended the payment to him. "Here you go. You'll find all the cash inside. Full payment for a month's rental."

He took the envelope. His fingers slid over hers. A surge of heat and awareness flooded through her.

Well, hello, trouble.

Haley yanked her hand back.

He didn't count the money. Just stared at her. "I can help you."

Her stomach knotted. "What makes you think I need help?"

His lips thinned. Then... "I can tell when a person is running."

"I'm not running. I'm at my destination." *But thanks, Sheriff Sexy, for making me nervous.*

"Are you in trouble with the law?"

Oh, jeez. "If I am, would I confess that to a sheriff?"

His lips quirked. "Probably not."

She shook her head. "I haven't done anything wrong. I'm just a woman who wanted a vacation and decided to go someplace new." She wondered if he would call her on the lie.

She was even holding her breath as she waited—

"Good night, Haley."

He turned and headed for the front door. She stood, rooted to the spot, in the middle of the cottage. He reached for the doorknob. Stopped. Looked back at her. "Welcome to Point Hope."

A little dot on the map. A random place that she'd found because the name had intrigued her and because it had been so very far away from her home.

Spencer's deep, dark eyes pinned her in place. "I promise, you'll be safe here."

Such a strange promise to make. Did he realize that she *never* felt safe? Not anymore.

But he opened the door and walked away. She rushed forward and locked the deadbolt. She spun around and stared at the cottage. Everything seemed cheery and warm. And quiet. So incredibly quiet.

Haley slid off her coat. Dropped it on the back of the couch. Then she pushed up the sleeves of her shirt. Time to get busy unpacking—

She stilled. The bruises were still visible on her left wrist. Dark bands that circled her skin. A shiver slid over her.

He won't find me here.

He probably wouldn't even look for her. She was long gone from his life. And soon, he'd be nothing but a bad memory for her.

A nightmare that she'd finally escaped.

She yanked the sleeves back down and reached for her suitcase even as Spencer's words seemed to ring in her ears...

"I promise, you'll be safe here."

She knew better than to believe a man's promise. She also knew better than to trust Spencer Lane. After all, she'd been burned by a handsome face before. Sometimes, a man could look gorgeous on the outside, but inside...

He was a real fucking monster.

***

She was totally lying to him. Did Haley think he couldn't see her lies? This was far from his first ball game, and he knew the whisper of a lie when he heard it, even when the lie fell from lips as sexy as hers.

Spencer went back to the main house, booted up his computer, and he had the main details of her life in about five minutes.

Turned out…Haley Quick *was* her real name. When she'd hesitated over saying her last name, he'd thought she might be giving him an alias. Maybe she'd hesitated because she almost *had* given him a fake name.

But, no, Haley Quick was real.

She'd shut down her social media pages. Tried to erase her digital footprint, but he found her. After all, he had connections that most people didn't. And he used those connections without a hint of remorse. Hacking into a few government resources that showed him…

Haley Quick. Age twenty-four. Graduate of NYU. Single. No children. An up and coming gallery manager who had organized many high profile shows in the past. No criminal record. No outstanding warrants.

No red flags.

Maybe she was a woman who'd just come down south to escape the winter snow. A woman who wanted a quiet vacation.

Spencer thought of the fear he'd seen on her face. In her eyes.

And maybe I'm fucking Santa Claus.

Haley Quick was running scared, and he didn't like it. Not one damn bit. He rubbed his chest as he stared at the computer screen. Distantly, he could hear the waves crash onto the beach below. In his mind, he saw Haley. Beautiful Haley. Lying Haley.

If Spencer had his way, there would never be fear in her eyes.

Never.

CHAPTER TWO

"You're Santa Claus." Haley took a step back and eyed the red hat and red coat. "I think you need a little more fluff, Sheriff Santa."

He smiled at her.

Oh, jeez. She felt the impact of that smile all the way through her body. They were in the town's small bar, one that had holiday music blaring from old speakers. Mistletoe was hung everywhere. Seriously, everywhere. She'd been dodging it all evening. The place was loaded with old, vintage decorations, and the crowd was obviously feeling ever-so-merry.

"What can I get you, Santa?" Haley lifted a brow as she waited for his order.

His smile slipped. "You're working here?"

"Obviously, your detective skills are killing it. Yep, I'm waitressing."

"Since when?

"Um, an hour ago?" Since she'd realized it would be a good idea to start earning more cash for her new life.

Spencer blinked. The man had ridiculously long lashes. Black and so thick. "I thought you were vacationing?"

"Even vacationers need extra spending money." She gave a fake shrug. "I saw the sign in the window, asking for help, and figured, why not?" Haley grabbed a bottle of beer and pushed it down the bar top toward a waiting customer. "I worked a bar back in my college days."

He sat down on the stool in front of her. Glowered.

Well, someone looked like a grumpy Santa. "No Eggnog Surprise for you," she murmured.

A low whistle followed her words. The whistle hadn't come from Spencer.

A brown-haired guy with a wide smile and a reindeer sweater sauntered toward the bar. "I must be dreaming, because I swear I am looking at an angel—"

Spencer put one hand on the fellow's chest and stopped the guy mid-pick-up line. "Get your ass back to your table, Sean. Your wife is only gone for two days. She'll be back before you know it."

Sean instantly deflated and scurried back for his table.

Haley couldn't help but smile. That had been fast.

Spencer watched the guy walk away and then turned back toward Haley. "He's a dick."

"Duly noted." She saw a patron motion for another beer near the end of the bar. Briskly, she popped the top on a bottle and sent it sliding toward him.

A woman cheerfully called out, "A sleigh bell!"

Haley nodded. Yep, the bar's signature drink. Well, one of many, anyway. She got busy mixing the vodka and Sprite. It fizzed nicely as she added cranberry juice and a cherry.

Spencer gave a loud and unhappy sigh. "Guys are going to hit on you all night in this place."

"Right. They have been." She looked up. Pasted a smile on her face. "I can handle them."

He glowered again. Those full lips of his turned down as his jaw tensed. "You don't need to handle them. They need to back the fuck off."

She passed the sleigh bell to her customer. After the lady headed for her friends, Haley put her hands on her hips and turned to the grumpy Santa. "You haven't told me what I can do for you yet."

His lips parted. Before Spencer could reply—

A loud voice began, "Oh, I will tell you what you can do for me, sweet—"

Then...the voice stopped.

Just stopped.

Because Spencer had lunged up from his stool. "Watch the fucking tone with her."

The guy immediately bolted. Haley had a quick impression of red hair, pale skin, and frightened eyes.

Spencer rounded on her. "Drunks. Out of town drunks and local bozos. Why the hell would you want to work in the bar?"

"Because the tips are stellar." Because the owner hadn't cared about references. Because it was a fast job and the money would come in handy.

Spencer's dark eyes hardened. He sat back down and sure didn't look happy about it. For the moment, she ignored him and got busy with the other customers. But she could feel his stare on her. All suspicious like.

When she had a moment to breathe, she glanced back at him. "I'm sure you've dug into my background by now."

No confirmation. No denial.

Haley gave him a slow smile. "Did you find out that I'm a serial killer?"

"No."

"Ah...a wanted felon, at least?"

"No."

Her eyes widened. "Just a woman on holiday?"

"I highly doubt that."

She laughed. The sound slipped from her. It was strange, but that was one of the first real laughs she'd had in ages. "You sound so disappointed. Sorry you couldn't solve the mystery, Scooby Doo."

His dimple winked at her. *Oh, Jesus. He had a dimple.* How had she not noticed it before? A dimple in his right cheek. Kind of a slash, really. Maybe not a full dimple. Way, way cute.

"That's okay," Spencer rumbled in that toe-curling voice of his. "I'm just getting started."

If he dug too far...

What would he find?

Or...who would find him? "Leave it." Her voice had dropped as she leaned toward him. Suddenly, she was very, very serious, and her laughter was gone. "I want to be someone new here. Let me be her."

His brow furrowed. "Haley? What—"

"It's time for Christmas Karaoke!" Maureen O'Claire called out. Maureen owned the bar. She was a lady with bright red hair and a glowing necklace of Christmas lights—she was also the lady currently standing on the bar's small stage in the middle of a spotlight. She gripped a microphone in her hand as she preened for the crowd. Maureen had revealed that she was pushing seventy and currently on her fifth husband. Her laughter was loud and wild, her smile infectious, and her holiday spirit? Oh, on a scale of one to ten, Haley would score it a solid twenty.

"Who wants to be our first volunteer?" Maureen's expectant gaze darted around the crowd.

And Haley did not know why, she had no clue what little devil inside prompted her to shout, "Sheriff Lane!"

Silence.

Immediate. Thick. Consuming.

Maureen blinked.

Uh, oh. Everyone's attention was suddenly on Spencer...and Haley. She squirmed because all of that focus had not been her plan. And as for Spencer? His eyes were on her. His stare was blazing with an emotion that she couldn't quite name. All the moisture in her mouth vanished.

"Excellent idea!" Maureen boomed. "Spence, come get this party started!"

There were hoots. Yells. Whistles. Claps.

Spencer very, very slowly smiled at Haley. "You're coming on stage with me."

"Oh, no, I'm not," she whispered right back.

"Yes, you are." He reached across the bar and his fingers circled around her wrist.

Haley couldn't help it. She hissed out a pain-filled breath.

Instantly, he let her go. "Haley?"

"Sheriff Lane! Get up here!"

More yells and claps followed Maureen's call.

He ignored them all. "What happened?"

He'd seen her bruises. She yanked down her sleeve. "Nothing. Get up on the stage. Everyone is waiting."

"Let them wait." His eyes glittered. "What happened to you?"

She shook her head.

"Whose ass do I need to kick?"

God. Everyone was watching them. Barely moving her lips, she whispered, "Sheriffs aren't supposed to kick asses. You uphold the law, remember?"

He leaned closer to her. "If someone hurt you, I'm kicking his ass."

"Sheriff Lane!" Maureen gave a nervous laugh. "We're ready for you!"

He still didn't move.

Haley rushed from behind the bar. Too many eyes were on them, and she was *not* talking about her bruises now. She grabbed Spencer's hand and tugged him from the bar stool. "Get up on the stage."

He leaned in close to her. "Only if you promise to tell me what the hell is going on." His voice was a low growl. "I'll go, but you do *not* leave this bar. You wait for me. Then you tell me who the fuck hurt you."

She turned her head and looked into his eyes. "It's nothing."

"I know a man's fingerprints when I see them."

She backed up. And realized—crap, the way they were standing, it must have seemed very intimate. People were giving them knowing glances, and she felt her cheeks sting. This was bad. So bad. "Get on the stage," she urged.

"Tell me everything."

No, she'd tell him just a little. "*After* you get the eyes off me." Being the center of attention wasn't something she wanted. She should have thought of that before she'd spontaneously opened her mouth and said he would sing karaoke.

His hard jaw tightened, but Spencer gave a grim nod. "Don't even think of leaving before I come back."

Where the heck did he think she could go? If she ran back to the cottage, she'd be on his property. She glared at him.

He pointed at her. "Don't. Leave."

He turned and made his way to the stage. She could see tension in his body. His broad shoulders were stiff. His movements were tight and jerky. But when he climbed up onto the small stage and

Maureen beamed at him, Spencer managed to work up a smile.

Catcalls filled the air. The folks in the bar burst into loud applause. Obviously, the sheriff was popular with the locals.

Haley backed away. She retook her position behind the bar as she pressed her sweaty palms to the front of her apron. An apron that had been designed to look like a Mrs. Claus outfit. The last thing she wanted to do was explain any of her secrets to the sheriff. *The sheriff.*

"I didn't know you were involved with Spence."

Haley jumped.

The other waitress—Keri—smiled at her. "Sorry. Did I scare you?"

"No, I'm just jumpy." A new personality trait that she hated. Music had begun to play, and her curious gaze darted back to the stage.

"How long have you two been together? I mean...I guess I should've put it together when I heard you were living with him but..." Keri's words trailed away.

Probably because Haley was gaping at her.

"What?" Keri blinked. "Is something wrong?"

"I'm not *living* with him. I'm staying at his cottage. He's my landlord." And he was singing. The man could seriously *sing.* His voice was deep and low, and it wrapped around her and made her want to rush toward him. He was doing Elvis Presley's *Blue Christmas,* and the sheriff was rocking it. Holding tight to the microphone, swaying and smiling for his crowd. As she stared at him, Haley felt her lips curl. He was wearing his big, red coat, his Santa hat was perched sideways on his head, but he just seemed so damn sexy and—

No. Do not go there. Stop. Stop right now.

"Uh, huh…" Keri grabbed two bottles of beer and put them on her tray. "Landlord? Right. You're staring at him like he's the best present you've ever seen—a present you can't wait to unwrap—because he's your *landlord*."

Haley's cheeks didn't just sting. They burned. "That's not…" She cleared her throat. "I didn't realize he had a good voice, that's all. He's talented."

Keri laughed and leaned toward her. "That's what's called a fuck-me voice. A man who gets all deep and sexy like that…well, he can fuck me all night long."

Okay. Haley was not sure how to respond to that one, but she really didn't like that Keri wanted Spencer to fuck her all night long. "He's the sheriff," she heard herself say all primly. *Primly.* She'd never been prim. "I'm sure he's not into—"

"Dirty, hot, awesome sex?" Keri grabbed another bottle of beer. "Trust me, he is. The guy's an ex-Navy SEAL, did you know that?"

"Uh, no." She hadn't known, and what did that have to do with dirty, hot, awesome sex? And why did she suddenly have the visual of herself having dirty, hot, awesome sex with Spencer? Haley waved her hand near her face in an attempt to cool her hot cheeks. The bar was crowded, after all. It was normal to be warm. The warmth had nothing to do with Spencer. Or the idea of dirty, hot, awesome sex with him.

"He's dangerous. Deadly. Strong," Keri said with a faint sigh. "Those SEALs, they are all about adrenaline. Living on the edge."

"He's living in Point Hope." It was hardly the criminal and danger mecca of the world. Wasn't that why she was there? Haley grabbed a cloth and swiped it over the top of the bar. "And you know what? I think I'm over the whole danger stage of my life. I like quiet."

Spencer was wrapping up his song. Smiling. She was half-surprised the cheering women up front weren't throwing their panties at him. The chicks needed to calm down. It was karaoke night. Not a rock concert.

Oh, no. No. Am I jealous?

Keri hummed in appreciation as she glanced over at the stage. "Well, I like Spence, and if that man ever gives me the go-ahead, I'll ride him all night long."

Haley's mouth dropped as Keri swung away and headed to deliver her beers. Haley's eyes narrowed on the other woman. Keri was attractive. Tall, with thick, black hair and an hourglass figure. After she dropped off her beers, Keri made a point of heading toward the stage and Spencer. She put her hand on his chest and leaned close to him.

Haley fisted the cleaning cloth.

I am so jealous. Jealous over her landlord? Ridiculous. She turned away and marched for the storage area. She didn't want to watch Keri put the moves on Spencer. She had plenty of other things to do.

Things that didn't make her want to rip a cleaning cloth into teeny, tiny pieces.

***

"I told you to wait for me." Spencer shut the door to the storage area. He didn't want to be disturbed for this conversation. When he'd come off the stage and Haley hadn't been behind the bar, a surge of panic had pulsed through him.

She turned at his voice. "I was just restocking the whiskey." She held a bottle in her hands. "Not running. You can relax."

No, he couldn't. He yanked the Santa hat off his head and stalked toward her. As he approached, Spencer saw her stiffen. "Don't," he bit out.

Her eyes were huge. "Don't what?"

"Don't be afraid of me." He didn't like her fear. Not one bit. "I'm not going to hurt you."

Her tongue swiped over her lower lip. "I don't know you. I don't trust people I don't know."

"Got issues with authority figures, huh? Another cop screw you over?"

She just stared back at him. Didn't even blink.

Well, that's a hell yes. Spencer cursed. The last thing he wanted to do was make her more defensive. He kept thinking about her bruises, and they pissed him off. *No one should be hurting her.* "Did the guy who put those bruises on you...was he a cop?"

"No."

He waited for more information. She didn't say a word. "Haley," he growled.

"Spencer," she fired right back.

He could only shake his head. "I want to help you."

"I don't need helping. I'm fine. Okay? I get that you're a SEAL, and you're all big and bad and—"

"Who've you been talking to? Who told you I was a SEAL?"

She blinked. Her green eyes were incredible. The kind of eyes that stared straight into a man's soul.

She didn't answer his question.

"Who told you I was a SEAL?"

"Um, Keri?"

He nodded. A puzzle piece slid into place. "Because you were asking about me?"

"No! I wasn't! She was asking! No, I mean, she was telling." Haley shook her head. "She wanted to know if we were involved, and I told her that we weren't. That you were just my landlord. Nothing more."

"Nothing more," he repeated carefully.

Haley gave a quick nod. "Exactly."

Not so exactly. "Don't see how the SEAL part came up."

Her cheeks turned the cutest shade of pink. "I do believe she mentioned that part after."

"After?"

"After I told her we weren't involved."

"Because *you* were asking about me?" He was trying to figure her out. The woman was a constant mystery to him, and he wanted to know her secrets.

"Because I was curious about why she'd made a certain assumption about you."

His head tilted. She sure was holding tight to that bottle of whiskey. A death-grip if he'd ever seen one. "What assumption had she made?"

Her lips clamped together.

Wow. This had to be good. "Haley." He loved her name. "What assumption did Keri make?"

"That you liked hot, dirty sex." Her eyes flared. "Oh, God, did I just say that?"

He nodded. "You did."

Her eyes closed. "The floor can't open and swallow me, can it?"

He glanced down at the very solid-looking floor. "I don't think it will."

"Right." Her shoulders straightened. Her eyes opened. "For the record, Keri is the one who thinks you like hot and dirty sex. I asked why she would assume that, and she said it was because you were a SEAL." She winced. "Something about SEALs and danger and adrenaline and—look, can we stop talking about this? Please?"

"Absolutely." *We will totally revisit this.* "You can tell me who put the bruises on your wrist."

Her breath blew out. "You don't let go, do you?"

"You're in my town." He turned serious. "You're obviously running from something— someone. If you need help, I am here."

She peered down at the bottle in her hands. Haley bit her lower lip. "I just wanted to get away for a little while."

"Did your boyfriend put those marks on you?"

"I don't have a boyfriend." Her head snapped up. "No lover. No anything right now." A hard exhale. "I had a bad relationship. It ended months ago."

"That bruising is fresh. It's not from months ago."

"I-I was mugged before I left home. The guy grabbed my wrist. I jerked away. That's how I got the bruises."

He had the feeling she was giving him a very condensed version of the story. A version that left out a lot of facts. "Tell me the bastard was arrested." But Spencer knew he hadn't been. When he'd done his search on Haley, he hadn't found any indication that she'd filed a police report on anyone.

"He got away in the crowd. After that, I decided maybe it was time for me to get away, too. Time for a change." One shoulder lifted. "So here I am."

Yes, here you are.

She swallowed. "Now, if the interrogation is over, I need to get back to work. You're blocking my path."

He moved to the side.

Haley started to walk past—

"You don't need to be afraid of anyone or anything. No one should ever put bruises on you." *And if an asshole tries, I will kick his ass.* "When you decide you're ready to tell the rest of the story..." Because he knew there was a whole lot more she was leaving out. "You find me."

Haley cleared her throat. "There is no rest. The story is over."

He hoped so. *No one should hurt you.*

She reached for the doorknob.

"Keri is right."

Haley froze.

He strode closer to her. Didn't touch her. Wouldn't, not until she asked for his touch. But just so they were clear... "I do like hot and dirty sex."

"Uh..." Haley glanced back. She licked her lower lip one more time.

He loved her mouth. "But I also like slow and tender sex." His voice deepened. "It all depends on who you're with, don't you think?"

"I think..." Her gaze was on *his* mouth. Her voice had turned husky. "I think I have to get to work. *Now.*" She yanked open the door.

Rushed out.

Spencer rolled back his shoulders. He still held the Santa hat. He shoved it into his pocket as he followed Haley to the main bar area. A couple was up on the stage, singing about *The Twelve Days of Christmas*. Everyone was laughing and drinking. And a few guys were already heading toward the bar, probably because they'd caught sight of Haley. They weren't closing in because they were thirsty. Well, maybe the jerks were. But not thirsty for booze.

Haley looked sexy as hell in her boots, tight jeans, and red sweater. The apron she wore was cute as could be. Her blonde curls danced over her shoulders as she got to work making drinks. The men were smiling at her. Their eyes were drifting all over her, and his own gaze narrowed on them. He was discovering that where his new tenant was concerned, Spencer felt quite protective.

So protective that he was going to do a little more digging. He had some favors that could be called in—favors that would be performed by people who knew how to get intel without arousing suspicion from anyone. Haley was running hard and hiding. If danger was stalking her, he wanted to be prepared.

As he watched, Spencer saw one of the eager jerks at the bar nudge his friend. Haley had just darted from behind the counter and she was making a drop-off at a nearby table. The fellow at the bar rose quickly, and Spencer saw that his eyes were on the mistletoe hanging from the ceiling.

Mistletoe that Haley was just about to walk under.

I don't think so.

Before the guy could reach his destination, Spencer was there. The fellow was so intent on Haley that he didn't even notice Spencer. The man bumped right into him. Spencer recognized Zane, the owner of the local car lot.

Spencer lifted a brow. "That eager for a kiss, huh?"

"What?" Zane tried to maneuver around Spencer. "No, I was trying to get, um, I was, uh—"

"I know what you were trying to get." *Asshole.* Zane was a total player. "Now I want *you* to get back to your seat. You're not kissing Haley, mistletoe or no freaking mistletoe, got me? She's off-limits."

Zane hurriedly backed away. "Sorry! My bad. Didn't know she was with you."

Well, now you fucking do. But he bit those words back because...she wasn't. She wasn't with him. He was simply looking out for her. She'd obviously had a bad time, and the last thing she needed was some douche sniffing around after her. Spencer turned around and found himself staring straight into Haley's green eyes.

Had she heard the dumbass's comment? Probably. He needed to set the record straight because the last thing he wanted was for Haley to believe that he was lying about her. "Listen, she's not with—"

"Spence!" Keri called out. "You're under the mistletoe! Don't you *dare* move!" She rushed toward him, moving up fast behind Haley.

Haley narrowed her eyes. "You're under the mistletoe."

"I—" Shit. *I was trying to make sure the idiot skulking away didn't kiss you.*

"That means you have to get kissed," she told him softly. "That okay with you?"

"Uh, yeah. Yeah, it's—"

She shoved the drink tray onto the nearest table. Grabbed the front of his red coat and yanked him toward her. She shot onto her toes, and Haley's lips pressed to his.

Everything stopped around them. He didn't even hear the music. The crowd was gone. The voices and laughter faded. There was just her. Haley's lips were soft and parted, and yes, he took a taste. His tongue swept into her mouth, and desire freaking exploded within him.

His arms curled around her body. He hauled her even closer to him. And that light, tentative little kiss became something a whole lot hotter. He feasted on her mouth, and she kissed him back with the same wild ferocity. Her hands were on his shoulders now, hauling him closer, and he wanted to lift her up, get her to wrap those long legs around him and—

Haley jerked back. Her breath heaved in and out. In and out.

His heart almost burst right out of his chest.

She stared at him with shock on her face. In her eyes.

Then the clapping started.

So did the whistles.

Her face flushed that delicious pink that he was starting to adore, and Haley grabbed the tray she'd put down before she hurried away. Spencer scanned the smiling faces. All right, so he didn't have to worry about the assholes hitting on Haley anymore. Because after the kiss, everyone was assuming that he and Haley were hot and heavy. But he didn't want her embarrassed. Not even for a moment. "Mind your own damn business, everyone," he snapped. "Nothing to see."

Keri sidled toward him. "I disagree. That was... plenty to see."

It had been plenty to feel, too.

"Knew you were involved," she added with an incline of her head. "Could tell by the way you watched her when you came into the bar. Landlord, my ass."

"I am her landlord." Spencer glanced over his shoulder. Haley was busy behind the bar, and she didn't look up to meet his gaze.

Keri gave a throaty laugh. "Yes, I'm guessing you're that and a whole lot more."

Haley looked up at Keri's laugh. Her gaze locked on his.

He'd seen fear in her eyes before. Seen it and hated it. But this time, when she looked at him, Spencer saw desire.

And he knew the same need was blazing in his own gaze.

The kiss had taught him one very, very important lesson. Okay, two lessons.

Lesson one...Haley Quick could sure as hell kiss.

Lesson two...He wanted her in his bed. The sooner, the better.

CHAPTER THREE

Haley hurried out of the bar, her boots rushing over the sidewalk, as snow fell down onto her.

Wait. Hold up. Haley tilted back her head and squinted. Sure, the temperature had dropped a little bit, but it still had to be in the sixties. No way was snow actually falling on her head. It couldn't be. She lifted a hand and caught a bit of the snow on her fingertip.

"Bubbles," Spencer's deep, rumbling voice told her. "Since Mother Nature doesn't give us the real thing all too often, we have to improvise down here." He pointed to the balcony on the left.

A bubble machine was up there, blasting down its fake snow.

As she watched, more of the small bubbles fell down, raining on the street.

"Practice for the big parade," he added as he ambled closer to her. "People in town like for things to be perfect."

She dropped her hand and tried *not* to look at his mouth. She failed, though. Miserably. Her gaze went right to his mouth, and she immediately thought of the kiss they'd shared.

Of the way heat had blasted through her whole body.

Of the way that she'd plastered herself to him.

Of the way his mouth had felt against her.

Of the way...she wanted more.

"Everything okay?" Spencer asked in the low, sexy voice that she knew would haunt her dreams that night.

"Fine." She sidled away from him. A little distance between the two of them had to be a good thing. The more distance, the less temptation. She hurried down the sidewalk.

He followed.

As soon as she turned the corner of the building, he turned, too. Haley spun to face him. "Stop it!"

Spencer frowned. "Stop what?"

"Following me. I don't like it, and I don't need—"

He pointed behind her. "My motorcycle."

His what now?

"My motorcycle," Spencer repeated as a smile played at his lips.

Dammit. She was looking at his mouth again. It was wrong for a man to have such gorgeous lips.

"My motorcycle is parked right there. I wasn't following you. I was going for my bike."

She looked back. Saw a big, black beast of a bike. Her head swung toward him. "Where's the patrol car?"

"I'm off duty. I don't drive it when I'm off duty." He motioned toward his Santa coat. "Didn't notice I wasn't in uniform?"

"This town is...eccentric." She'd definitely noticed that during the day. "You're the seventh man I've seen in a Santa coat in the last hour. I figured it *was* part of the uniform."

He laughed. Why did he have such a warm and sexy laugh? She rocked back on her heels. Around them, thousands of small, clear lights filled the trees that lined the streets. The town was old-fashioned, seriously, like something from a greeting card. The streets were as close to cobble-stone as she thought it was possible to get. The storefronts all shone merrily with their decorations. And the trees—the trees on either side of the streets had obviously been carefully decked out. She wondered how many hours and hours it had taken the city employees to cover all of those trees in the soft holiday lighting.

"It's not part of the uniform. I was at the elementary school earlier, doing a reading for the kids. That's why I'm still wearing the coat."

Oh, God. He'd read for small children. Of course, he had. Could the man be any more perfect?

And he rides a big, black motorcycle.

Her eyes narrowed as she frowned at him. "Stop it."

Spencer looked around. "Stop what?"

Stop being sexy. "You know what you're doing."

His dark gaze focused on her once more. "I have literally no clue."

She pointed at him. "You're too good to be true." He kissed too good to be true, as well. And if there was one thing she'd very clearly learned from the life-altering disaster in New York...if a guy seemed too good to be true, he was.

"You keep saying I'm good." Spencer shook his head. "No one is one hundred percent good." He closed the remaining distance between them. Stood right in front of her. All big, strong and handsome—damn him. "Trust me, I've done plenty of bad things in my life." The shadows of pain and anger whispered beneath Spencer's words. "There are some things that you can never forget."

Her heart ached. "I'm sorry."

"For what?"

She rolled one shoulder. "For bringing up bad memories." No, it was more than that. "I'm sorry that you hurt." Her hand lifted, and she squeezed his arm.

He stiffened. His gaze moved to her hand. Then very slowly, his stare tracked back to her.

Okay, I should stop touching him. Only, her fingers didn't seem to get that message. They went right on touching him. Maybe stroking him a little bit. *Woman, stop!*

On the third try, she yanked her hand away. "It's late. I should get home."

He nodded. "How about a ride?"

"On your motorcycle?"

His dimple peeked at her. "Unless you want me to go and find the patrol car..."

"No!" Hard no. She didn't want to be riding around town in the patrol car.

"Then the motorcycle it is." He headed around her and offered her a helmet that he picked up from the bike. "Safety first."

She plunked the helmet on her head as he climbed onto the motorcycle. She bit her lip and nervously studied him. "You know what you're doing? Like, this isn't secretly your first time to drive a motorcycle, is it?"

He revved the engine and tossed her a smile. "It's your first time to ride, isn't it?"

"Yes. Back home, my preferred mode of transport was the subway."

He leaned toward her. Conspiratorially, Spencer told her, "We don't have those here."

She pressed her lips together to smother her smile. After a moment, she managed, "I did notice that."

He took her hand. "Climb on behind me."

A bit hesitant, she did.

He put her arm around his waist. "Hold on tight."

She settled her arms—both of them—at a better position around his waist.

"How about we go the long way home?" Spencer asked. "Ready for the scenic route?"

"Um..."

Too late. They were off. The motorcycle seemed to shoot forward, and she tightened her light hold to a full-on death grip around him. The lights whizzed past them and soon they were away from the downtown area and winding along the twisting road that faced the bay. Heavy, thick oak trees were around them, and their thick limbs stretched overhead. The enormous limbs were weighed down by moss. Moonlight glinted off Mobile Bay as she looked into the distance. They were up on the bluff, and the water gleamed below them. The longer they drove, the more her fear vanished. She found herself relaxing even as she kept holding tightly to him. And with every curve...

She was smiling.

Even laughing.

She felt free on the motorcycle. Free with him as they took the old roads and the wind rushed over her. He wasn't speeding. Wasn't being some kind of show-off. He was just driving her and letting her feel...

Good.

All too soon, he was turning toward his house—and her cottage. He opened the gate and then drove through. When he braked in front of her cottage, Haley realized that she was still holding his waist. Her arms were curled around him, no, correction, her whole body *curved* around him. So she'd gotten a wee bit clingy on the ride. Whoops. Haley finally pushed back and hurried off the bike. She could feel his gaze on her as she fumbled with the helmet.

"Not so bad, was it?"

"Not bad at all." She handed him the helmet. "Thanks for the ride home."

"Anytime." He reached for the helmet. His fingers brushed hers.

Her breath caught. Why did his touch send that spark of awareness through her? She yanked her hand away from his and immediately put *both* of her hands behind her back. "Good night." She backed away.

He remained on the motorcycle. "Are we going to talk about it?"

"It?"

"Uh, hmm." Now he put down the kickstand. Slowly rose. Headed toward her.

The lights from her cottage blazed behind her. She'd realized that morning that he had the exterior lights set on a timer. It was nice to come home to the lights and not total darkness.

"It." He kept his arms at his sides. "The kiss."

Her hand rose and tucked a lock of hair behind her ear. "You were under the mistletoe."

"And I do appreciate you joining me there."

His voice had gone all sensual on her. In that moment, she could still taste him.

"I was about to leave the bar—after our little talk in the storage room..."

Like she needed any reminder of that talk. *Dirty, hot sex.*

"Then I saw one particularly bold dumbass decide he'd cut you off by standing under the mistletoe. Guess he thought he'd luck up and get a kiss."

She didn't remember any other guy. She only remembered him. "He didn't luck up."

Spencer took another step toward her. "No."

This was intense. The air felt thicker, and her skin was warm.

"Why did you kiss me, Haley?"

"Because you were under the mistletoe. We just established that." She turned away. Reached for the door.

"You could have ignored me. I wasn't going to push you. I might want you like hell, but I wasn't going to—"

Haley spun back around. "Say that again?"

His hands clenched at his sides. "I wasn't going to push you. That's not who I am. I'm not—"

"No. You said that you want me."

"Baby, after the kiss, I think it was obvious to everyone there that I was fucking wild for you."

He'd just called her baby. She wasn't his baby. They weren't involved. They were... "You're my landlord."

"Haley..."

"I don't...I need this place, okay?" The cottage. The town. The anonymity. But she was also starting to wonder...

Could I need him, too?

"The place is yours." His voice had roughened even more. "And you don't have to do a damn thing with me, if that's what you're thinking. You staying here is no way dependent on you kissing me or fucking me."

Wow. Okay. He'd been direct. "Good to know."

Spencer leaned toward her. Didn't touch her. Instead, he put his hand on the door behind her head. "I want you."

Breathing was a little tricky.

"When *you* kissed me, I thought you wanted me, too."

She had. She did.

"I want to know why you kissed me. And don't lie and say it's just because I was under the mistletoe. The thing about me is…I don't like lies. Fucking hate them, in fact."

Then you'll hate me. Because she'd already told him more than her share of lies. And she'd tell him more. But not right then. In that moment, she'd give him the truth. "I kissed you because I wanted to kiss you. I…didn't want Keri to kiss you." Keri and her talk about dirty, hot sex with Spencer.

Keri could back the hell off.

"Why would you care if she kissed me?"

"I have no idea."

She expected him to laugh at her. She didn't even understand what was happening herself. Instead of laughing, Spencer nodded. "Fair enough." A pause. "Want to know why I was under the mistletoe?"

"You told me already. You said some guy—"

"I didn't want you kissing *some* guy. I wanted you kissing me. I wanted to know what you tasted like ever since the first moment I saw you. You were standing in the middle of the street, looking like the cutest thing I'd ever seen…"

"I was about to get run down by elves," she whispered.

He laughed. "When I got you out of their way and we were on the side of the street, I realized how wrong I was about you."

What?

"You weren't just cute. You are absolutely beautiful."

Her lips parted.

"I wanted to taste you, and that's why I was under the mistletoe tonight. But I made a mistake."

Oh. Right. She straightened her spine. "Because you're my landlord and—"

"Screw being your landlord. I told you, that doesn't matter. It has nothing to do with what happens between us."

What happens...she could imagine plenty happening. "I have this annoying habit," she whispered. "I pick the wrong men."

He stared into her eyes. "You think I'm wrong?"

"You are wrong for me." She knew it with certainty. He was the *sheriff*. That spelled all kinds of trouble. No matter how amazing his kiss made her feel, no matter what sort of reaction her body had to him, he was wrong.

She couldn't afford to let him get close.

"I see." Spencer nodded. He stepped back. "Strange. Because when we kissed back at the bar, I've never thought a woman felt more right to me."

Her breath caught. That was...sweet. Romantic.

He offered her a slow smile. "You have a good night, Haley. And don't forget, if you need me, I'm right next door." He turned away.

Headed down the little path.

She stood in front of her door. She should go inside. Call it a night. But... "That's it?" Her hand flew up and slapped over her mouth. She had *not* just said that.

He whirled around. His expression told her that...yes, she'd said it.

Her hand dropped. "I mean...good night."

He kept staring at her. "That's it...until you want more."

Her heart lurched in her chest.

"Because I'm not going to push you, Haley. I think you've been pushed enough in your life. You want me? Well, you know where I am." He pointed. "Right next door."

Warmth spread through her. "I think I was wrong about you."

His hands were loose at his sides. "Oh?"

"You *are* a good guy. I guess they do exist." She just hadn't come across one before. "It's nice to meet you."

His hands went to his hips.

"Good night, Spencer."

She unlocked her door, headed inside, and for the first time in ages, Haley truly felt safe.

***

Well, shit.

Spencer stood on the lit walkway, his hands on his hips, and his eyes on the closed cottage door.

When they'd first met and he'd been trying to reassure Haley, he'd told her that she didn't need to be afraid of him because he was one of the good guys.

She hadn't believed him then.

And he hadn't believed his words would come back to bite him in the ass so quickly. They had.

Because Haley Quick—the sexiest woman he'd met in ages—had just put him in the *nice* guy zone.

Sure, sure, she'd called him a *good* guy, but he knew what she meant.

Sonofabitch. She might as well have slapped him in the friend zone. He whirled away. His body was tight and hard and he needed a very icy shower...

She thought he was *nice*. Fucking hell.

CHAPTER FOUR

This was so embarrassing. Especially after the night they'd had so far but...

Haley lifted her hand and rapped against Spencer's front door. She quickly shoved her hands behind her back and tried to school her expression. The man had just left her twenty minutes ago. Right after she'd told him that basically—nope, *nothing is going to happen between us*. Because it couldn't happen. Could not. If he got too close and learned her secrets, she'd be royally screwed—

The door swung open.

Screwed. She was well and truly screwed.

Her lips parted. Her heart raced. And her eyes dropped.

Spencer was wet and wearing a towel. Only a towel. A white towel that he'd hurriedly knotted around his lean hips and the towel appeared to be in major jeopardy of falling. One little tug, and Haley was sure it would drop.

She forced her gaze to jerk away from the top of the towel. From the fabric that simply needed a tiny tug to come loose. Her stare lifted, and she saw abs. Abs for freaking days. The man must work out like a beast because he was ripped. Ripped enough to make a woman drool. Or moan. Maybe both.

Definitely both.

Water droplets snaked down his abs. Such lickable abs.

Look up. She made her eyes rise even more. Shoulders. There. She'd look at his—wow, his shoulders were even broader than she'd thought before. Wide and strong.

"Haley?" He waved his hand in front of her face.

Crap. *Focus.*

Spencer took the hand he'd just waved and shoved it through his wet hair. "What's the emergency?"

"Shower." Wonderful. She'd managed to croak one whole word because, obviously, she was amazing.

"Yeah, yeah, sorry." He glanced down at his body.

So did she.

No wonder Keri had been all on Team Spencer. Most of the women in the town were no doubt Team Spencer.

"I was in the shower," he continued gruffly. "I'd just gotten out when I heard you knock. I thought it might be an emergency, so I rushed to the door." His gaze flew back to her. "Is it an emergency?" His stare was flat and hard. "Is something wrong? Did something scare you?"

"No."

He waited.

She should say something else. Jeez. What was wrong with her? She'd seen naked bodies before. He wasn't even completely naked. He was just wet. In a towel. And ripped. So, so ripped. "You should...put some clothes on." She shook her head. "No, I'll just come back. It can wait." She spun on her heel—

He snagged her hand. "Just come inside."

Haley glanced back at him.

"I'll put on clothes. You come inside. You tell me what's wrong."

"It's really not a big deal." He had faint calluses on his fingertips. They were slightly rough against her skin, and his touch was so warm.

Spencer let her go. "Big enough of a deal for you to come knocking." His hand dropped to his towel.

She did *not* look down again.

"Come on in," he told her as he turned and headed into the house.

His back was just as strong and muscled as his front. He had a tattoo on his left shoulder. It looked like... "Is that a trident?"

His shoulders stiffened. "Yep."

Beneath the trident, she saw a faint, red scar. Actually, there was another scar on his back, too. Lower down. She found herself hurrying forward, and her hand rose to touch his back. Her fingers skimmed over his skin—

Spencer whirled around and grabbed her wrist. His grip was tight, but not at all painful. "Probably shouldn't do that," he gritted out.

"I—"

"Dammit. Your wrist." He immediately eased his hold, and his fingers moved to brush carefully over the fading bruises there. "I didn't mean to hurt you."

"You didn't."

His fingers caressed her skin once more. Did he feel the way her pulse was suddenly racing?

Probably.

She cleared her throat. "I shouldn't have touched you. I'm sorry."

He'd been staring at her wrist, but at her words, Spencer's gaze rose and his stare pinned her. "You saw the scars."

"Yes."

His lips quirked. "Don't sound so sad. They don't hurt anymore."

But they'd obviously hurt very badly once. "You were shot."

He let her go. "Just so you know, the towel fell when I grabbed you."

Her gaze whipped down, then immediately back up. She whirled around and gave him her back.

His soft laughter followed her. Then... "I'm covered, but so that doesn't happen again, I'm going to put on clothes."

She'd left the front door open when she followed him inside. Haley hurried toward it. Shut it. Flipped the lock.

The sound of his footsteps padded away.

She decided it was time to breathe again. She sucked in a deep, heavy breath. Let it out. Took about five more deep breaths before she turned around and stared at—

Wow. A huge Christmas tree. Had to be at least sixteen feet tall. The thing was *massive.* Spencer's den had one of those crazy, tall ceilings—at least two stories. There was a snaking, wooden staircase that led upstairs, and the massive tree was right next to it. The tree hadn't been decorated yet. The tree just waited. The scent of fresh pine filled the air.

She took a few steps toward the tree. Her hand reached out to touch one of the branches.

"Sorry. I'm decent now. You don't have to worry about any other flasher scenes."

Her hand yanked back. Haley turned toward Spencer. He stood a few feet away, clad in a pair of jeans that hugged his hips and powerful thighs. His feet were bare, and *come on*, the man even had good-looking toes. Tanned feet. Big feet. The big feet fit, though, going along with his big—

"Like the tree?" Spencer asked with a wave of his hand.

He hadn't put on a shirt and his muscles flexed with the movement.

"Haley?"

She nodded. "I...it's almost as big as the one at Rockefeller."

Spencer laughed. "Doubtful. It was supposed to go at the high school, but there was a mix-up and two trees were delivered. Didn't want the farm to lose out on the money, so I bought it and had it delivered here." He headed toward the tree. "You probably think it's crazy for me to have that tree here, huh? A giant tree and just me in the house?"

She looked back at the tree. "I think it's quite beautiful." Her voice had softened. She hadn't thought she needed Christmas this year. This year was supposed to be about surviving. Escape. But... "I don't think it's crazy at all."

"Great. Then you can help me decorate it tomorrow."

She could help him do what now?

Haley slanted him a suspicious glance, but he gave her his wide, reassuring smile. God, the man was too gorgeous. Gorgeous men were trouble. Trouble. Even *nice* gorgeous men.

"Want to tell me your emergency?" He took another step toward her. "What sent you running to my door?"

"I..." She cleared her throat. "It's not a big deal. It could wait until tomorrow. The, uh, hot water stopped working in the shower." She hadn't been able to get it to heat up. "I just was coming by..." Her voice trailed away.

He winked at her. "Because I'm the landlord and you want me to fix that shit right away?"

"Um, yes, please."

He laughed. "You don't ever have to say 'please' to me. I'll take a look right now." Spencer started to turn away.

She bounded toward him. Touched his arm. "No, it can totally wait—"

She'd *meant* to touch his arm. Her fingers had missed her goal. She'd wound up touching his chest and now her hand was doing a crazy lingering thing that could not be good. No way. No day. "It can wait," Haley repeated softly.

"No. You want warm water, so I'm getting it for you."

Was his voice deeper? Darker? Seemed that way. She pulled back her hand. Fisted her fingers. A few moments later, they were leaving his place and heading to her cottage. He'd snagged a t-shirt and running shoes on his way out. She led the way, but as she got closer to her cottage, her steps slowed.

She stared at the little cottage. Then her slow steps stopped.

"Haley? What's up?"

Her gaze remained on the cottage. "I shut and locked the front door when I left." Lights blazed from inside, and the door was wide open.

He didn't ask her if she was sure. Didn't ask if she hadn't left in a hurry and made a mistake. He grabbed her hand and immediately pulled her back.

"Wait, I—"

"No waiting." He lifted her over his shoulder. Seriously, Spencer hoisted her up and put her over his shoulder and her mouth dropped open because that was the last move she'd expected. Haley got a fast and up-close view of Spencer's ass as he rushed back to his place. In a flash, he unlocked the door and deposited her inside.

His eyes were cold. His stare flat and hard. "You stay here." He disappeared into the study on his right for a moment, then came back out with a gun in his hand. "Lock the door behind me and *stay here*."

"Spencer—"

"If someone is in your place, I don't want you anywhere near the cottage. Stay here."

"But—but shouldn't you call for backup or something?"

He frowned at her. "Sweetheart, I am backup."

That was a crazy badass thing to say and she opened her mouth to tell him that, but it was too late. He'd already left. Her fingers were shaking when she locked the door.

***

Spencer's steps were dead silent as he entered the cottage. He'd been trained to move stealthily, and he knew how to secure an area. He took his time on the search, not wanting to miss anything and not planning to give any intruders the chance to jump him. As he made his way through the cottage, nothing seemed out of the ordinary. No furniture overturned. No signs of a search or robbery.

The cottage was quiet. Still. One by one, he checked the rooms until he was in Haley's bedroom. His gaze darted to the left and right. He checked the closet. Under the bed. Her bathroom. Everything was clear. And, again, everything seemed undisturbed.

He took a step back. Haley had unpacked her suitcase. Her clothes hung neatly in the closet. Two pairs of shoes were carefully positioned on the closet floor. She had a few make-up items on the bathroom sink.

Everything seemed normal. But...

His head turned. The door that led to the little patio area was closed. Spencer strode toward it, and his hand lifted toward the lock.

Broken.

The lock had been broken on the door, so that anyone who might want to come into Haley's bedroom—anyone who wanted to sneak inside from the patio—could just waltz right in. *While she was sleeping?*

Fuck, no.

He opened the door and stepped outside. The moon gave him enough light to see down below—the winding steps on the wooden staircase that led down to the small beach and the bay. The long dock that snaked out over the water. No one was there. At least, no one that he saw.

But every instinct he had screamed at him that someone *had* been in the cottage that night. And the broken lock in her bedroom...

That was bothering him the most.

Okay, so maybe the intruder had *gotten* in that way. Gotten in through the easiest lock, realized there wasn't anything too valuable inside and run out the front door but...

The TV wasn't taken. None of the appliances were stolen. And they were all high end.

But the intruder *could* have come through the back, tried to find a quick grab and then run out the front door when he hadn't seen anything small enough for a fast snatch and grab.

Or...

Or the intruder didn't want to take anything. He'd been looking for someone. He'd been looking for Haley, and when she hadn't been here, he'd left?

Spencer didn't like the options. None of them. And fucking especially not the last option. He did another sweep. Then he headed down to the beach. He'd grabbed his phone when he left his house, and he used it to call the sheriff's station now. He wanted the cottage checked for prints. Sure, a *smart* thief would use gloves, but in his experience, thieves weren't always smart.

Sometimes, they were dumbasses.

After he finished his call, he continued the search. The waves crashed into the shore as he looked along the beach. He used the light from his phone to sweep over the sand. If anyone had come that way, he'd see footprints.

There were none. No tracks at all in the sand.

He glanced back up at the stairs. At the lights that shone from his house and from the cottage. He'd left Haley up there. What if the intruder hadn't left? What if he'd just been biding his time and waiting for her to be alone again?

Spencer bounded back up the stairs. He was damn thorough as he made his way back to the main house. The property's front gate was closed. Secured. There was a camera out there, so he'd be checking it ASAP. Spencer circled back to the house, and he kept the gun in his hand. He reached for the doorknob—

The door yanked open.

Haley stood there. Her eyes were wide, and her face was too pale.

"I didn't see anyone." He entered. Put the gun down on a nearby table. Secured the door. "I've got a crew coming by to check for prints because someone sure as hell *was* in the cottage. The door in the bedroom had its lock broken. I'm just fucking glad you weren't there when—"

She hugged him. Threw her body against his and hugged him tight. "I'm glad you were with me," she muttered. "Very, very glad."

His hands closed around her shoulders. And he wondered what would have happened if Haley *had* been in the bedroom when the intruder slipped inside...

Just what might the sonofabitch have done to her?

Spencer's hold tightened on her.

CHAPTER FIVE

"You're staying here."

Haley turned toward him. She had her hands tucked in the back pockets of her jeans, and her loose sweater slid off one shoulder. "Is your team done with the cottage?"

"Yes." Though they'd turned up nothing. "Even got new locks on the doors."

She gave a decisive nod as her hair slid over her shoulders. "Great. Then I can get out of your way and—"

He moved into her path. "You're staying here."

She cut him a narrowed glance. "That sounds like an order." And her voice sounded like she was less than pleased to be receiving an order from him.

Too bad. "That's because it is. Someone broke into the cottage. *My* property. You could have been hurt while you were there, and that would have been on me." Rage burned beneath his skin. He hated the thought of her in danger. "You asked about a security system when you first arrived, and I should've had it put in today." He'd screwed up. She'd almost paid the price. "I assure you, the company will be here first thing tomorrow, and you'll be safe. Until then, you aren't getting back in the cottage. You're staying with me."

She backed up a step. "That's very...gentlemanly of you and all—"

Gentlemanly? Great, they were back to the *nice* category. He growled, "I'm not feeling fucking gentlemanly tonight. The door that was broken led straight to your bedroom. You could've been hurt."

Her breath caught. Something flashed in her eyes, an emotion he couldn't quite name. "I get that you feel responsible because you own the cottage, but this isn't on you."

Who the hell else was it on? "*My* property. You're staying here." He wasn't going to debate this. Her safety came first.

But she straightened her shoulders and jutted out her cute chin. "Right. The cottage is yours. I'm not."

I'd damn well like for you to be. He barely bit back those words. Now probably wasn't the right time for them. Correction, it definitely wasn't the right time for them.

"You can't tell me where to stay or what to do. So, thanks..." She stepped around him. "But I've got—"

"You're scared." Time to cut through the BS.

She faltered.

"No, make that terrified. When we went back to the cottage, and the door was open, I could see the terror. Hell, I could practically smell it on you." He reached for her hand. Carefully, he lifted her wrist. The bruises had faded more to a yellowish color. "It's all related. You're running. You ran from the bastard who did this, and now you're afraid he's found you."

"He hasn't," she retorted quickly. Her voice was a bit sharp.

Ah. So I'm right.

"He *hasn't*." She tugged her wrist away. "I left and I didn't exactly leave a forwarding address. There is no way he found me this quickly."

Spencer crossed his arms over his chest. The better to not grab her. "You trying to convince me of that? Or yourself?"

She raked a hand through her loose curls. "I heard your deputies talking. They figured it was probably some punk kid. They mentioned that you get the occasional break-in around here. Even small-town USA has crimes. It's the holidays, and one of your deputies said the intruder could've been looking for expensive gifts to grab. Since none were there, he ran as fast as he could."

A few things nagged at him. Like the fact that..."The intruder wasn't caught on the camera near the gate."

"Yes, because he knew how to avoid it. Even punk kids can avoid certain things." Her words came out quickly. "There are woods on either side of your property. He could have darted through there and made his big escape."

"That's certainly possible." There *had* been a few other holiday break-ins. He didn't like them, but they'd occurred. An unfortunate holiday situation...people swiping expensive presents and running into the night. They also had encountered a few front porch pirate situations. Again, he freaking hated those, but they happened even in his town. Yet, tension nagged at him. And when his instincts talked, he listened. "Or something else could've happened. Something tied to the past you're determined to hide."

Her hand was shaking as it fell back to her side. "Look, I'm not some criminal. I haven't broken any laws."

"I know." Spencer tried to make his tone gentle.

He must have failed.

"That's right. You checked me out. Right after we met." Her eyes widened. Her lips parted. She rushed up toward him. Stopped just inches from him. "You been doing more digging on me, haven't you?"

He winced. "Guilty."

"How the hell could you do that?"

Seriously? "Uh, 'cause I'm the sheriff? Because it's my home?" *Because I don't like it when you're fucking afraid?*

"You thought I was dangerous?" Hurt flickered in her eyes. Unfortunately, that emotion was too easy to read, and it made him feel like an absolute jackass.

"No," his voice softened as he answered. For her, he was trying to be soft. She wouldn't get how very alien that was for him because she didn't know about his past. "I thought whatever—whoever—was chasing you might be dangerous. I wanted to help you."

A furrow appeared between her eyebrows.

"That's the same reason I want you to stay here tonight. Because I want to help." There was actually a whole lot more to it than that. "I don't want you over there alone, not until I think things are more secure. Even if it is some jerk teen, I don't want him scaring or hurting you. This house is plenty big. You'll have your own room. You stay there, you stay safe, and we can figure out everything else tomorrow."

She nibbled on her lower lip. "Tomorrow..."

He could practically see the wheels spinning in her head, and Spencer knew that she was thinking about running. All she had to do was pack her bag and slide out of town. If she thought the trouble from her past had found her, it would be incredibly easy for her to run again. "Don't," he rasped.

Haley's gaze held his. Such deep, dark green eyes. "Don't what?"

"Don't run. Stay." *Stay right here with me.* "I can keep you safe."

"But why? I am nothing to you."

Now he had to swallow. "Not true. I'm your landlord, remember? You're my tenant. It's my responsibility to protect you." He cleared his throat. "I'd do the same for any tenant. Not like I'm giving you special treatment."

Her long lashes swept toward her cheeks as she seemed to consider his words. "I suppose so."

Great. "You can take the room next to mine. It's upstairs, just go down the hallway on the right. Second door. Mine is the first."

Her lashes lifted. "You're being really nice."

Wonderful. "I think I fucking hate that word."

"What?" A quick, startled laugh. "Why?"

"You'll figure it out." Spencer rolled back his shoulders as he tried to banish the tension that had gathered there. "It's late. We should both get to bed." His crew had been very thorough, and it had taken them a long time to turn up their absolute jackshit.

"Right." She didn't move.

Neither did he. His gaze had dropped to her mouth again.

She licked her lips.

Fuck.

He turned on his heel. "Yep, definitely time for bed. Definitely time to—"

"Thank you."

He stopped. Spencer was at the stairs and his hand had reached for the bannister. "What are you thanking me for?"

He heard her soft steps then turned to find her right behind him. She gave him a bright smile. "For being a hero when I needed one. It's a nice change for me."

I can be whatever you want.

She eased past him and climbed the stairs. He was immediately given a killer view of her ass. He should probably look away.

But then, she hadn't looked away when he'd answered the door in his towel. In fact, she'd seemed to enjoy the view. His lips quirked at the memory. Of course, that was the moment she looked back.

"What is it?"

She'd caught his grin. "Sorry about flashing you earlier. Didn't mean for the towel to drop."

He heard her fast inhale.

"I'll make sure it doesn't happen again. You know, since we're being professional. Landlord and tenant and all."

She was on the stairs a little above him. Because she was a few stairs up, they were on eye level. Mouth level.

Kissing level.

"Don't want to...cross any lines," he added gruffly.

"No." So soft. "That would be bad."

Too bad I have the feeling it would feel incredible.

She held his stare, then glanced up.

What was she looking at? "Haley?"

"Just making sure there's no mistletoe above me." Her gaze came back to his. "There isn't."

"No. Nothing there. No reason to kiss." Except that her mouth obsessed him.

She leaned forward.

But caught herself. Stopped. "No reason." She pressed her lips together. After a moment, she told him, "Have a good night, Spencer." She turned away.

He didn't move as she climbed the steps. His dick was hard in his jeans, and all he wanted was...*her.* "It's Spence."

She was at the top of the stairs. She reached the landing and frowned back at him.

"Friends call me Spence. Tenants can call me that, too."

Haley gave a nod and a faint smile. "Good night, Spence."

He stayed rooted to the spot until he heard her close the door to the guest room. Then he released the breath he'd been holding. She wasn't interested. He would back off. Leave her alone.

Even though she'd be starring in his dreams that night.

***

"I think I found her, boss." The voice was low. Gruff. He held the phone a bit tighter and said, "You're not gonna believe where little Ms. Fancy wound up."

"Cut the shit and *tell* me," Drew Bradley demanded.

"Alabama. A little dot on the map. She's staying in some bayside town, and she's all alone."

Music blared in the background. The boss must be at one of his clubs.

"Say it again," Drew ordered.

"Point Hope, Alabama. I tracked her movements here. Wasn't hard. It's like amateur hour." Sure, she'd done a good job of using cash so that there hadn't been a credit card trail to follow, but when he offered the right people money—like the guy at the train station or the fellow manning the bus terminal—he'd hit pay dirt.

The fact that Ms. Fancy had a killer body and an unforgettable face? That helped. It made her stand out in the crowd. People who stood out were easy to remember and to track.

"Want me to make a move?" He'd already gone into her cottage in order to be sure he had the right lady. When dealing with a guy like Drew, it didn't pay to make careless mistakes.

"No, you keep watching her. You keep eyes on her. *I'll* come and deal with her myself." Drew hung up on him.

Francis Callaway frowned at his phone. "You're welcome, asshole. Happy to find your missing girlfriend for you. No, no, I don't need a bonus for a quick job during the holiday season. Not like I got an ex-wife waiting on alimony. Your thanks is more than enough." He shoved the phone into his pocket. "Dickwad."

But Drew was a very, very wealthy dickwad. A guy with a ton of cash and a million connections, some that weren't always on the right side of the law. It would be good to have a man like Drew owe him a favor.

So he'd watch the pretty lady. He'd make sure she stayed in town. And if she tried to run before Drew arrived to claim her, then Francis would stop her.

No matter what, his target wasn't going to slip away.

***

She couldn't sleep.

Haley stared up at the ceiling. The bed was soft. The mattress was fresh and obviously new. Moonlight drifted through her window. She could hear the faint rush of waves against the shore. A soothing sound. She should've been asleep.

She wasn't.

Because...

What if he's found me?

Her asshole ex. The whole reason she'd lost the life that she'd loved back home. A guy who should have been perfect. Everyone had told her that Drew was perfect. Handsome, charming, successful. He'd said all the right things at the beginning. And, sure, there had been some whispers that he might be tied to the darker world in the big city, but...who believed whispers? Not her. Oh, no. She didn't fall for gossip.

I do, now.

Now she knew the truth.

She'd broken things off with Drew six months ago. Everything had gone straight to shit when she found out just how bad her ex truly was. The kind of bad that had dirty cops working on his side. That had people turning their back on her. The kind that had her running because she'd seen things she shouldn't.

Now she'd had a break-in at the cottage. Could be nothing. Jerk kids. Some would-be robber. But what if...what if it was more? What if it was him?

She had to get out of that bedroom. Because if she stayed in that bed, letting her mind spin as she stared at the darkness, she might go crazy. Haley hopped out of the bed. Her bare feet curled against the wooden floor. She'd go downstairs. Grab a glass of water from the kitchen. No, check that, she'd go for milk. A nice, soothing glass of milk. She'd peek in Spencer's fridge and, hopefully, he'd have milk. Surely, he wouldn't mind if she got just a small glass?

The guest room door gave a faint squeak when she opened it. Spencer had gotten his crew to bring pajamas over for her—well, her pajamas consisted of comfy jogging shorts and a loose, soft blue t-shirt. When she walked toward the stairs, she realized how incredibly quiet the house seemed. So still.

She put her hand on the bannister. The wood was smooth and solid beneath her fingers as she made her way down the stairs. A few of the stairs creaked beneath her weight, and she winced every single time because she was afraid she'd rouse Spencer. She'd already been enough trouble for him. The last thing she wanted to do was wake him.

She made it to the kitchen. Her eyes had adjusted to the darkness so she could easily see the fridge. She opened the door, and—*yes, success!* She reached for the carton and a few moments later, she'd flipped on the counter light so that she could snag a mug and pour some milk. She had a quick flash of her childhood as she drank the milk and—

"Guess I'm not the only one who couldn't sleep."

Holy mother of God. She hadn't heard a *sound.* Like, no creeping stairs. No rustles. No footsteps. Nothing. He was suddenly just there. The mug slipped from her hand and shattered on the floor.

"Don't move."

He hit the light switch on the wall, and the kitchen was flooded with illumination. Not just the little bit of light that had come from the counter area, but all of the overhead, recessed can lights spilled a soft glow down on her.

On her...

On the broken mug at her feet.

At the puddle of milk currently spreading across his tiled floor.

"I am so sorry." She started to crouch and reach for the broken shards. "I didn't mean—"

"Haley, what part of *don't move* did you miss?" He caught her hands. Then scooped her into his arms. Held her as if she weighed nothing. She didn't, by the way, the guy was just strong. Sexy strong.

He didn't have on a shirt. No crime there, she totally approved, and his jeans hung low on his hips.

He was warm and muscled and still holding her. "Y-you don't have to do this."

"You might cut yourself. That's why I didn't want you to move. Hold on." He turned, took a few steps, and put her down on the nearby countertop. "You okay? No shards hit you when the mug fell?"

She smiled. "I'm really okay. No cuts. Just sticky feet." Her smile faded. He stood right in front of her with his tousled hair and intense eyes. "I'm sorry about the mess. I didn't mean to break your mug, and please tell me it's not one that you are super sentimental about—"

"It was my dead father's mug. He drank from it every single day."

Her stomach clenched. "I can fix it! Give me some super glue and—"

Spencer sent her a toe-curling grin. "It's a dollar mug that I got at the school yard sale last year. Forget it."

Her heart was racing. "That is not funny."

"Are you sure? I've been told I'm hilarious."

"I—"

"Stay here. Do *not* think of moving. Those toes get cut, and I won't be a happy man."

He cleaned up the mess in a blink. She sat on the bar, swinging her legs and admiring the fact that, seriously, he must work out a whole lot. A very, very lot.

"Ahem."

He'd stopped cleaning. She had no idea when. His hands were on his hips, and he was just a few feet away.

Her cheeks burned. She'd been ogling him. Caught in the act. How unstellar. "I need to get back to bed."

"Are you sure? If you're still thirsty, I can give you another mug."

"No, no, I need to get back to bed." She pushed away from the countertop and her toes hit the floor. Before she could take a step—

She was in his arms again. Why did it feel so good to be in his arms? "You don't need to do this. I can easily walk on my own."

His gaze dipped to her mouth. "I could've missed some shards. Just in case, I'll carry you back to the stairs."

Her arm looped around his neck. "I think I'm probably the worst tenant you've ever had."

A soft rumble of laughter. "Like I told you before, you're the only tenant I've ever had. I just posted the cottage online, and you were the first person to request a stay." He reached the stairs. Lowered her onto the step. He turned away—

"I'm sorry if I woke you," Haley blurted.

He glanced back at her. "You didn't."

"You were already awake?"

A slow nod.

"You were having trouble sleeping?"

His lips parted, but he seemed to think better of what he was going to say. He slowly turned to fully face her. The air seemed to thicken between them. She needed to say something. Anything. Or maybe she should run up the stairs. She didn't, though, because...

She wanted to stay with him a little longer. The kiss...that crazy kiss at the bar. It would not get out of her head. Surely it hadn't been *that* good. Not as good as she thought. Not so good that arousal had flooded through her whole body and she'd clung to him as tightly as possible. It had just been...the drama of the moment. Having all the attention on them. Her nerves.

He cleared his throat.

Her gaze whipped up. Wonderful. First, he'd caught her ogling his abs and now he'd seen her staring at his mouth. First tenant for him...and worst tenant for him.

"Want to tell me what you were thinking about?" Spencer invited.

She shouldn't. She'd already said there were lines they wouldn't cross. But...

But if I'm leaving in the morning, does it matter what I do tonight? And, unfortunately, as she'd lain in bed and stared at the ceiling, as fear had started to swirl within her, she'd realized that she needed to keep moving. Find a different place. Just in case she had been traced to Point Hope.

So why not do what she wanted that night? Why not just see if the kiss had really been...all that? "I was thinking a second kiss wouldn't be as good as the first."

His thick eyebrows climbed. "That really what you were thinking?"

"Yes." She licked her lower lip. "No way was the kiss as good as I thought it was."

He took a step toward her. His right hand reached out and curled around the bannister. "You think the kiss was good?"

A shrug. "Yes." *It was body melting, toe-curling, where-the-hell-am-I-when-it-was-over* good. "But it was probably just a fluke."

He laughed. "No, no, don't worry. You won't hurt my self-esteem any."

Oh. She gave a wince. "I didn't mean—" Haley stopped. Squared her shoulders. "How about we try a second time?"

If possible, his eyes seemed to darken even more. "You're saying you want me to kiss you."

She absolutely was. Haley nodded. "Just to see, you know, a scientific inquiry kind of thing."

He leaned closer to her. His delectable scent curled over her. "I thought you didn't want us mixing up our relationship."

"Yes...um, don't think that rule applies any longer." *Because I'll be cutting out of town as soon as I can get a driver to come and pick me up in the morning.* She put her hand on his chest. Loved the way his warm skin felt beneath her touch. "So let's try for scientific inquiry."

His jaw hardened. "Bullshit."

That wasn't exactly the romantic response she'd expected. "Excuse me?"

"You want me to kiss you, and it has nothing to do with a scientific inquiry." His mouth came nearer, but he didn't press his lips to hers. "You just want my mouth on you."

So guilty. "Don't you want my mouth on you?"

"Fuck, yes, but I'm not gonna lie about it. I'm not gonna lie to you, and I don't want you lying to me."

That was unfortunate. She'd already lied to him. Would lie again, too. Dammit. "Never mind. We can just—"

His left hand curled around her waist. His right was still on the bannister. "Tell me what you really want."

"I want your mouth."

And he gave it to her. His lips met hers in a hot, passionate kiss. The kind of kiss that a woman felt in every cell of her body. That rare and wonderful kiss that was so good you found yourself moaning. And maybe scratching your partner as your nails dug into the arms of the man who was kissing you.

He wasn't hesitant. He was confident. Seductive. His lips and tongue were amazing—no other word for it. Spencer wasn't some bumbling kisser. He was a man who kissed like he damn well knew what he was doing. Not too wet. Not too hard. Seducing. Claiming.

Panty-melting.

She wanted more. So much more.

He caught her lower lip between his teeth. Gave a sensual nip.

She moaned again.

Then his tongue was thrusting back into her mouth. She met him full force. Her body pressed to his as she tried to get as close to him as possible. Her breasts were aching, the tight nipples thrusting against the cotton of her shirt, and she knew he had to feel them pushing against his chest.

Haley was so turned on that she wanted to rub her whole body against his, and it was all just from a kiss.

A simple kiss.

He lifted his head.

Her breath rushed out.

"I don't know what it was like for you, Haley." His voice was deep and hard. A sensual rumble. "But for me, the second time was just as fucking fantastic as the first."

She licked her lips and tasted him. But Haley shook her head. A very definite no.

A furrow appeared on his forehead.

"It wasn't as fantastic," she told him seriously. Her voice had turned way husky. "It was even better." How was that possible? Shaken, aching, she spun away from him. "Good night, Spence." *Spence.*

She hurried up the stairs.

"I think you're right. It was better." A pause. "Kinda makes you wonder what it will be like next time."

She almost tripped.

"Sweet dreams, Haley. I'll see you in the morning."

No, he wouldn't. Because she would be long gone when the sun rose.

CHAPTER SIX

Spencer crossed his arms over his chest as he stood near the gate at the front of his property. A quick glance at the lighted dial of his watch showed him that it was nearing six a.m. He figured he wouldn't have much longer to wait...

Then he heard the grinding. A very distinct sound.

Right on time.

The grinding came for a few more moments, then Haley ambled into view. The sun was just starting to rise. Faint streaks of red and gold slid across the sky. Haley's head was down, and her blonde curls tumbled over her face as she pulled the big, rolling suitcase behind her. The wheels were grinding over the pavement. He waited a bit longer, and she still didn't glance up, so...

"You need a hand with that?"

Her head whipped back, and she stared at him with wide eyes. Her breath heaved in and out. In and... "Jesus! Are you trying to give me a heart attack?"

Are you trying to sneak away when my back is turned? Instead of asking that question, he merely said, "I was trying to give you a hand with your luggage. It appears that you are...going somewhere."

Her lips clamped together. She kicked the suitcase a bit behind her, as if it hid the freaking thing. The move would have *almost* been adorable, if she hadn't been trying to leave him.

Haley didn't respond.

He sighed. "You're running away."

"I am not. I am walking out to the road because my ride should be here soon."

He lifted an eyebrow.

"I called one of those ride share services. The friendly fellow will be arriving any moment." She bit her lower lip. "You realized I was going to leave? Leave, not run."

You're running, baby. You're terrified, and I need you to trust me. "I figured it out last night when you kissed me." He dropped his hands and stalked toward her.

Her shoulders stiffened.

"No." Spencer shook his head. "Not gonna happen. You don't ever need to be afraid of me." He waved toward the road. "You want to leave, you do it. Your choice." *Always, your choice.* He closed the rest of the distance between them and stopped in front of her. "But you want to stay, if you want to have someone on your side who will keep you safe from whatever nightmare is following you, then you choose to stay with me. You choose me, got it?"

Her head tilted back. "You don't know me."

"You sure about that? Because I know you like to drink a glass of milk to help you sleep. I know your mouth is soft and sweet, and I've never gotten lost in a kiss the way I do with you."

Her cheeks flushed.

"I know you like to listen to the sound of the waves, and I know that when you smell a Christmas tree, you smile just for a moment, before you catch yourself. And I know—unfortunately, I know—what it looks like when you're afraid."

She swallowed. Fiddled with the suitcase.

"You came to my town afraid. Last night, the break-in spooked you even more because you think your past caught up to you. But you don't trust me enough to help you. You want to run." Now he shook his head. "You don't have to do that. Take a chance on me. I can help you."

A car slowly rolled to a stop near the gate. The driver opened the door. "Uh, I'm here for Haley Quick?"

She didn't look at the driver. Her gaze stayed on Spencer. "I wish I'd met you before." There was longing in her voice.

He wanted to grab her, hold her tight, and not ever let her go. Instead, he locked down every muscle in his body. "You've met me now. Fuck the past."

She pushed up on her toes and kissed him. Her lips were open, warm and sweet, and that electric charge he felt whenever they kissed surged through him. Kissing her ignited a white-hot need within him, and he wanted to stop playing the fucking gentleman and just *take*.

But she was backing away. "I didn't know it could feel like that. Every time..." Her voice was low, just for him as she confessed, "I kiss you, and everything goes crazy."

Didn't she get that crazy could be good? It could be exactly what she needed.

"You don't want me in your life, Spence."

Yes, he fucking did.

She stepped around him, rolling that damn bag with her. He heard her check the driver's info out, and he was glad she was being safe. Reviewing the tag number, making sure this was the guy who was supposed to pick her up, doing everything right.

But...

She's still leaving me.

Spencer marched forward. He took the bag from her. Put it in the car. Then he stared down at her. "Come back to me."

Her eyes widened.

"When you get on the road and you realize that you don't have to keep running, come back to me."

Her lower lip started to tremble. She caught it. Bit it.

And he backed away. He didn't say a word as she climbed into the car and the nervous driver winced.

"Sorry, man," he muttered as he appeared super uncomfortable. "Didn't realize this was a break-up scene. Getting dumped during the holidays sucks but—"

"Screw off," Spencer told him flatly.

"Well, merry Christmas to you, too, buddy." The man gave him a cheery wave with one finger and climbed into the car. A few minutes later, the vehicle was heading down the road.

Haley was gone.

***

"So you want to get dropped off at the nearest bus station?" The driver's voice was all chipper as he adjusted the radio and holiday tunes filled the car. "I'll have you there in no time."

She glanced back through the rear windshield. She didn't see Spencer any longer. He was gone.

"Broke up with the boyfriend and you're heading home to family, huh? Good thing. Family is where you should be during this time of the year."

She didn't have any family. Her parents were dead. She didn't have a home.

She had...

"Come back to me." Spencer's voice whispered through her mind.

Her hand lifted and her fingers touched her lips. The last kiss had been a mistake. She should have stayed away from him. Now she could feel him. Now she could taste him. Now...

"Take a chance on me." Why couldn't she get his words out of her head?

"Miss?" The driver cleared his throat. "You good back there?"

Good? Nope. Not even close.

"You changed your mind? You know where you want to go?"

She knew. She wanted Spencer. She'd said that he didn't know her, and his response had made her insides quiver. Had anyone ever said sweet things like that to her?

And she'd realized that she knew him, too.

She knew the people in the town respected him. Knew that he went out of his way to keep everyone safe, even diving into the path of oncoming elves. She knew that he had a killer voice and that he could kiss ever-so-amazingly well under the mistletoe...and everywhere else, too.

She knew he wasn't afraid to jump into action when a threat appeared. Knew he was chivalrous enough to carry a lady so she wouldn't step on broken shards of a mug. Knew that he was one heck of a handyman because his home repairs had been super impressive to her.

Knew that he had a wild side because he liked to drive his motorcycle...and because he'd been a Navy SEAL.

Knew that he had abs for days. Days. Nights. Weeks.

Knew that he hadn't pushed her. Hadn't pressured her.

Knew that he'd watched her drive away, but told her to come back to him.

"Ahem." The driver cleared his throat once more. "Does the silence mean we should keep heading for the bus station or did you have another destination in mind?"

Haley blinked and her head turned so that she wasn't looking back any longer. After all, what was the point in looking back? There was nothing good to see in the past. "I know exactly where I'm going."

***

"You seem a little...extra pissy today, Spence."

Spencer glanced up from his computer and narrowed his eyes on the deputy who'd just spoken. Deputy Titus Malone beamed back at him. Titus had been working at the station for the last year, and the guy was a good deputy. Not just good, but amazing. He didn't take shit from anyone, he always arrived for his shift on time, and the fellow genuinely loved his job. Wins all around. But today...

"Don't start with me, Titus."

"Is this about that trouble at your place last night...or, rather, trouble with the lady at your place last night?" Titus wiggled his brows.

Spencer let out a long sigh as he leaned back in his chair. "You don't want to go there."

Now Titus winced. "Aw, man, that bad, huh? Look why don't you come with me to Maureen's bar? I know you're off duty. Let's get out of here. You can't be moping around this place all night."

Why not? Wasn't like anyone was waiting at home for him.

"Do not be a buzz kill. I need you to be my wingman." Titus nodded briskly. "Got my eye on a certain lady, but you know it always helps when you come in with a good wingman at your side."

Like Titus needed a good wingman. The ladies were crazy about him. They whispered and giggled about how he looked just like the actor Shamar Moore. Titus kept his head smoothly shaved, and his dark eyes twinkled...even when he was busting perps. His grin was infectious, and damn if even the bad guys didn't start to like him.

"Come on," Titus urged as his voice turned wheedling. "I bet they will even let you sing karaoke if you ask nicely."

"Fuck off," Spencer grumbled.

Titus only laughed. "Bro, get your lovesick ass out of the chair. Let's move."

If Titus wasn't his best friend, Spencer would have told him to fuck off yet again. But they'd been SEALs together. They'd survived a nightmare together, and Titus—despite his easy smiles—had a world of pain inside of him. He was as close to Spencer as a brother, and Spencer knew the guy was trying to get him out of his funk.

A fucking funk. He was down because Haley had left him. They'd just met. Yes, they had explosive chemistry. Yes, she made him feel alive for the first time since he'd come back to the US after his deployments but...

She was gone.

And I'm worried that trouble is chasing her.

"You look like you lost your best friend, man. It's sad. So sad." Titus lifted his hands. "Because your best friend is standing right here." He pointed to himself. "Now get your ass up and come with me to the bar. Don't make me ask again."

Fine. Fine. He stood. Grabbed his old, beat-up jacket. He'd already changed out of his uniform hours ago, and now he wore jeans and a black shirt. He shouldered into the jacket.

"That's what I'm talking about," Titus said approvingly. "One woman is not worth this much angst."

"Angst?" His eyes turned to slits. "You did not use that fucking word."

Titus turned away. "Yeah, well, glad your *angsty* ass is up."

The man was such a sonofabitch. The kind of sonofabitch that you always wanted at your side because he looked after you. Spencer threw an arm around Titus's shoulders. "All right. All right. Who's the lady you're after tonight?"

***

There were a lot of strangers at Maureen's bar. Most of the visitors came in the spring for the big arts festival. Then others headed to town for summer vacation.

Strangers during the holidays? Well, they were usually in town because they came to visit family members. Point Hope received a few snow birds, too, but most of the birds preferred to head on down to Gulf Shores or Orange Beach and stay directly on the Gulf of Mexico, not on the bay.

When they entered the bar, Spencer immediately took stock of the faces there. The locals. The newcomers. He was always assessing threats, a leftover habit from his SEAL days. Back then, you always had to know where your threats were coming from. If you made a mistake, people could die.

But this place was far, far from his dark past. There was no blood and death in the cheerful bar. There were no men with guns waiting to fire. No attacks from enemies. There were just people singing. Dancing. There were holiday lights twinkling.

And...there was a gorgeous blonde woman with curling hair and green eyes dressed in tight jeans and a loose red sweater. She stood behind the bar, and she tossed him a nervous smile.

Spencer blinked.

That particular blonde wasn't supposed to be there. She'd *left* him that morning.

Titus slapped him on the back. "For historical accuracy, it should be noted that I am the greatest wingman of all time."

Spencer swung his head toward his friend. "How—"

"Happened to stop by earlier and saw her." A wink. "You're welcome." His attention drifted to a nearby table and a group of ladies who gave him delighted waves. "Ah...duty calls. Got to go."

He strode away.

"You're *off* duty," Spencer muttered. But, yeah, he was going to owe Titus. He'd give the guy a case of whiskey for Christmas. Spencer's gaze swung back to Haley.

She was staring at him.

He couldn't look anywhere but at her. He crossed the room in an instant and stood against the bar.

Her smile came quickly. "Hi."

"What the hell are you doing here?"

Her smile dimmed.

Okay, shit, he needed to dial things back. Way back.

"You're upset that I stayed?" She started to back away.

His hand flew out and curled around her wrist. "I'm thrilled you're here. Just thought—all day—that you were gone." And he didn't want to let her go again. If he let her go, he was afraid that she might vanish. How could he have missed someone—so much—that he'd only just met?

He was in serious trouble. The kind of trouble that wrecked a man's life.

His trouble glanced down, and her long lashes hid her green gaze from him. "I was going to leave, and then I realized you were right."

Look at me, baby.

Her lashes lifted.

"I am glad you're here," he told her softly. His thumb brushed along her inner wrist. "I would love to know what made you decide to stay."

Her pulse gave a quick jerk beneath his touch. "I decided it was time to stop running."

You need to tell me what you're running from. Because...hell, maybe he'd been digging deeper into her life that day since he'd been so freaking worried about Haley going off on her own. Whatever waited in her past was bad, and he hated for her to be afraid. By nature, he was a fixer. He wanted to help make things better for the people around him.

He wanted to do everything possible to make Haley's life better.

"I decided that I needed to give Point Hope a better try." She smiled at him. "I hear the town has one really amazing Christmas parade. Something about an army of elves on bikes. Don't want to miss that."

He found himself smiling back at her. "You know we're trying to break the world record for the number of elves on bikes this year."

Her eyes widened. "Are you serious?"

He laughed. "I'm glad you're here." Very, very glad. He'd felt hollow all day, but now that he was with her, everything seemed right again. "You know, I bet we could put you in that parade if you wanted. Something tells me you'd be cute as hell with a pair of elf ears."

Before she could respond, someone called out to her, asking for a drink.

"Hold that thought," Haley murmured. She hurried away.

Spencer made a mental note to tell Haley that the hot water had been fixed in her cottage. He'd worked on it, in case she came back. He settled down on the barstool and spun around, letting his gaze sweep over the crowd. Titus was...occupied. Well occupied by three women. Couples were leaned in close together. A table to the right had a group of women obviously enjoying a ladies' night, and laughter spilled from them. Behind the ladies...

Spencer tensed. *What's up with that?*

Behind the ladies, a man slouched at a table. His back was pressed to the wall, and a half-empty drink waited in front of him. The guy didn't seem to be interested in the drink. Or the festivities in the bar. Instead, his attention was focused...

Spencer followed the stranger's glance...

On Haley.

On a Haley who smiled as she talked to the customers at the end of the bar.

Spencer's gaze darted back to the stranger. Something about the stranger's focus didn't sit well with him. The man wasn't watching Haley with admiration or attraction. Just a single focus that set off alarm bells for Spencer.

So that shit was going to be investigated.

He rose from the stool and made his way across the bar. Friends called out greetings, and he waved to them as he ambled toward his prey but...

The guy's gaze flickered to Spencer, and he tensed.

You should tense. I'm coming for you.

The man rose quickly. Tossed some cash down onto the table and made for the door.

"Hey, Spence!" Keri curled her hand around his shoulder. "Tell me you'll be singing tonight."

He shook his head. "Sorry, Keri, but I told Titus the microphone was all his."

Her eyes lit up. "Oh, I *love* it when he sings." She immediately took off toward Titus.

Yeah, Titus *hated* to sing. But he did have a soft spot for Keri, so Spencer was sure his buddy would be winding up on stage soon.

Spencer glanced back toward the stranger. The table was empty. Dammit.

The bar's door was closing, the little bell overhead jingling. Spencer hurried forward. The fellow running out—right then—was suspicious as hell. Spencer didn't get stopped again as he rushed outside. But when he made it to the street...

His prey was gone.

Spencer had catalogued the fellow when he saw him...Dark, receding hair. A thin frame. A nose that appeared to have been broken. Oversize clothes. Stubble on his jaw. When he'd gone for the door, Spencer had realized the man stood at about six feet tall.

And he'd hauled ass. Seriously, hauled ass.

Spencer's gaze went to the left. Then to the right.

A few people were walking on the street, and the lights in the trees were as merry as ever. But the mystery guy was gone, and that did not sit well with Spencer.

The bell jingled behind him as the door opened. "Spence?"

His shoulders stiffened at Haley's voice. He schooled his expression before he faced her.

She stood in the doorway, her head tilted, and her curls sliding over her shoulder. "Is everything okay? I turned back around and saw you running out."

He wasn't so sure everything was okay. He didn't like that the stranger had vanished. *Major red flag.*

She took a few steps forward, and the door swung shut behind her. "You're mad that I stayed?"

He caught her hand in his and pulled her closer to him. Both because he wanted her close and just in case any threats were out there. "Hell, no, I'm not mad," he told her gruffly. "I'm glad you're staying."

A smile teased the corners of her lips.

"I spent the whole day thinking that you were gone, and I was certain I'd missed out on something special."

"You say really nice things."

He groaned. "You called me *nice* again." Did she not get that was the kiss of death to a guy? What was he gonna have to do in order to show her—

She shot onto her tip toes, wrapped her hands around his shoulders, and hauled him toward her. Her mouth met his in a crash of need. He didn't hold back. He wanted her—wildly, damn near desperately—and Spencer needed her to realize that. He wasn't playing some game. He wanted her naked and screaming his name.

She kissed him with a wild abandon that he loved. A passion that made him crave her all the more. His hands locked around her hips, and he wanted to lift her up, to hold her and let her wrap those gorgeous legs around him as they fucking forgot everything else.

But...

A car passed, honking excitedly.

But this wasn't the place.

His head slowly lifted.

"I think I like nice," she whispered. "It's a good change for me." A pause. "I promised Maureen that I'd work until ten tonight. Any chance you want to meet me after?"

Hell, yes. "Yeah, I'll be here."

She smiled at him again, the kind of smile that made a guy think it was just for him, and then she hurried up to the bar's door. He watched her go because a man sure as hell knew to enjoy a view when he had one. The door closed behind her, and once he knew she was safely inside...

He spun around just in time to see the shadow moving near the bookstore. The bookstore's windows were decorated with a whimsical display of reading snowmen, and the light from the display provided enough illumination for him to see...

Got you.

Spencer took off running across the road. He heard his prey give a fast, hard curse as the man scrambled to escape.

Not happening.

Spencer caught the fellow just as he darted around the corner. Spencer slammed him against the nearby brick wall. He lodged one forearm against the guy's throat. "Who the fuck are you?"

A gasp. The man's coat opened as he struggled, and Spencer caught sight of the bulky object there. An object in a holster. A gun.

In a flash, Spence had taken the gun from him. Aimed it at the fellow. "Let's try this shit again," Spencer snarled. "Who the fuck are you and why are you watching Haley Quick?"

The man lifted his hands. "Let me..." he panted. "Show...ID."

"*I'll* get the ID. You keep your hands up." Spencer reached forward. Patted him down and pulled back out—

Fuck.

There was enough illumination from the lighted trees around them to easily see the star within the circle...the identifying symbol of... "You're a US Marshal?"

"Yes." Stronger. Rougher.

"What in the hell do you want with Haley?" Spencer's gut had tightened because this shit was not going to be—

"I want to protect her."

CHAPTER SEVEN

Spencer stalked around his desk and glowered at the US Marshal who'd just taken a seat in his office. "Talk," Spencer ordered as he glanced down at the ID he still kept.

US Marshal Fenton Callaway. Spencer had already made plans to thoroughly check the guy out because, yeah, he wasn't exactly a trusting sonofabitch.

Fenton sighed. "You don't have clearance to hear everything I've got to say."

Oh, that was cute. Spencer laughed and tossed the ID back at the fellow. "I'm the sheriff here. You're in *my* town. I have clearance for every fucking thing that's going on."

Fenton gave a little hum.

What. The. Hell?

Spencer leveled a hard stare at him. "You don't want me to tell you to talk again..."

Fenton quickly swallowed. "Look, it's obvious, you're, um, involved here. Like, personally involved. And I get it. Haley is hot. Smoking."

Spencer felt his body stiffen. *Don't deck a marshal. Don't...* "Watch yourself."

Another swallow. One so loud that Spencer heard the click. "Yes, so, personal involvements don't work out. You need to step back."

"From *what?*"

"From her, of course! Who else are we talking about?"

Spencer rolled back his shoulders. "I get the game."

"This isn't a game. I realize it's high above your paygrade, but you should take my word for it and just—"

Spencer's laughter stopped him.

Fenton's cheeks flushed. "Did I say something funny?"

"You don't know my paygrade." *Asshole.* What a dick thing to say. "And you don't know me. Don't come into my town and treat me like I'm some hick who can't handle a case. Because if I remember correctly, I was the one who got the drop on you. I pegged you as a stalker with one glance at the bar."

Fenton immediately shot to attention in his chair. "I am *not* a stalker! I was protecting her, just like I told you! I was doing my job." His face scrunched up. "Not trying to get in her pants— which is what I think you were doing."

"Do you want me to beat the shit out of you?"

Fenton's wide-eyed glance swept around the too quiet station. "You...you can't do that. You're the *sheriff*..."

"I'm off-duty." Spencer waited for the man's gaze to lock on his. "And either you talk or I go over your head and find out from your supervisor exactly why you're in *my* town, stalking *my* tenant."

Fenton shot to his feet. "You don't have to call anyone! Dammit! Look, I'm not here officially."

And I'm not going to officially kick your ass...but it will still happen.

"I...felt sorry for her, if you want to know the truth."

"Why would you feel sorry for Haley?"

"Because she got a raw deal! She brought in her evidence, enough evidence that should have buried her ex, but you throw in a few bad cops—cops too eager for a quick take—and add in some folks in the DA's office who conveniently helped the other team...and all of sudden, the case that should have been fool-proof is nothing but ashes."

Case? What case? When he'd been looking into Haley's past, he hadn't found ties to a case.

Fenton was still talking. Still fuming as he said, "And the person you've got with the balls to come forward? It's Haley. Only instead of getting the federal protection she was promised..."

"Witness protection," Spencer muttered. He'd figured that part out. Why else would a marshal be involved? He hadn't thought for one second that Haley might be a fugitive. Marshals were mostly involved with fugitive apprehension and witness protection. Since he didn't buy that

Haley was guilty of a crime, option two made more sense to him.

"Yes, yes, witness protection. The folks in charge told Haley that she'd get a new name and a new life, but someone with power—someone like her jackass ex—pulled his strings and her new life vanished. She was left alone in the city with his thugs closing in and, hell, is it any wonder she cut and ran?"

Spencer's hands had fisted at his sides.

"So...yes." Fenton raked a hand through his thinning hair. He sat down again, slouched in the chair, and wrinkled his clothes even more. "Yes, I tailed her a bit. I wanted to make sure she wound up safe and not in some hole in the ground. The whole case vanished from public record, and I didn't want her vanishing, too."

The case vanished from public record. Well, that explained why Spencer hadn't found it in his search. But cases didn't usually vanish, not unless someone with a whole lot of pull was yanking on strings. Spencer sucked in a deep breath. "I want the name of the ex."

"Look, I told you, buddy, this is way above your—" Fenton stopped as he stared into Spencer's eyes. "Fine. Your funeral. You want the name? It's Andrew Bradley. Drew Bradley. On paper, he looks clean as a whistle, but you listen to your girl, and she'll spin a different story. One that will give you nightmares."

The name wasn't familiar. He'd been digging into Haley's life, but he hadn't turned up the guy. So many secrets had been hidden. Secrets that someone had wanted to bury.

Dammit, he was going to need to call in some more favors on this case.

Fenton's chin jutted toward his chest. "I came down here to make sure she's safe."

"She is," Spencer said flatly.

"'Cause she's sleeping with you?"

"I don't like you, Fenton. You should know that."

Fenton huffed. "Well, I don't like you much, either. You freaking attacked me in the street, and you're lucky I don't have you up on charges right now."

"Why don't you try to press charges and let's see how that shit works out?"

Once more, Fenton rose to his feet. His glare turned his eyes beady. "I'm getting out of here. You wanted to know more, I told you more. Now I've got a motel room waiting in the next town." He rattled off the address of the place over in Daphne, Alabama.

Everything the joker said made Spencer suspicious. "Why aren't you staying in Point Hope?"

"Didn't want to stay here, because just in case *I* was followed, I didn't want to lead the bad guys to Haley."

"Uh, huh. Good of you to think ahead."

"Now that I know she's okay, I'll be getting back on the road first thing in the morning. It's one long haul back home for me."

Another piece that didn't fit. "You're going to leave without ever talking to Haley?" Fenton had been in the bar, watching her, but not approaching her?

"I just needed to see for myself that she was okay." He seemed to take Spencer's measure. "If things go to shit here, do you think you can keep her alive?"

"Absolutely."

A grunt. "You're a confident prick. I'll give you that."

"I *will* keep her safe."

"Good." Fenton tipped his head to Spencer and shuffled toward the door. "That's all I needed to know. Merry freaking Christmas."

Spencer waited for him to leave the office. Waited for the door to close, then he reached for his phone. He'd made some good friends over the years. Both while he'd been a SEAL and after. One friend in particular would be coming in handy for him right about now.

Eric Wilde.

Eric Wilde ran Wilde Securities, *the* best security and protection firm on the East Coast. Spencer had done some work for Eric, back in the day, before he'd decided that he wanted to return to the home he'd left so long ago.

Because it was late, he didn't bother calling Eric at his office. Instead, Spencer dialed his buddy's private line. His eyes stayed on the door. The phone rang once, twice...

"Spence, you tricky bastard. Long time, no see."

Spencer's lips curled. "What the hell are you talking about? I was at your wedding not too long ago." He still couldn't believe Eric had settled down or that the guy had looked so completely obsessed with his beaming bride.

And, hell, Eric wasn't just a husband now. He was a father. Talk about going all in...and Spencer knew Eric couldn't be happier.

"Yes, well, you need to come for a visit. Or, you know, I still have that position open for you—"

"I'm not *looking* for a job. In fact, I have a job for you."

"Tell me that again?" Eric's voice sharpened. "You got a problem? You want a team down there?"

"I want information first, and I know how very good you are at acquiring information."

"I'm the best." Not arrogance. Just truth.

"That's why I called." Tension had gathered at the back of his neck. "I need you to do some research on a few names for me."

"All right."

Just like that. No questions asked. Just...*all right*. Because that was the kind of friend that Eric was. They'd met on a mission gone to hell. Eric hadn't been a SEAL, but he'd helped to save the lives of Spencer and other members of his unit. Hell, Eric had saved a whole lot of units when he'd been working with Uncle Sam. Eric was a good man, a good friend, and Spencer knew he could count on Eric completely.

It's good to have friends you can count on in this world. "First, a man named Andrew Bradley. He's up in New York—"

"I know where he is." Now Eric was even grimmer. "The man is bad news. Folks have been trying to lock him up for years, but he's slippery."

"So I hear." Slippery and dangerous. "The next guy is US Marshal Fenton Callaway. The guy just walked out of my office after he sang me a song and delivered a fancy dance."

"What was he singing about?"

I'm not betraying her. I'm trying to help her. He'd tried to get Haley to confide in him, but she hadn't. Now he had to learn as much as he could to ensure her safety. *Still feels like a fucking betrayal.* Spencer's back teeth had clenched. With an effort, he gritted out, "Haley Quick. The marshal told me that she's Drew's ex and that she could be in danger."

A low whistle.

"I want to know how much danger. I need to know what I'm facing so I can protect her."

"Like that, huh?"

"Exactly like that." *Like I will do anything for her.* "Someone broke into Haley's place last night, and I'm not just going to sit around while she's threatened."

"You've never been the sit-on-your-ass type."

Hell, no. "I need to know who is coming for her. If I know the enemy, then I'll be ready to kick ass."

"I'll get everything I can," Eric assured him. "You want manpower, too?"

"I've got Titus. I can count on him."

"Hell, yeah, you can. Despite my efforts to recruit him, he hasn't decided to join my team."

No, not yet. But Titus didn't always like to stay in one place too long. And Spencer figured that one day—a day too soon—his friend would head out again. Titus often seemed to be searching for something...he just didn't know what it was.

"How fast can you get me this intel?"

"Dude...it's *me*. You'll have everything you need to know by dawn."

Hell, yes. Hell, *yes*.

***

She pushed open the bar's front door. The bell jingled overhead, and the sound of laughter followed Haley as she stepped outside. The air was slightly brisk, a chill she hadn't expected, and she found herself pulling her coat a bit closer as she headed down the wooden steps...

And toward the man who waited near the motorcycle.

A wide smile curved her lips as she approached Spencer. Seeing him made her happy. And it was crazy and foolish and she should probably have been a million miles away, but the truth was that Haley was tired of running.

"Hi," she told him as she stopped close to him.

"Hi."

"Thanks for coming back by. I mean, I appreciate it, and I—" *I am rambling*. But she was stupid nervous, like she was on a first date or something. And she wasn't. This wasn't a date.

Was it?

He handed her a helmet. "Got something I want to show you, New York."

She took the helmet. Laughed. "Did you just call me New York?"

"It's where you're from, isn't it? I can hear it in your voice, slipping in and out."

He climbed onto the bike, and she slid in place behind him. Her thighs hugged his legs even as her arms wrapped around his stomach. He was warm and strong and, damn, but the man smelled *good*.

"What do you miss most about New York?" he asked her.

"Snow." She shook her head, then realized he couldn't see the movement. "Sometimes, I hated it...like when you had inches for days and days and you had to slog through it, but...it's Christmas, you know?" She hadn't exactly had a ton of Christmas spirit lately. "There's just something about seeing snow at Christmas that makes you feel good."

"Thought you might say something like that." He had the motorcycle growling to life. "Hold on tight."

Like she had to be told. She was already holding on tight, thank you very much, and definitely enjoying the ride. He zipped through town, driving them beneath the soft lights and under the swaying wreaths that hung high above the streets. He didn't head toward his house, but instead took her through the town until they stopped at what she realized was a park, one framed by enormous oak trees. The limbs sagged with heavy moss. Lights were on inside the park, giving it a faint glow.

"Why are we stopping here?" Haley asked as curiosity filled her.

He kicked down the stand. Turned off the bike. His head turned so he could see her. "Got something I want to show you."

Um, okay. That was all mysterious.

Haley hurried off the bike and put down her helmet.

He stood next to her and extended his hand. "Trust me." He winked at her.

The thing was...she did trust him. Her fingers curled over his. They headed toward the gate. The *locked* gate. "Umm..."

"Don't worry, I have a key."

She'd been *umming* because she'd just realized the park was named after him. *Lane Park*. "So the name, that's not a coincidence—"

"My grandfather donated the land for the park. One of the reasons I have a key."

The gate swung open.

She lost her breath.

All of the trees in the park had been carefully decorated with glowing, soft white lights. Just like the trees along the downtown streets. "This must have taken forever."

"It definitely took a while, but the city council considers the lights to be a tradition. And the families love it."

She could see why. Sure, there was no snow, but those beautiful lights made it seem like a winter wonderland.

"The park opens for families tomorrow night. It was just shut down while the last of the decorations were being put up. We'll have a big party here, and then families can come walking through the park for the rest of the holiday season." He guided her to a spot underneath a big oak. There were glowing ornaments hanging from the oak tree.

She laughed as she stared up at them. They were beautiful. The whole place was like something from a dream.

"I'll be right back. Don't move."

"What? Spencer?" Her head turned.

He'd ducked behind a nearby oak.

And a moment later...

Snow. Snow came drifting gently toward her. She reached out her hand, and, no, it wasn't bubbles this time. It was honest to goodness snow. In Alabama.

It might have just been the best present of her life.

"Thought you'd like it." He came back to her side. His hand lifted beside hers and snowflakes landed in his broad palm. "It's part of the festivities for tomorrow night. We'll have snow machines set up all around the park so that kids can play. Hell, they'll even make snow angels, too. The snow won't last long, but—"

"But it will last long enough to make them happy."

He nodded. He shook his hand, and the snow drifted from his fingers. Then his fingers rose to her cheek. His touch was cold, and she shivered, but she liked it. Him...and the cold.

"Are *you* happy?" Spencer asked her.

She was. But... "I could think of something that would make me even happier." A pause. A breath. One that pulled in some courage for her. "Kiss me."

His mouth immediately took hers. God, would she ever get used to the way the man could kiss? Such intensity, such focus, and such freaking sexiness. He tasted and took, and she was moaning and rubbing against him. He was kissing her in some kind of picture-perfect scene that seemed far too good to be true. But if this was a dream, then she was going to dream as big as she could. "Take me home," Haley whispered against his mouth.

He stiffened. Pulled back. "You want to go to the cottage?"

Precious. He wasn't getting it. "I want to go back to the cottage with you." She'd stayed for this. For him. Because sometimes, there were things out there—people—who were so good that you couldn't leave without experiencing them to the fullest.

She wasn't leaving without having her time with Spencer. "I want you." So much for lines and not crossing them. "You...you want me?"

"Fuck, yes."

Haley laughed. When she was with him, she felt so happy, and she loved that. He was kissing her, she was kissing him, and she loved that they were—

He lifted her into his arms. She wasn't even going to pretend, Haley found it hot as hell when he lifted her up so easily. Strong was ever so sexy.

After a long, hot moment, Spencer raised his head, stared into her eyes, and—

Everything plunged into darkness.

Every light in the park flashed off in an instant. The darkness was complete and total as

Spencer's hold tightened on her. *"What in the hell?"*

Fear snaked through her. Suddenly, even in his arms, she didn't feel so safe. She knew what could wait in the darkness. She'd been threatened in the dark before, and she didn't want to be vulnerable again. Not *ever* again.

"It's okay. I've got you." His voice was low and soothing. He was still holding her in his arms as he walked straight forward. "I'm taking you out of here."

"Spencer…"

"A transformer could have blown. We have a lot of power running out here." His voice *almost* seemed normal. Almost. But there was a faint edge there that put her on guard. "Good thing you and I tested things out for the town. We can get the lights fixed before tomorrow night. You'll be the town hero."

Doubtful. But they were beyond the gates now and there was light. He put her down next to the motorcycle. He reached for his gun.

His gun.

She hadn't even realized he'd had the holster on under his coat.

"I want to check things out," he told her in that too calm voice of his. "You stay at the bike. I'll be right back." He turned for the darkened park once more…

And the lights inside flooded back on.

CHAPTER EIGHT

"Yeah, yeah. So what you're saying is no transformers blew? No fuses went out? You can't find a damn thing?" Spencer's voice was low as he kept his gaze on the closed bedroom door. They were back at the cottage, and he wanted answers. "Then why the hell did the lights turn off?" His hold tightened on the phone he held to his ear.

"I don't know," Titus muttered back. "Maybe it was some fluke."

Maybe. Or maybe it had been something else. "Get the other deputies to run some patrols through town and out near my place."

"You think Haley's in danger?"

"I think I'm not going to be leaving her side tonight." Because he didn't buy a fluke explanation. Not with what the marshal had told him.

And I don't trust that guy, either. Fenton had been shifty as hell. The fellow had just been *staring* at Haley in the bar. Why hadn't he approached her?

"You need me?" Titus asked. "Because if you do, I'm there. I can come out and keep guard at the gate."

"No, no, I put in extra security today. I'm good." *I meant it, I'm not leaving her side.* "Just get the patrols to swing by. If I have trouble, you'll damn well know about it."

The bedroom door opened. Haley stood there, her bare toes curling against the floor. Her coat was gone. She wore her red sweater and the form-fitting jeans. There were pink spots of color in her cheeks, and her red lips gleamed.

Gorgeous. "Got to go," Spencer told his friend. "Thanks, Titus." He dropped the phone onto the nearby table, right next to his holster and weapon.

"Any word on the park?"

"Titus says everything is fine there. Things should be in order for the big night tomorrow."

She nibbled on her lower lip. Then Haley seemed to reach some sort of conclusion. With interest, he watched as she squared her shoulders and lifted her chin. She marched toward him. Very determinedly.

He lifted one eyebrow when she stopped right before him.

"I meant what I said."

Spencer waited.

"I want you."

"And the fact that I'm your landlord...?"

"Has nothing to do with it."

He was fighting the urge to grab her and hold tight. They needed to clear the air. *Then I need her.* "I thought you didn't want to cross lines."

"I thought you did," she threw right back.

Ah... "Guilty." He grinned.

She didn't smile back at him. "I don't have the best of experiences with men. The last guy I was with turned out to be a serious liar. Very bad news. You think a guy might be Prince Charming, and it really sucks when it turns out that he's more of a Captain Hook."

His hand lifted and his fingers slid beneath the thickness of her hair. "I promise, I'm no Hook." He bent and his lips brushed over hers.

That was all it took. His mouth on hers. Her taste. Her scent. *Her.* Desire surged through him. The kiss had started as a gentle caress. All tender as he tried to use finesse to seduce her, but, in about two seconds, the fucking finesse was gone, and he was kissing her with frantic desire. Kissing her with the wild need that she stirred in him.

He growled against her mouth. Wanted to get *everything* from her. Her taste was insane. Sweet and hot. Her lips were heaven. The way she moved her body against him, rubbing and arching, drove him to the edge. Her hands were on his shoulders, and she was so responsive that he was going out of his head—

Spencer forced himself to let her go. To step back. To suck in a breath, but he just still tasted her. "You sure?" *Sure you want this? Want me?*

Her smile made his heart lurch in his chest. "I'm sure that I want you."

Hell, yes. In the next instant, he had her in his arms. He carried her back into the bedroom. When he entered, he saw that she'd lit a candle on the nightstand, and the soft light filled the room. He lowered her onto the bed. Took a step back and yanked his shirt over his head.

"I have to tell you," Haley confessed, "I may be in love with your abs."

What do I have to do…so you'll be in love with me? No, fucking wrong thought. Wrong question. This wasn't about love. It was sex.

His hands went to the waistband of his jeans, but Spencer stopped. He'd keep the jeans on, at least until he'd had time to stroke and lick every inch of her.

She sat up on the bed. "Spencer?"

"You've got on way too many clothes." He sounded guttural. Savage.

"Oh. I can fix that." She yanked off her sweater. Tossed it across the room. Revealed a silky red bra. "Better?"

Much. But still too many clothes. He climbed onto the bed. Made sure not to put his weight on her, but kept his palms against the mattress to brace himself as he leaned over her and kissed her. He enjoyed that sexy mouth of hers. Her mouth was heaven. He savored her lips and then he kissed a path down her throat. Over her collar bone. Down, down he went. He kissed the tops of her breasts and got rid of her gorgeous bra.

Her breasts were full. Her nipples tight. When he drew one nipple into his mouth, sucking hard, she moaned and surged up against him. His legs were between hers, and she was riding his jean-covered dick. Pushing up. Sliding her body closer and closer.

He eased back.

"Spencer!"

He smiled. "Just helping you with the too-much-clothing situation." He reached for the snap of her jeans. Pealed the jeans and her red underwear off her long legs. Her skin was like freaking satin beneath his touch. So smooth. Of course, he had to caress her. Had to kiss her. Kiss the inside of her thighs. Slowly work his way up to her bare sex.

Her gasp filled his ears. Her hands grabbed for his shoulders.

His mouth took her.

He licked and sucked. He teased her clit and strummed her with his tongue. He enjoyed every gasp, every moan, and every arch of her body. He couldn't get enough of her. *More. More. Take.*

Her body tensed. "Spencer, I'm about to—"

Hell, yes. He drove his tongue into her. Retreated. Blew against her clit. Licked. Pushed into her with his fingers even as his mouth kept working her, and she cried out in pleasure beneath him. The orgasm tore through her body, making her shiver and arch, and he lifted his head so that he could see her face.

Absolutely beautiful.

He licked his lips. *I will be having more.*

Her lashes had closed as her breath panted out. As he gazed at her, Haley's lashes slowly opened, and her stare caught his. Every muscle in his body was locked down tight as a ravenous need pulsed through him. His control held on by the tiniest of freaking threads. His cock was about to shove out of his jeans as—

"You've got on way too many clothes," Haley told him, her voice husky as she gave him back the same words he'd said to her moments before. "But don't worry, I can fix that."

She pushed him back. He went willingly as she rose above him and her hands went to the top of his jeans. He'd kicked his shoes off—he had no clue when—and she unsnapped the jeans and pulled down the zipper.

He was a commando kind of guy, so his heavy cock sprang toward her. Her soft hands closed around him, stroking him from tip to base, over and over, and he had to lock his back teeth because it felt so good.

Then she put her mouth on him.

And it was about a million times better than good.

She licked and teased with her tongue. Her lips feathered over the broad head of his cock before she opened her mouth wide and took him in, sliding her lips over him and squeezing the base of his dick at the same time with her hand.

She felt like paradise, and there was no way he'd last. Hell, no. He wanted her too much. "Haley..." A growl. A rumble. Barely human. "I need *you*."

Her head lifted. The soft glow of the candle fell on her face. "You've got me."

And I want to keep you. A dark, possessive thought that whispered through him.

She bent as if to put her mouth back on him. *No.* He caught her, rolled her back and pinned her beneath him on the bed. "Baby, as much as I freaking love your mouth, I'm about to explode, and I want to do that buried balls deep in you."

"I like that plan." She nipped his lower lip. "I took the liberty of...ah...picking up condoms earlier today. They're in the nightstand."

He nearly knocked the nightstand—and the candle—over as he yanked open the drawer. He kicked his jeans out of the way and got the condom on in a flash. He went back to Haley, settling between her spread legs and pushing his cock against the entrance of her body. He didn't sink into her, not yet. His hands caught hers. Held tight.

She stared into his eyes.

Smiled.

He sank deep.

Fucking heaven.

And he lost it. Lost all control because she felt incredible. A haze of lust and need took over. He withdrew, thrust, withdrew...drove so deep. Her legs wrapped around his hips, and she urged him onward, pushing against him and tipping back her head.

He had to kiss her neck. Had to lick and bite. Had to pound into her again and again.

"Spencer!" Haley yelled his name as she climaxed. He felt the contractions of her sex around him. A tight, white-hot paradise.

He drove into her again. *Haley.*

The orgasm nearly obliterated him. Pleasure slammed through every cell of his body. A release that went on and on, and when it finally ended and he could suck in a breath, Spencer looked at her.

The candlelight flickered over her face.

She was smiling. "Just so you know, I'm going to want to do that again."

A rumble of laughter vibrated in his chest. "Hell, yes." He pressed a kiss to her neck and enjoyed her shiver. "Hell, yes."

***

"It's *Jingle Bells*," Haley whispered sleepily.

Spencer pulled her closer against him. He was comfortable as fuck, her soft body pressed against his side, and he had no intention of opening his eyes and—

"I hear *Jingle Bells*," she murmured. "Don't you?"

His eyes flew open. Hell. He did hear *Jingle Bells*. Because his asshole of a best friend had reprogrammed all the ring tones on Spencer's phone earlier that day. He'd caught Titus in the act but hadn't taken the time to fix things.

Jingle Bells played again, and Spencer rolled out of the bed as adrenaline surged through him. The bedside clock told him it was two a.m., and a call at this time? No way it was good news. "I'll be right back."

The covers rustled. "Is everything okay?" Nervousness had her voice rising a little.

Okay? Probably not. Good thing it was dark so she couldn't see his expression. "You just rest. I'll find out what's up." Naked, he padded to the den and snagged his phone before the familiar tune could play again.

He saw Eric Wilde's name on the screen. Eric calling in the middle of the night? *No, everything is not okay.* Spencer put the phone to his ear. "What's happening?"

"He isn't real."

Spencer's eyes narrowed. His gaze had adjusted to the darkness around him. "Who isn't?"

"Your US Marshal. I had this shit checked and triple checked. There is no Fenton Callaway who works for the US Marshal's office. Hell, I only found two Fenton Callaways in the whole United States. One is an eighty-eight-year-old veteran living in Colorado, and the other is a sixteen-year-old kid in Arkansas."

"Then who did I talk to today?"

"I don't know, man, and that's the reason I'm calling you right now." Eric's voice was flat and hard. "Everything else checked out. Andrew—Drew—Bradley is one real piece of work. My contacts told me he is involved in the criminal world up to his damn eyeballs, but he has connections and power, and nothing is sticking enough to keep him in jail. Your Haley Quick was supposed to testify against him, but the case fell like a stack of cards. It completely disappeared from the books. She's on her own, and when I did some poking around, I learned that she quit her job, packed up her apartment, and left town *right* after she got mugged in the street a few days ago."

"Mugged?"

"Yeah, well, that's what the cops described the attack as. She was found screaming for help near the subway station entrance. Her purse was gone, and, according to my sources, she was sporting injuries. The next day, she was in the wind."

And running to Point Hope.

"I'm sending backup down to you," Eric said.

"I have Titus—"

"And, like I told you, this guy Drew Bradley is seriously bad news. You've covered my back before, so now I'm covering yours. I'll have two agents there by morning. I'll fly them in on a private plane, and they'll land at that little strip right outside of town. I'll tell them to check in with you, but otherwise to stay out of sight. At least until we know exactly what we're dealing with."

He forced his jaw to unclench. "I appreciate the help. Thanks."

"You know you don't need to thank me," Eric grumbled.

"Send me the bill."

"Uh, no, *not* going to happen—"

"Wilde Securities protects the rich and famous. I know how much you charge for your services, and *you* know I can cover payment. Send me the freaking bill."

"You're an asshole."

Spencer was too furious to smile. "If that SOB isn't a marshal, then who the hell is he?" *And why was he stalking Haley?*

It was time for Spencer to find out. *Lie to me once, shame on me.*

Lie to me twice?

I'll make you fucking sorry.

***

Spencer stalked back into the motel's small parking lot. It wasn't a big surprise that "Fenton" hadn't been in the motel over in Daphne. A bullshit name, a bullshit location. Spencer was going to make certain that an APB was placed for the guy—he'd issue a description and see what could be discovered.

His gut told him that "Fenton" was still in the area. He was still in the area because Haley was in the area. The man was interested in her, knew everything about her, and the only reason he'd been skulking around Point Hope?

Haley.

The dumbass had made mistakes, though. He'd lied to the sheriff. He'd impersonated an officer. He'd just given Spencer the perfect reason to have the jerk locked up...

As soon as Spencer found the man.

Time to get the search started. Time to send out the rest of his team.

And time to go back to Haley and get the truth from her.

CHAPTER NINE

Her hands gripped the warm mug while she stared out at the bay. The waves pounded at the shore, rising and falling, and in the distance, she saw a sailboat slowly weaving through the water. The sun had just started to rise, and both shadows and light drifted over the waves.

"Haley!"

She turned at Spencer's call and found him hurrying down the wooden steps to the beach. She'd taken a walk to clear her head and to enjoy the pounding of those waves while he'd been gone. But as he approached her and she saw the grimness of his features, worry slid through her.

"It's bad." She nodded. "Very bad." The kind of bad that made a woman take a step back. Which she'd just done.

After Spencer had taken his phone call, he'd told her to lock the doors and reset the alarm, then he'd rushed out. Hadn't given her explanations. Hadn't stopped to say, *"Why, thanks, Haley, for the most amazing sex of my life. You're awesome."*

Would that have killed him?

So when he stalked toward her, all grim and determined, there was only one conclusion...

Very bad.

"I was worried when you didn't answer at the cottage." His voice was rougher than normal.

"I was just taking a walk." The mug felt heavy in her hands.

He looked to the left. To the right. The stretch of beach was deserted.

"We need to go inside and talk." A muscle jerked along his hard jaw.

Uh, oh. "Spencer..."

"I know, okay? I knew last night. And it's time to stop pretending. You're not on a damn vacation. You're running scared, and I'm worried your past has caught up with you."

The wind had a faint chill, but suddenly, her body seemed to be ice cold. *I knew last night.* "Back up."

He frowned at her.

"You knew last night? *What* did you know last night?" Before he'd made love to her, what had he discovered? No, no, they'd had sex. Just sex. This wasn't about love.

But...

It had been about trust.

"You lied to me, Haley, and I found out about the lies. There is no more pretending."

He seemed rough. Darker than he'd been before. His voice was thick and his body hard with tension. He kept glancing along the beach as if looking for threats, and she realized that he was battle ready. The friendly, charming guy she'd met was gone. There was no easy grin on his face. He looked intense. Dangerous.

"You're going to tell me everything. Then I'm going to figure out what the hell to do."

Her eyebrows shot up. "You're going to figure things out?" Okay, this was a really crappy morning-after situation. Great sex, then implosion. Because, at that moment, she felt like *he'd* been lying to her. If he'd discovered the truth about her last night, why hadn't he said anything?

Because he thought I wouldn't have sex with him? Because he wanted to screw me?

If he'd told her that he knew the truth about her life, if he'd put everything on the table and made the hard demands that he was making right then, would she have slept with him? Or would she have turned away?

"Haley, we need to get inside. I want to know *everything.*"

"I thought you already knew everything."

That muscle along his jaw jerked again as the waves beat behind her. "I know your ex-boyfriend is a criminal. So when you said you had bad experience with men, yeah, I got that was a freaking understatement of the century."

His words *hurt* her. Haley sucked in a sharp breath. She stumbled back.

Spencer's eyes widened. "Haley, no, look, I didn't mean it that—" He reached for her.

She lifted her hands, as if to stop him, but she was still holding the mug so she wound up lifting that, too, and—and it shattered. The mug shattered in her hands even as there was a weird whistle in the air around her. For a moment, she did not understand what had just happened. Why had the mug shattered? It hadn't fallen. She still even gripped the handle, but liquid was dripping down her arm yet it...it wasn't coffee. It was red, red like—

"*Gun!*" Spencer roared. In the next instant, he'd launched at her. He shoved her down and shielded her with his body just as something hit the ground near her, sending sand shooting into the air.

Her brain seemed to have frozen. From the instant the mug shattered until Spencer covered her with his body...everything froze. But when the sand erupted into the air, awareness and understanding flooded through her.

Someone is shooting at us. Shooting at them from a position high on the bluff.

"Can't stay here," Spencer snapped as he kept her covered.

Covered with his damn body! He was using himself as a shield, and he couldn't do that. If he got shot...*no*. Haley tried to roll over—she was on her stomach, she needed to get on her back—and push her way free of him.

"Not fucking happening, baby. To get you, he'll have to go through me."

That was the last thing she wanted. "No!"

"We have to move, now. Understand? I'm covering you. You stay with me. Run as fast as you can—I'll keep up—and get under the stairs. Ready?"

Absolutely not. She was not ready to run while someone was shooting at her. She was also not ready to die—or, worse, have Spencer die trying to protect her. No, thank you. She'd be good without all that. But—

"*Let's go.*"

She leapt to her feet with him. He curled his body around hers—jeez, he needed to *stop* that shielding crap—and they ran fast for the stairs. She felt sand erupt behind her and she heard that whistling sound again. There were no bangs or bams as if a gun had been fired. Why didn't she hear those noises?

Spencer locked one arm around her waist and heaved her up against him, and then the guy seemed to *throw* her under the stairs before he hurtled after her.

The sand provided cushion for her as she slammed down. She rolled over, spitting out some of the grains that had gotten in her mouth. "Spencer—"

He had his gun out. "He was shooting from the bluff. Based on the angle, I don't think he can reach us from here. We're too close to the base of the bluff for him to get a clear shot, and the stairs provide cover for us." He leaned forward a little as his gaze swept the area. "My phone is in my side pocket. Get it and call for backup."

She scrambled forward. Her hand sank into his pocket—

"Other pocket," he growled as he kept his gaze—and his gun—directed toward the top of the bluff.

Her fingers fumbled, brushed against something big that was *not* a phone, then she was reaching around him—and ignoring the sting in her arm—as she searched in his other pocket.

"*Haley,*" he groaned her name. "Don't play."

"Does it look like I'm playing? Your pocket is tight!" Haley snapped back at him. Not her fault she was accidentally fondling him. She yanked out the phone. "Do I call nine-one-one?"

"Call Titus. He'll get a team out here. Tell him we have a shooter on the bluff. To haul ass."

Right. She'd met Titus at Maureen's. Big, muscled, and friendly. "Uh, I'm going to need your code to get in the phone—"

He rattled off the code. She found Titus in his contacts, called, and gave him the information.

"Are you fucking serious?" Titus demanded as soon as she slowed down to let him respond.

"Yes, I am fucking serious." She looked at her arm. Winced. "I also think I'm fucking bleeding, so will you please hurry?"

Spencer's head whipped toward her. "You're hit?"

"I'm on the way," Titus promised her at the same moment. "You stay down. Spencer will keep you safe."

Right. Because Spencer kept using himself as her human shield.

"*You're hit?*" Spencer asked again. His voice had gone positively lethal. Such a cold, savage growl.

She put the phone down on the sand and tucked her legs underneath her body. Not like there was a whole lot of room down there. Her gaze darted to her arm. Her sleeve was a bloody mess. "I'll live."

He growled again. "I'm going to kill the sonofabitch."

He sounded like a stranger. This wasn't the guy who laughed about elves on bicycles or who sang karaoke in a Christmas-covered bar. This man was hard and dangerous and chilling in his intensity.

She inched back.

"Don't."

Haley stilled. Her gaze lifted, and she realized that he was staring right at her.

"Don't move from beneath these stairs. We're safe for now." His lips flattened. "I want to chase the sonofabitch, but I can't be certain it's only one shooter. If I go after him and leave you alone..."

She would be a sitting duck. She got that. "I-I didn't hear gunfire."

"Because the shots came from up on the bluff, probably from a gun that was silenced."

She'd just been shot at. Haley looked at her arm. No, she'd been *shot.* "It stings like a bitch."

He reached for her arm.

She jerked back.

"Baby, I need to see the damage."

"You need to keep your eyes open for the bad guy. You look out there, and I'll take care of my arm."

Did his lips curl? Just for a moment? But he swung away to look for the bad guy. She gingerly peeled back her sleeve. It hurt because the blood had caused the sleeve to stick to her wound. But...

"I don't think it's a bullet wound." It was a deep cut. "Maybe...maybe I was cut by the broken mug? Like a shard or something?" It was a jagged cut, and she was pretty sure she'd need stitches. But it wasn't a bullet wound. She wasn't lying in a pool of blood on the beach. She wasn't dead. *Win, win, win.*

She ripped the bottom part of her shirt—the part that looked the cleanest—and she wrapped it around her forearm, hissing a little at the pain. But at least that would help things, wouldn't it? On TV shows and in movies, people were always binding bad cuts.

Then she inched toward him. "What can I do?"

His gaze locked on her. "Stay the fuck alive."

"At the top of my to-do list." Haley sucked in a shallow breath. "Do you have a backup gun on you or anything?"

He reached down near his ankle and came back up with a small, black gun. "You know how to use this?"

"I aim at the bad guy, and I pull the trigger."

"*After* you take off the safety."

"Right. Yes. Of course." *The safety.* People talked about those in TV shows, too. Her hand closed around the gun.

"Someone tries to kill you, Haley, you *shoot* him."

The gun trembled in her grasp.

She stayed pressed close to Spencer, holding the gun, barely breathing, until she heard the scream of approaching sirens.

Thank God, it's the cavalry.

***

"I can't believe the shooter got away from you, Spence." Titus shook his head. "How is that shit even possible? Are you losing your touch? I swear, back in the day, you could stalk up on your enemy without so much as a whisper of sound and you could put your knife to—"

Haley's eyes were the size of saucers. Beautiful saucers, but *still* saucers. She was sitting in the back of an ambulance, an attendant was examining her arm, and Haley appeared far, far too pale.

"Shut the fuck up," he muttered at Titus.

"But, man, *how* did the guy—"

"Spencer didn't want to leave me," Haley said, voice husky as her eyelids flickered. "That's why the shooter got away. Because Spencer stayed with me."

He sure as hell had stayed with her. *Run and risk a second guy coming up and attacking her?* No, staying with Haley had been what mattered.

The EMT cleared his throat. "She needs stitches." The EMT was Dodge Clinton, a guy who'd gone to high school with Spencer and played on the football team with him. "We need to get moving and take her to the hospital."

He hated that she'd been hurt. When he'd seen the blood on her, he'd flipped the hell out.

Spencer grabbed a young deputy walking by—Cody Waller—and shoved him toward the ambulance. "You ride with her to the hospital. You stay with her every moment, got me?"

Cody's eyes were almost as huge as Haley's. "Yes, sir."

The shooting was a big damn deal. The first shooting the little town had experienced in, shit, he didn't know how long. Cody looked nervous but determined as he swallowed a few times and climbed in the ambulance.

Spencer wanted to go with her. He didn't want to leave her side. But he also needed to search the area. He stared hard at Haley. There were so many things he wanted to say to her, but he didn't exactly want to bare his soul in front of their audience.

"Thank you," Haley told him quietly as she notched up that ever so adorable chin of hers. "You saved my life today."

"You don't need to thank him." Titus slapped a hand on Spencer's shoulder. "It's all in a day's work for our sheriff."

Spencer growled at him.

Haley frowned. A little furrow puckered between her brows. "I am grateful. But you should never have put yourself at risk for me."

Uh, oh. He knew where this was going. With that in mind, Spencer figured he might as well go ahead and clear the air and screw the audience. Spencer jumped into the back of the ambulance.

"Oh." Cody blinked. "Did you change your mind, Sheriff Lane? Are you going instead of me?"

"You are not running," Spencer told Haley.

Haley swiped her tongue over her lower lip. "No, I'm about to ride away in an ambulance."

His eyes narrowed on her.

"Uh, Spence," Dodge mumbled. His freckled features scrunched up. "You're kinda in my work space, buddy. Gonna need you to jump *out* of the ambulance so I can take my patient to the hospital."

Spencer didn't move, not yet. "When you're done at the hospital," Spencer said as his eyes locked with Haley's, "the deputy is going to bring you back to me."

She started to shoot off the gurney.

Gently but firmly, he caught her shoulders and pushed her back. "You need your stitches."

Her chin notched up.

"You're coming back to me as soon as you're cleared at the hospital. We have things to discuss." Like the lies she'd told him. And the guy who'd just tried to kill her.

"You're acting like a different person," she whispered. "All bossy and controlling."

Dodge laughed. "Different? That *is* Spence. Describes him to a perfect T. Back on the football field, we used to call him Captain Control."

"You're not helping," Spencer tossed at the guy. Seriously, Dodge could keep some shit quiet.

But Dodge just shrugged. "And you're still in my way. We need to get moving."

Yes, fine, but he had to make sure Haley didn't run from him. "Promise me," Spencer urged.

Her gaze dropped.

He caught her chin between his thumb and forefinger and gently tilted her head up. "Haley, promise me."

Her eyes were such an insanely beautiful green. "I have a deputy dodging my steps. Not like I have a choice, do I?"

"With me, you always have a choice." He wanted her to choose him. "I'm going to find the shooter. I will stop him."

He let her go.

She grabbed for his hand. Held tight. "Don't you dare get hurt, understand me?"

"Sounds like you care."

She dropped his hand. Surprise flashed on her face, but she quickly schooled her expression.

He winked at her. "Don't worry. I'm pretty hard to kill."

"I don't want you killed *or* hurt!" Her words followed him as he jumped from the ambulance.

He grabbed the door and started to swing it shut. But he paused. "That's because you care." Slam. He reached for the second door. His gaze swept from Cody to Dodge. "Watch over her." *Slam.*

A few moments later, the ambulance rushed down the road.

"Ahem." Titus had been standing at his side as Spencer watched the ambulance drive away. "What's our next move, Captain Control?"

Spencer slanted him a glance. "Best friend or not, I will deck you if you call me that again."

Titus laughed.

Spencer shook his head. "The next move...it's that we find the bastard who tried to shoot *my* Haley. We find him, and we stop him."

Titus wasn't laughing any longer. His voice lowered as he asked, "You think it was that fake marshal?"

"Let's say he's suspect number one, and I also want to know where the hell Andrew Bradley is right now." He needed the exact location of Haley's infamous ex.

Titus nodded. He started to turn away, but Spencer caught his arm. "When I saw the blood on her, I thought she'd been shot."

Titus winced. "Aw, man, I—"

"Shot on *my* watch. You know I'm not going to let that shit happen again. I am not going to lose someone else. I will do everything in my power to keep her safe."

Sympathy shone on Titus's face. "That wasn't your fault. The way shit went down overseas, that wasn't on you—"

"My team. My responsibility." His mouth had gone dry. "I won't let her get hurt."

"You don't know her, Spence. I mean, you met her a few days ago. Look, let's take a step back. Let's make sure you're fully ready for—"

"I know her. She's mine, Titus. And, next time, I will fucking destroy the fool who comes for her with a gun." It was a grim promise. He let his friend go and stalked toward the woods that lined the bluff. But as he approached the woods, a black SUV braked to a stop near the edge of the road. His gaze lingered on the vehicle.

The passenger side door opened first. A tall, dark-haired male exited, wearing battered jeans and an equally battered-looking coat over his shirt. He moved toward the front of the vehicle, put his hands on his hips, and surveyed the scene.

The driver exited more slowly. A woman, wearing black dress pants and a crisp, green top. Her hair was dark and thick, and she moved with ease even in her two-inch heels. She met the man near the SUV's hood, and her gaze—

Went straight to Spencer. When their eyes met, she gave a little smile.

The agents from Wilde Securities had arrived on the scene. Spencer took a detour so he could meet them. The woman's smile stretched as he approached.

"Spence, nice to see you again." She stepped forward and gave him a quick hug.

Over her shoulder, Spencer noticed that her partner narrowed his eyes at the contact.

"But I wish the meeting had been under different circumstances." Blair Kincaid pulled back and studied him with her pale blue eyes.

"The circumstances suck. The last thing I want is some asshole shooting wildly in *my* town." His gaze locked on Blair's partner.

The guy smiled, flashing perfect, white teeth. "Heard a lot about you." He offered his hand. His assessing gaze belied the warm smile. "I'm Linc Dalton. At your service."

Linc had a strong grip. Spencer could appreciate that, and he sure appreciated the backup.

"Looks like we came after all the action." Linc's hand dropped back to his side as he nodded toward the activity behind Spencer. "What in the hell happened?"

"A shooter tried to take out Haley Quick this morning." Spencer's voice roughened as he remembered the attack. "He didn't succeed, but the bastard got away. Now we're trying to track him."

"Could be long gone," Linc replied. "If he missed his target and he knows the authorities are searching for him, guy could be miles away by now."

"Or he could hiding out until he finishes the job." Spencer had to choke down his fury. "Which he is *not* going to do." He walked back toward their waiting SUV. "As far as anyone else is concerned," Spencer said, keeping his voice quiet as the agents moved to shadow him, "you two are just tourists who saw all the activity and stopped by out of curiosity."

Blair nodded.

"You're in town for the holidays," Spencer continued.

Linc immediately reached for Blair's hand. Twined his fingers with hers. "Darling, I love spending the holidays with you."

She jerked, then gave him a look hot enough to burn, but she didn't pull away.

Spencer thought the hand-holding was a nice touch. Anyone taking a glance in their direction would see a couple, not undercover partners.

"Wish the vehicle had been a little less obvious," Spencer muttered as he raked their ride with a quick glance. "A black SUV screams, *I'm an undercover agent.*"

Blair winced. "I know, but I swear, it was all they had at the rental agency."

Spencer pointed down the road, as if he was giving them directions. "Haley is on her way to the hospital. She had to get stitches, and I sent a deputy with her." His hand dropped. "But I'd sure feel better knowing that you two had eyes on her." Protection was their business, and he wanted to make certain that Haley was safe.

"Thanks for the help," Linc said loudly as he gave a quick nod. "See you around, Sheriff Lane." He tugged on Blair's wrist, and a few moments later, they were driving away in the SUV.

Spencer spun on his heel and marched for the woods. Haley would be well protected. He knew he could count on the Wilde agents.

Now to find the bastard who'd shot at *his* Haley.

CHAPTER TEN

Haley strolled down the sidewalk, and her gaze darted to the businesses and their cheerful storefronts. The windows were all lit up, glowing with decorations. Snowflakes were falling in one window, paper flakes that fluttered in a continuous stream. In another window, little, mechanical elves slowly climbed up a wooden ladder as they carried colored lights on their backs.

And at the next shop...

"It's our Christmas shop," Cody told her quickly. "It's called Three-sixty-four. It's open every day of the year, except Christmas."

Heavy, white columns lined the exterior of the building, and green garland surrounded the windows. The front door was manned by two life-sized nutcrackers.

She started to take a step inside.

"Miss..." Cody blocked her path and appeared distinctly uncomfortable. "You know the sheriff is waiting to see you."

True. Spencer was waiting, and she was avoiding him. The young deputy with his close-cropped, black hair had been her shadow ever since she'd gotten out of the hospital. Now, Cody was walking with her every step of the way as she headed for the sheriff's station.

Or as she *delayed* heading to the sheriff's station.

"They didn't find the shooter." She knew this because she'd overheard Cody talking on his phone.

But he still shook his head. "Not yet. The search is still ongoing—"

She turned away. Her gaze danced down the street. A couple had paused near the sushi restaurant. The tall, handsome male had his head tilted attentively toward the pretty brunette with him.

"And since the search is still ongoing, you don't need to be out in the open like this," Cody continued doggedly. "Sheriff Lane is waiting and you need to—"

She whirled back to him. "Do you think I'm in danger out here?" Surely, no one would shoot at her in town? And if the person did...Oh, God, innocent bystanders could get hurt. She needed to move, fast, and get out of there.

"I think we need to get to the sheriff's office." Cody straightened his thin frame. "Now."

"But—"

"Sheriff Lane," he began.

She heaved out a breath and put her hands on her hips. "Yes, I know, Spencer is waiting on me, and he gave strict orders for me to come to his office, but I—"

"He's behind you," Cody whispered.

What?

She whipped around. Yep, he was behind her. With one eyebrow raised and his hands loose at his sides.

"This isn't the sheriff's station," he told her.

Whoops. Caught in the act. His expression was so hard to read. She tried a fake, bright smile. "I was heading to see you. Just got distracted—"

He reached for her hand. His touch was so careful as he lifted her wrist and peered at the bandage on her forearm. "How many stitches?"

"Only seven. It wasn't a big deal."

His gaze lifted. Held hers. "It's a big deal to me."

Oh, boy. When he got that intense look about him, Spencer was so damn sexy.

"We need to talk, Haley. In my office." He glanced over at Cody. "Thanks for looking after her. I know you have a shift later, so go get some rest."

"Yes, sir." Cody left in a fast, relieved rush.

Spencer kept his hold on her as he began to walk down the street. She basically had no choice but to move with him.

"What's wrong, Haley?"

What was wrong? Oh, so many things. "Well, someone tried to kill me this morning. The day didn't exactly have the best start."

She slanted a quick glance at him and noticed the hardening of his jaw.

"Then I realized that the guy I'd had sex with last night—he knew all about my big, bad, dark secrets."

An elderly man with stark white hair and a rather charming Santa beard had just strolled out of the bookstore. At her unfortunately loud announcement, he stopped. Stared.

His wife—Haley assumed the lady with him was the guy's wife—immediately elbowed him in the ribs. "Come on, Frank. Let's go."

Blushing, Haley picked up her pace. "It would have been good if you'd told me the truth *before* we had sex."

Spencer stopped.

She did, too.

He turned toward her.

She retreated. Why? She had no clue. But she stepped back as he closed in and put his hands on either side of the bricks behind her.

"You didn't tell *me* the truth, baby."

Okay, fine, she hadn't but... "You're the sheriff. You're the *good* guy. We talked about this—"

"Sweetheart, even good guys can have a damn dark side."

She tried again, "If you had just told me—"

"Told you—what?" His voice was even lower. His body even closer to hers. "That I knew your ex was a crime boss and you were running scared from him?"

"Yes. That."

"*You* didn't tell me." His voice was so rough and sent a shiver sliding over her. "You were the one who didn't trust me. I knew your secrets, and I didn't care. Don't you get that? I want you. I don't care about your past. Actually, scratch that, I do care."

A fist seemed to squeeze her heart.

"I care because I'm pissed as hell that someone is targeting you. That someone wants to hurt you."

The fist relaxed. Her heart warmed.

His gaze searched hers. "You're not in this shit alone, you get me?"

"You don't have to take on my problems. I'm not asking you to do that—"

He kissed her. Leaned in close and locked his mouth on hers. She should probably not kiss him back, Haley knew that, but she did.

She grabbed his shoulders and held tight as her mouth opened beneath his. Their tongues met, desire exploded inside of her, and she forgot they were on the street.

She kissed him as desperately as he kissed her. She loved his taste. Loved the way he felt against her. When he kissed her, when their mouths met, she didn't care about anything else. Only him.

That was so dangerous.

His mouth pulled from hers. "Last night changed everything." His voice was even rougher. Grimmer.

"Last night..." *Keep it together, Haley.* "That was just sex. You don't owe me anything. I don't owe you anything."

His body stiffened. "I'm sheriff here. I protect everyone in my town." A pause. "You can sure as hell expect I'll protect *you*." He took a step back. His gaze had hardened. "Just sex, huh?"

Just phenomenal, mind-blowing, best-sex-ever. "Yes. So don't worry that I'm clinging or—"

"Fuck that. I want more. I want *you*."

She wanted him, too.

A friendly voice called out, "Hey, Sheriff Lane! Can't wait to see you at the park tonight!"

"Shit," Spencer groused. He looked over his shoulder.

She looked around, too. And realized that quite a few people had witnessed the show they'd put on. Her stomach knotted at the knowing glances thrown her way. Haley had a quick worry. Exactly *how* loud had she been when she announced, "That was just sex" a few moments before?

Spencer straightened his shoulders. The star on his chest caught the light and gleamed. "My station. My office. Now."

He was being all tough and fierce and *not* smiling again.

"We're clearing the air, Haley, and we're not doing it in front of half the town."

***

"That explains a few things." Linc Dalton popped a piece of chocolate in his mouth as he watched the sheriff glare at the folks on the street. "Damn." He savored the chocolate on his tongue.

"This stuff is incredible. Can you believe they make it on site?"

His partner shot him a glower. "I was with you when the lady at the chocolate store explained the process. So, yes, I can believe it."

His smile flashed. "You're jealous because the lady gave me a free sample."

"You could've shared the sample. I am your partner."

His gaze slid over her shoulder and noted the sheriff—and the hold that the sheriff had on Haley Quick. "They're sleeping together."

"Yes, I heard the announcement."

He laughed. They *had* been close enough to hear Haley's angry words. "I'm guessing their relationship is why we're here. The sheriff panicked because his girlfriend was threatened, and he wanted Wilde agents at the ready."

"Please." Blair rolled her blue eyes. "Spence doesn't panic over anything."

He thought of the too-familiar hug that she'd exchanged with the sheriff. Linc choked down the bite of chocolate. "You know him well."

"Eric wanted him to work at Wilde, but Spence wanted to come home." She motioned around the town. "Home has always been important to him. He left and joined the Navy, then became a SEAL, but his ties bound him to this place and the people here."

Oh, great. The dude was a freaking SEAL. He already knew that Blair had a tendency to fall for those guys in Special Forces.

She gave a light and totally fake laugh as she glanced down the street, as if he'd said something funny, but Linc knew she was just using a cover as she directed her attention at the sheriff and Haley Quick. "He's definitely involved with her," she murmured. "And personal involvements mean lines get blurred. Maybe Spence didn't think he could be objective enough on this one, so he wanted extra eyes. Sounds like a good plan to me." She looked back at him. "It's a very—*umm.*"

He'd just put a new piece of chocolate to her lips. "For you, darling."

Her eyes narrowed. She bit into the chocolate.

Two teenage girls hurried past them. "That is so sweet," the blonde girl said.

Blair chewed. Swallowed. "Sweet," she ground out.

He winked at her. "Shall we go and get our room settled for the night? The sheriff has the target at his side, so I think we can rest easy for a bit."

Her eyes turned to slits. "Did you just say *room*? As in singular?"

"We're a couple. Of course, we'd only have one room. Anything else would be suspicious."

"Suspicious," she repeated.

"Exactly what I said." She had a little bit of chocolate on her lower lip. His hand rose automatically, and his thumb brushed away the chocolate.

Her tongue happened to slide out at the exact same moment as she licked away the chocolate. She wound up lightly licking his thumb.

Fuck.

His gaze held hers. Had she felt that surge of heat? She must have—

She smiled ever so sweetly. "One room," Blair agreed. "And you'll be bunking on the floor." She turned away. Strode happily down the street.

Linc stared after her. "There is such a thing as one room with two beds. Full beds. Queen beds. It's a *thing*."

Why the hell did he have to sleep on the floor?

***

Spencer shut the door to his office. Flipped the lock.

Haley paced a few feet away. Nerves and tension rolled off her.

He sucked in a breath and caught her sweet scent. *Raspberries and cream.* He'd barely been able to keep his hands off her on the street. Okay, correction, he hadn't kept his hands off her. He'd kissed her, and he wanted to kiss her again. He wanted to get her out of the office and back to his place, but that shit wasn't going to happen.

Because he was pretty sure he had a freaking hitman lurking in his town.

"We aren't after a sniper. From what I can gather, the shots were fired from a standard 9 mm. It's your basic weapon of choice for a lot of folks. That's good for us. A trained sniper would've had a rifle up on that bluff, would have been equipped with a scope, and there is no way his shots would have missed."

She flinched. Paled. "What?"

He wasn't being tactful. At all. Mostly because this wasn't a time for tact. "You were attacked in New York."

"Uh..." She took a few steps toward his desk. Her hand dropped, and her fingers stroked idly over the wooden edge. "I was mugged."

"Bullshit."

Her head whipped up. "Excuse me?"

"You aren't going to lie to me." He stalked toward her. "Not if you want to stay alive. Not if you want me to catch the asshole who was *shooting* at you this morning." The same asshole he suspected of breaking into her cottage.

Her lips firmed. "You don't seem so easy going to me right now."

What was she talking about? "Easy going?"

"Yes, when we first met, you were all slow smiles and southern charm. I think you were trying to Matthew McConaughey me out of my pants—"

He held up one hand. "What?"

"You were deliberately seducing me. You were—"

"If you're saying that I wanted you from the first moment we met, hell, yes, I did."

She gave a slow blink. "That...wasn't what I was saying."

"Fine. It's what I'm saying. I wanted you from the first moment we met. I thought you were the sexiest woman I'd ever seen." He wouldn't lie. "And I never pretended to be someone I wasn't."

She sucked in a breath. "I did that."

"That's not what I meant." He raked a hand through his hair. "Haley—"

"I didn't want to lie." Her voice dropped. "I was trying to put that life behind me."

"What happened in New York? I need to know. Someone was shooting in *my* town this morning. I have to catch the bastard."

She nodded. "It's going to change things, isn't it?"

He had no clue what she meant.

"I understand. I do, really. And I'm so sorry that I brought danger here. I would *never* want anyone else hurt because of me. I don't think of this situation as some kind of game. I swear, I don't. I didn't think I'd be followed. I tried to be so careful. I traveled with cash. Switched buses and trains. Didn't use any credit cards." A faint line dotted her brow. "I don't know how he found me."

"Andrew Bradley." Her asshole of an ex.

A nod. "Drew." A slow exhale. "It has to be Drew. Or one of his men. No one else would care about me."

Not fucking true. Spencer cared. One whole hell of a lot. "You were involved with him."

Spencer recognized the jealousy burning through him. He didn't want to imagine Haley with anyone else. Especially not some fucking jerk who'd hurt her.

"Drew owned a few clubs in the city. That was how we met, you see. He wanted art work for the clubs, and I was the manager at a popular gallery. I helped him to pick out the art, and we hit it off."

He did not like this story, but he'd been the one to demand she tell him everything, so he was damn well going to listen.

"But six months ago, I saw him for the man he really was." Her small hand fisted against the edge of his desk. "The warning signs had been there all along, and I should have heeded them. I was suspicious of his work, of the connections...of the clubs, but he always had such ready, easy answers for me. Always convinced me that I was the one imagining things, that I was the one with too many suspicions. That I didn't trust him enough because of my past."

"He was gas lighting you." Spencer wanted to tear the jerk apart.

"Both of my parents are dead. I tend to...I don't let people get close. But I was tired of being alone, and when I met Drew, I thought...why not just see what happens? I ignored my fears and hesitations. I let him lead me into the dark, and I should have—"

"Stop."

She nodded briskly. "Yes, I should have stopped. I should have gotten the hell away from Drew sooner."

He wanted to see her eyes, but her gaze was directed down to the floor. "Look at me."

She swallowed, but didn't glance up.

"Baby..." He could feel her pain, and he hated it. "Look at me. Please."

Slowly, her gaze lifted.

"Stop blaming yourself, you understand me? I read his file. The guy was a master manipulator from the word go. You don't get to say this shit is your fault. That doesn't happen. From where I'm standing, *you* were the only one who ever got close to sending the sonofabitch to jail."

A broken laugh slipped from her lips. "That didn't work out so well. I realized too late that he had a ton of cops *and* people from the DA's office in his back pocket. Evidence disappeared. The other witness—a waitress at his club—turned up dead. Everything went to hell."

He searched her eyes. "Back up the story for me. When did you realize what a fucking asshole Drew Bradley really was?"

"When I stopped by Shade, his main club, late one night. A new piece of art had come in to my gallery, and I was sure it would be perfect for the place. I had his security code, so I went inside, not thinking a thing about it, not until I heard the voices." She bit her lower lip. "He was working a drug deal. And I'm not talking some small change thing here. He was talking about a million-dollar deal, distributing the stuff at his club. Acting like it was nothing." Haley shook her head. "I took out my phone. I recorded what he was saying. What the men with him were saying. Then I went straight to the police station."

"That took some serious guts."

"I was furious with him. And I hated myself for getting so close to someone like him."

"Baby..."

"My recording was the first piece of evidence to vanish. Not the last. Everything just fell apart, and soon, so did my whole life."

"And you came here." *To me.*

Her lips curled down. "I had to run. It wasn't safe for me in the city anymore, and when I saw your rental online, it just seemed perfect."

He was so grateful that she'd wound up at his place.

"When you trust someone, and the person betrays you so fully, it can rip you apart."

They needed to be clear on this. "Baby, I will never hurt you."

"That's an easy enough line to say." She wet her lower lip. "Drew told me the same thing. He promised he'd never hurt me. Then after the case was dropped, after I thought the nightmare was going away, one of his crew tracked me down just outside of the subway. The guy grabbed my wrist..."

Her fucking bruises.

"And he put a knife to my throat. He told me that if I talked to the cops ever again, he'd make sure I never said a word to anyone."

Rage nearly choked Spencer.

"Oh, God." Her long eyelashes flickered. "You're the cops."

"Haley—"

She pushed against him, and he stepped back. Haley hurriedly put some space between them. "I ran away and I thought I was safe, but if I was followed, if Drew's man saw me...then he saw me talking to the cops. That's why he shot at me. I was warned, and I didn't listen."

"Haley..."

"I should have kept going." She barely breathed the words. "After the break-in at the cottage, I knew that I should leave and not look back. I was in the car, I was driving away." She spun, giving him her back.

Silence filled the room. He wanted to go to her. To put his hands on her shoulders and pull her against him. Instead, Spencer didn't move. "Why didn't you leave?"

"You know."

"Maybe I want to hear the words."

"I ran all the way from New York..."

"And yet the bastard still found you. Don't you see that it doesn't matter how far you go? He *will* keep hunting you." Spencer paused. "*Why didn't you leave Point Hope?*"

"Because I was tired of running." She looked back at him. "And I wanted..." But her words trailed away.

Baby, say it. He needed those words so badly.

"I haven't wanted another man in the six months since I broke up with Drew. Since I realized that the guy I'd fallen for was a monster in a fancy suit. And then I met this new man, and the first thing he did was save me from being run down by elves. Elves." A weak laugh.

I will save you from every threat.

"I wanted you," Haley told him quietly.

Yes. That was what he'd been so desperate to hear.

"I met you and I started to feel something inside again. Something other than fear. You made me laugh. You made me feel safe. And when I kissed you, my toes curled. I know it sounds stupid, but they did."

"Nothing you could say to me would sound stupid." His voice was gruff. Too rough.

"I didn't want to put you in danger." Her gaze held his. "I promise, that is the last thing I wanted. When we were on that beach, and I realized the bullets could hit you, I was terrified."

"How do you think I felt when I saw the blood on your arm?"

She looked down at the bandage. "Barely a scratch."

"Bullshit."

Her head whipped up.

"I should have done a better job of protecting you. Next time, I will."

"This isn't *your* fault."

He was the sheriff. His town. His job. "You're in my town." *You're mine now.* "And I protect what belongs to me."

"I don't belong to you." She turned to fully face him as she wrapped her arms around her stomach. "I shouldn't stay. I shouldn't—"

He had to tell her. Voice tight, he revealed, "Haley, I think a hit has been placed on you."

She blinked.

"Last night, I saw a man watching you while you worked at the bar."

"What?"

"I confronted him, and he told me that he was a US Marshal. That his name was Fenton Callaway and that he'd been helping you in New York."

A quick, negative shake of her head. "I don't know any marshal named Fenton."

"That's because Fenton Callaway isn't a marshal." No way to soften the truth. "I suspect he's a hitman who came to make sure you never turn on Andrew Bradley again."

CHAPTER ELEVEN

"Relax," Spencer told her as his hand brushed carefully along her shoulder. "You are completely safe here."

She was out in the open, at Lane Park, and the lights in the trees were shining, the snow was blowing, kids were making snow angels, and high schoolers were singing Christmas carols. It was supposed to be a festive and fun event, but she was about to lose her mind. "I shouldn't be here."

A hitman. Jesus! A hitman?

"If a hitman is in the area, if he's coming after me, then I could be putting everyone here at risk." She'd tried to tell him that before, over and over, but he'd insisted that she come with him. She kept her voice low as Haley added, "This is a terrible idea."

"I have the park secured. There are deputies patrolling every sector, and I've got some undercover help checking the crowd."

Undercover help?

"I want you at my side," he added. "I feel better when I can keep an eye on you."

"It's not your job to babysit me every moment."

"I don't think of it that way."

She glanced to the left. A hot chocolate station had been set up near the oak tree over there.

"You are safe here. The people in this park are safe." He pointed to the thick trees and then to the brick wall that surrounded the park. "Getting access to this place isn't that easy—especially not with my teams patrolling. This is probably the most secure area in the town."

Her breath slid out. "I just...the kids are safe, aren't they?"

"They are. And so are you." He nodded. "The tree lighting should begin in the next few moments, and then we'll be able to sneak away."

"Uh, the trees are already lit."

"Not the big one."

They were all big. The oaks were massive. They'd probably been there for hundreds of years, and they were most definitely lit.

The high schoolers stopped singing.

A lady in a long, red dress rang a bell.

"She's the librarian, Mrs. Wu. Been a fixture here forever," Spencer murmured.

Mrs. Wu moved to the center of the park. All eyes seemed to be on her. "I know what you all came to see." She smiled. "So without further ado...it's time to illuminate our town's tree!"

Lights flashed on. So many different colored lights flashed on right in the middle of the park. A wide smile curved Haley's lips as she stared at the lights and at the tree that she hadn't even noticed last night because she'd been so distracted by the snow and Spencer.

It was at least a twenty-foot tall Christmas tree, completely decked out. A tree that still grew in the ground and it was absolutely gorgeous.

Haley spun toward him. "You did not show me that tree last night."

He grinned. "I was saving it as a surprise. I know you like big trees...thought it might make you feel more at home."

The snow machines kicked up a notch.

Her gaze darted back to the tree. "It's beautiful."

"Yes. Stunning."

Her head turned toward him. His eyes were on her.

"You...you're talking about the tree."

"Sure, it's pretty, too. You, though, you're stunning."

Her body felt a little warmer. "You are, too. I mean..." Jeez. "Thank you."

That dimple of his slid out, then disappeared. "High school seniors decorate the tree every year. It's a tradition. Mrs. Wu watches them in action, then they do the big reveal for everyone to see."

"Impressive."

"We try." He stepped a little closer to her. "So did it work?"

She couldn't look away from him. "Did what work?"

"Does the place feel more like home to you?"

It was starting to feel more like home than anything else ever had before. Except she didn't think that feeling had to do with the tree or the snow. She thought it might all be due to Spencer.

His radio crackled. He was wearing his sheriff's uniform, and the radio was strapped to his side. He lifted the radio, talked into it quickly, and she heard the response from his deputy that the area was "All clear."

Some of the tension slid from Haley's shoulders. It had truly been one hell of a day. Every time she thought of those gunshots and she thought of how close Spencer had been to being hit...

A shiver slid over her.

"You're cold." He immediately shouldered out of his jacket and slid it around her shoulders.

It wasn't even close to cold out there, but his jacket was cozy and it carried his crisp scent. He pulled the edges closer and smiled down at her. His head started to lower—

The radio crackled again.

"Duty calls," Haley murmured. "I think I'll grab a hot chocolate."

He pulled out his radio again as she headed the few steps over for the hot chocolate. She smiled at the teens manning the booth and slipped a few bills into their donation jar.

Someone bumped lightly into her arm. Haley glanced over.

A woman smiled at her. "I'm so sorry." A little wince. "I think I was overeager for the hot chocolate. Didn't mean to hit you."

"It's fine." Haley reached for her cup. Thanked the teens.

The woman got her hot chocolate as well. "You all really put on a fun show." There was no accent in her voice. "So glad my fiancé convinced me come down here before the holiday."

"It's not my show." Haley glanced at the kids making snow angels. "I'm just visiting, too."

"Well, then it's nice to meet another traveler. I'm Blair." She offered the hand *not* holding the hot chocolate.

"I'm Haley." She gave a quick handshake.

"How long are you in town, Haley?" Blair asked.

Haley hesitated. The woman certainly looked harmless enough, but Haley wasn't exactly feeling the urge to trust strangers. "Not sure." She sipped her hot chocolate.

"I'm only here for a few days. It's nice to meet folks, you know?"

"Um." She took another sip. *I am so damn suspicious.*

Blair laughed. "My fiancé just got involved in a snow ball fight. I'd better go pull him out before all the kids attack him." She inclined her head toward Haley. "It was great to meet you."

"You, too."

Blair hurried away.

Haley tightened her hold on the cup as she watched Blair pull a tall, muscled guy out of a snow ball fight. Well, Blair tried to pull him out.

At the last minute, he turned and nailed her with a snow ball.

Haley laughed. Okay. She'd definitely overreacted. They were simply a couple at the park, having fun. They weren't stalking her or anything like that. She had to get a grip. It was just hard considering—

"We found him."

Spencer's voice was low and grim.

Haley's gaze whipped up to him.

"Titus said our pretend marshal was spotted a few minutes ago. He's down near the town's main pier. Titus is keeping him in sight until I get down there."

"You mean, until *we* get down there."

Spencer blinked. "Uh, no, that's not what I meant—"

"I'm going with you, Spencer." She was adamant on this. "I will stand back, I will let you and Titus do your jobs, but I need to see this man."

His jaw hardened. "I don't fucking want him anywhere near you."

"If he shot at me today, then I want to face him."

"Dammit."

"Please, Spencer."

"You're not going down to the pier. He's probably armed, and I'm not risking a shot hitting you while we take the SOB into custody."

Her heart raced in her chest.

"But you can go to the station. I'll bring him there. Once he's secured—once he's locked down and not a threat—then yes, you can see him." He motioned to a nearby deputy. Then glanced down at her. "I will meet up with you at the station."

She grabbed his arm. "Be careful."

"Always."

***

The sonofabitch tried to run. Why did they always run? Just once, couldn't the bad guy raise his hands and surrender? And make everything one hell of a lot easier? But no, when Spencer called out a warning and told the jerk to freeze, the fake marshal spun and immediately ran.

The fellow wasn't at the town's main pier when Spencer arrived. Instead, he'd been hurrying down the old path that trailed near the small beach. At Spencer's shout, though, the dumbass took off, obviously trying to make it to the shelter of the trees where he thought he might be able to escape.

Not happening.

Spencer ran as fast as he could, and he launched at the perp. His tackle sent them hurtling off the path, and they crashed into the sand. Spencer flipped the man over, and the SOB made his night by trying to take a swing at him.

Spencer dodged the swing and punched back with his own attack. A hard hit that slammed into the guy's jaw and had his head plunging against the sand. Before the idiot could move again, Spencer had his gun aimed at the fellow's forehead. "Hello, Fenton."

"Fuck me." A snarl of frustration.

"No, you're not exactly my type." It was dark on that stretch of beach. Plenty of shadows, plenty of places to hide, and "Fenton" had probably been counting on that fact to avoid detection.

"Get the hell off me!"

"Why'd you run? I believe I told you to freeze, and as a US Marshal, you should understand the importance of following an officer's order."

No response.

"Oh, wait..." Spencer hauled the jerk to his feet and kept the gun aimed the whole time. "You're *not* a US Marshal. You're just an asshole who tried to shoot an unarmed woman this morning."

"What? No, no!" The fool *lunged* away. He tore from Spencer's grasp and ran—

Spencer sighed. And watched as Titus stepped from behind a nearby tree and clotheslined the jackass. The perp slammed straight into Titus's extended arm and fell back down.

Spencer closed in. Now both he and Titus had their guns on the guy.

The man spat out sand.

"You're under arrest," Spencer told him. "You impersonated an officer of the law and you freaking *shot* at—"

"I haven't shot at anyone! Someone stole my gun right out of my motel. I swear it!"

Spencer hauled the man to his feet. "I don't want your bullshit."

"I'm not giving you bullshit!" Sand rained off him as he straightened. "I didn't shoot anyone!"

"Then who the hell did? Who the hell took aim at Haley Quick this morning?"

The guy's mouth dropped open, but he didn't offer up anyone else's name.

"Yeah," Spencer snarled. "That's what I thought. Your ass is getting locked up. *Right now*."

***

"You can't do this shit!" The prisoner grabbed the bars of the holding cell in the sheriff's station. "I have rights! You don't just get to lock me up and—"

"Impersonating a US Marshal is a crime." Spencer had already bagged and tagged the guy's fake ID *and* his real ID. "But then I suspect you know that, don't you, Francis?" Francis, not Fenton. Fenton had just been a BS name.

Francis Callaway tightened his hold on the bars. "Look, so I got a little overzealous with my job! I didn't expect some Podunk sheriff to spot me watching my target in the bar. I needed a cover story."

"Podunk," Titus muttered from his position a few feet away. His back was pressed to the wall, his arms crossed over his chest. "That's just insulting. I happen to think we are fucking *charming*."

Francis cut him a nervous glance, then turned his attention back to Spencer. "Look, you're sleeping with her. I get it. I understand how it all went down. She's hot, you get to score with her, so maybe you started feeling all possessive and you got a little crazy—"

Spencer took a step toward the cell.

Titus let out a low whistle. "Oh, first you insult his hometown, now you say shit about his girl. You keep on, and you're going to dig yourself a hole so deep you will *never* come out."

Spencer didn't look away from the perp. "He's already done that. He got in too deep the minute he shot at Haley."

"No!" Francis jerked his hands back and made a quick time-out gesture.

A friggin' time-out sign? Seriously? Were they playing a game?

"I didn't shoot anyone, I told you that already! I was hired to find her when she split from New York. To tail her. That was all!"

Like Spencer bought his story.

There was a knock at the door behind him. Titus moved to open it, and a few moments later, Haley was rushing toward Spencer. No, toward the cell.

He put out his hand, stopping her. "Don't get too close to the perp."

"I-I don't know him."

Spencer glanced over at Haley. She'd tilted her head and narrowed her eyes on the prisoner.

"He's not the one who attacked you back in New York?" Spencer asked.

"Attacked?" Francis backed up a step. "I haven't attacked anyone! I'm a PI! I was hired—"

"To stalk her. Yes, you already admitted that shit," Spencer snapped back. "But you didn't tell us *who* hired you."

Francis clamped his lips together.

"He is *not* seriously doing that shit," Titus announced. "He's not covering up for his boss when he's facing an attempted murder charge? Tell me he's not that stupid."

Francis wasn't talking.

"He's that stupid," Spencer announced.

Francis shook his head. "I give my client's confidentiality! And I haven't shot *anyone!* I'm not a killer! I'm a PI!"

"You're a creep." Spencer had seen his type before. "You stalked Haley and you ran back to your boss, Drew Bradley, and you told him exactly where to find her."

Haley pressed close to Spencer. With her gaze on the prisoner, she demanded, "Did you tell Drew where I was?"

Francis wouldn't look at her. "I want a lawyer. Even in Podunk places like this, you get lawyers. And phone calls. I want my phone call."

"Fine. We'll get you a lawyer. He'll be here first thing tomorrow." Spencer caught Haley's hand in his and turned away from the prisoner. "Have a good night, Francis."

"You aren't *leaving* me here!"

Spencer didn't look back at him. "Deputies will be on duty out front. I'll make sure one brings you a phone. Sweet dreams."

"There's a fucking toilet in the corner of the cell!"

"Yes, you're welcome."

"I'm not a criminal! I didn't do anything wrong! I'm just doing my job and I'm—"

Spencer sighed. "Impersonating a marshal?" He glanced over his shoulder. "Stalking a woman? And if you didn't pull the trigger on the gun this morning, then you were still damn well involved if *you* told Drew Bradley where to find her."

And there it was. Pay dirt. He saw Francis blanch.

"You did. You told him." Spencer shook his head. "Yeah, you're gonna need a lawyer." His hold tightened on Haley's hand. "Let's go."

Instead of leaving, she pulled away from him and marched toward the bars. "Drew is a criminal. You were working for him? You told him I was here?"

Francis wrinkled his face. "Lady, I was doing my job. Some guy said his girlfriend left him and she took some valuables with her. Simple story. How was I supposed to know it was a lie?"

"If you're any kind of PI," Spencer growled back, "then you know. You would have done some recon work on your client."

Francis swallowed.

"Or...maybe he's not a new client." Spencer considered this angle.

"That's what I was thinking," Titus added, voice flat. "Maybe our Francis is the Bradley bastard's go-to guy when trouble comes up. Maybe Francis here is neck deep in Drew Bradley's dirty business."

"I am *not!*" Francis was sweating. "I was only doing this one job. He pays well, okay? I got an ex-wife and alimony, and it was just a simple tail gig." His gaze darted to Haley. "I followed you, and I reported it. *That's all.* How many times do I have to say it? He didn't even want me to make contact with you. Just wanted me to keep an eye on you until—"

Now he stopped. Figured.

Titus shoved away from the wall. "Keep an eye on her until—*what?*"

"I am not a hitman! Okay? I'm not! I'm a PI, but I am not about to cross Drew Bradley." Francis swiped his hand over his sweaty forehead. "You know what happens when you do that shit?"

It was Haley who answered. "Someone tries to shoot you on a beach."

Francis made another swipe over his forehead. "Guy said he loved you. Okay? *Love.* So maybe it's not even him. Maybe he's trying to keep you safe, but people who are his enemies are closing in. Huh. What about that? Did you think about that?"

Spencer thought he was looking at a jackass. "Andrew told you to watch her until he arrived in Point Hope." It made sense.

And the widening of Francis's beady eyes told him that he was right. Sonofabitch.

"No!" Francis gave a vehement shake of his head. "No, man, I did *not* say that! I did not—"

"You didn't have to," Titus groused. "Shit was obvious on your face."

It was time for Spencer to give Francis something new to worry about. "Bet your boss will be pissed that you gave him up so easily."

"Seriously pissed," Titus agreed.

Haley stiffened.

"What? No, man, no, I didn't give him—" Realization dawned. "Oh, fuck me. You're gonna let him believe that shit? Can you even do that?"

Spencer smiled at him. "Sweet dreams."

He and Haley headed for the door. She kept glancing back over her shoulder.

"I didn't shoot at you, lady!" For someone who'd asked for a lawyer, the fellow was certainly being talkative as all hell. "Last night, I crashed in a motel—"

"We checked your motel this morning. You weren't there." Titus sounded annoyed.

"Yeah, not that one. That was total BS." He rattled off a name and an address. "I was in my room, ordering movies, and you know they put that shit on the bill. I had me a movie marathon last night, and you can check it out."

Great. The guy's alibi was that he'd been in his motel room watching porn.

"I'm not a killer! Shit, I wanted to cut out of this town, but I was told to wait for...for my boss to arrive. Okay? He just wanted me to keep eyes on the area until he could get here."

Haley's worried stare met Spencer's. "Drew is coming here?"

He might already be there. Slowly, Spencer turned and shook his head at the fool in the cell. "Don't you get it? He was going to pin it on you."

Francis rocked forward. "What are you talking about?"

"Her death would look suspicious. You get that, right? He told you to stay here because he was going to let you be the fall guy. He was setting you up for her murder." Spencer let that sink in, then added, "And we'll be sure to get you that phone call. Maybe you want to call your boss and tell him that I'm coming for him. I'm not going to stop until he's the one behind bars."

A rough and nervous laugh choked from Francis. "Good luck with that."

"I don't need luck. The bastard is going down and that's a promise."

He headed out with Haley, and Titus followed right behind him. When they were away from the holding area, Titus asked, "Think he'll be dumb enough to actually call his boss?"

"He damn well might be."

CHAPTER TWELVE

"I want to come inside, Haley."

She stood on the cottage's small porch, looking far too delicate and, dammit, breakable, as the lights near the door fell on her.

"Let me check out the cottage. I need to be sure everything is okay in there."

Haley gave a slow nod, sending her hair bobbing. "That's why you want to come in? To protect and serve?" She turned away and unlocked the door.

He followed her in and locked the door. He watched as she reset the alarm system, and then told her, "That's not the only reason. I want to fuck you, but I figured I shouldn't lead with that."

Haley swung toward him.

Okay. He probably should have worded that differently. Maybe used more tact, but—

She'd been dead silent on the ride home. Silent since they'd left that piece of shit jerk in the cell. Her silence was making him nervous. "Haley..."

"Do you really think Drew Bradley is going to personally try and kill me?"

Unfortunately... "Yes, I do." It was a possibility he couldn't ignore. Spencer had learned more about her ex that day. Off the books info that he'd gotten from Eric Wilde, and Spencer had discovered how twisted Drew Bradley's world truly was.

"He sent a goon after me in New York. Why not just send someone else now? I mean, maybe that PI is lying, maybe he was the one who pulled the trigger and maybe—" She stopped. Sucked in a deep breath.

"I already had a deputy check at the motel—Francis was watching his movies. Or *someone* was in the room ordering them. It's hardly an ironclad alibi, but the man seemed legitimately spooked at the idea he might be facing an attempted murder charge." Spooked. Stunned. Spencer was betting that after a night in the cell, Francis would want to cooperate.

Or maybe not. It depended on how much Francis feared Drew Bradley.

He let out a low sigh. "I want to check the cottage. Will you give me a few minutes?"

She nodded.

He hurried through the rooms. Checked under the bed. In the closet. Studied the windows and the locks, making sure nothing had been tampered with while they were gone.

Then he went back to her. Haley still stood in the middle of the den. Her head was tilted forward. She looked so fragile, and he hated that. He reached for her arm, and his fingers skimmed over the skin near her bandage. "I should have done a better job of taking care of you. I won't screw up again."

"I should have done a better job of staying away from you." Her chin lifted. "I won't screw up again."

Oh, hell, no. He did *not* like where this was going. "Haley..."

"You could have been shot today."

"I'm a sheriff. I could get shot *every* day."

Horror flashed in her eyes. Obviously, that had been the wrong thing to say. Very wrong. "What I meant..." He backtracked. "Risk is part of the job. Even if you and I weren't personally involved, I'd still protect you. That's what I do."

"You also keep secrets."

So do you, sweetheart. But he'd known this was coming. "I didn't tell you about the fake marshal last night—"

"Because you didn't think I'd fuck you?"

Tread very carefully. "Because I wanted you to tell me the truth on your own. I wanted you to trust me enough to do that. I also didn't buy his story, and I was looking for proof before I did *anything* else."

"I do."

She did...what?

"I do trust you." Her hands twisted in front of her. "That's why I'm still here. That's why I wanted you last night. I trust you, even though we just met, and I'm scared to death that I'm making another mistake."

"I'm not a mistake." The last thing he wanted to do was scare her away.

"I don't want you hurt." Her voice had gone softer. "I don't want you shot. I don't care if you're the sheriff or not, promise me that you won't get hurt because you're trying to keep me safe."

He was not going to make that promise. "I want to catch the bastard."

Her lashes fluttered.

"I believe he's in the area, Haley. I think he came down here for you. I want to catch him, and I want to lock him up."

"I tried that. It failed. He had the cops on his side. He had—"

"Because he was playing on his home turf. He's a long way from home down here. And I can promise you, he's not going to have me in his pocket. I will catch him, and we'll nail his ass. We've already collected evidence from the shooting on the bluff. We're lining up the pieces, and we will put him away." Then she wouldn't have to be afraid. Then she wouldn't have to run. "Give me a chance to do my job. I've got all eyes in the area hunting for this man."

"But what if it's not Drew? What if it's someone else he's sent for me? It could be a killer for hire. It could be anyone."

Yes, it could be, but... "According to Wilde Securities—"

"Wait, back up. Who is Wilde? Wilde Securities? I don't understand..." Her brows scrunched.

"Back when I was a SEAL, I met a guy named Eric Wilde. Eric could do nearly anything with tech, and it was his tech that helped to save my team when things went to hell around us."

Her eyes darkened.

"When I got stateside again, Eric was setting up his business, Wilde Securities. He normally guards the rich and famous, but he's got tech in basically every house in the world these days. He invented a security system that made him millions. The US government uses him, criminals are terrified of him, and there is no secret that he can't discover."

She nodded. "I see. So when the PI came to you last night, you sent Eric after my secrets."

Fuck it. "Yes."

She flinched.

He wanted to touch her so badly. Instead, he fisted his hands. "I asked Eric to dig into the life of US Marshal Fenton Callaway and Andrew Bradley. You were tied to them, so I knew he'd have to research you. I couldn't protect you without looking at them."

"And he found out that Fenton was a fake."

"He did. He also found out that Andrew Bradley is supposedly on a trip to LA, but when Eric dug more, he learned that the guy never checked into his LA hotel. At least, not personally. He had a virtual check-in. No one at the hotel has actually seen him. He went off the grid. The timing of that is too coincidental for me. I think he's trying to set up a cover story. I don't think he's in Los Angeles. I think he's here."

"To kill me."

"It's not happening." A hard vow.

"So you know all my secrets."

"No, baby, I don't know everything." He had the feeling he could spend the next twenty years with her, and she'd still surprise him.

"What happens now?"

It was late as hell and she probably wanted to crash. He stepped back. "I can sleep on your couch, if you don't want to be alone. Or if you don't want me here, I can go to the main house. The security system I had installed here is top notch, I swear. You'll be safe."

She stared at him. "I thought you said you wanted to fuck me."

Only every minute of the day and night. "Absolutely, but I was trying to be a gentleman and not—"

She kissed him. Grabbed his shoulders and pulled him toward her. *Hell, yes. Hell. Yes.* He locked his arms around her and drank her in. His mouth was rough and hungry on hers. Too demanding. But he couldn't hold back. He really had been trying to play the gentleman and give her space, but if she wanted him, he wasn't going to be a fool. He was going to hold on tight.

And never let go.

"I don't want you on the couch," she said against his mouth. "I want you in bed. I want you with me."

That was the number one spot he wanted to be in, too. A thousand times, yes.

He backed her up and took her mouth again. He nipped her lower lip and fucking loved the way she moaned.

Her shoulders hit the wall and her hips arched against him. He wanted more, so he lifted her up, holding her between his body and the wall. Her jeans were in the way. He wanted her against his cock. Wanted her silken skin against him.

He rocked against her, and she rode his cock through her jeans and his uniform. She kissed a path along his jaw, her lips feathering over the stubble on him. Then she put her mouth on his throat. Licked right along his pulse.

"Fuck." He carried her to the bedroom. Stripped in record time and then pulled off her jeans and shoes and left her in her shirt and underwear.

She smiled up at him. God, he would never get used to the sight of her smile. She caught the edges of her shirt and hauled it over her head. He hadn't wanted to move the shirt because he hadn't wanted to risk hurting her stitches.

She crouched on the bed, clad in her underwear, her body making his mouth water, and for a moment, he could only stare at her.

"I think that means it's my move." She slid to the edge of the bed. Put her hands on his hips. And then put her mouth on his cock.

Pleasure surged through him. Her mouth was hot and tight, her tongue knew just how to lick, she sucked and teased and—

He lost his control. It shattered as he pulled her away from his cock and tumbled her back on the bed. He knew he should be going slower. He knew he should be using more care. But he kissed her like a man possessed. His hands slid over her body, caressing and stroking. He wanted to touch every single inch of her. Wanted to have her moaning and screaming.

His hands pushed her thighs apart. His fingers dipped between her legs. Drove deep. Over and over and she cried out his name.

Not enough.

He grabbed for a condom. Ripped open the packet, rolled it on, and shoved his cock toward the entrance to her body.

"Now, Spence! Now!"

He plunged inside of her. She arched off the bed. He fucking touched heaven. He pulled back, thrust again. The bed pounded into the wall as he took and took and took.

She came once, a fast, hard release that squeezed his cock and made him even crazier. He pumped harder, faster, and grabbed her legs, looping them over his shoulders.

He was in a frenzy, needing her so much.

Spencer drover deep into her. Hard. God, she felt so fucking good. He kissed her. He was lost and obsessed. Consumed by his need for her.

She came again, buckling beneath him. Her body quivered, and the contractions of her sex sent him crashing into oblivion. The release was freaking amazing. It went on and on, and his breath heaved out as he rode the orgasm.

When it was done, he braced his body on his arms and stared down at her. His heart drummed madly in his chest. There were a million things he wanted to say to her, but he couldn't speak.

Her hand lifted and her fingers trailed across the stubble on his cheek. "Will you stay here with me tonight?"

He would do anything for her. And the truth of that was rather staggering. He withdrew, took a moment to ditch the condom before he went back to her, then Spencer slid under the covers and pulled her against him. He'd killed the lights, but the darkness seemed warm and comforting around him. Truth be told, he'd always liked the dark.

"Spencer, can I ask you something?" Her voice was low and hesitant. Husky.

"Anything." It was time for her to learn his secrets. He'd willingly share them with her.

"You were shot, weren't you?"

He'd known that, sooner or later, she'd ask about the marks on him. Since they'd pretty much seen every inch of each other's bodies, it would be hard for her to miss the scars he carried. "Three times."

She inhaled sharply and stiffened against him.

"Baby, it doesn't matter." He pressed a kiss to her temple. "I'm fine." There wasn't any sense telling her about how he'd once lain, covered in his own blood, choking on sand as it battered his mouth and he struggled to crawl forward and escape the enemy. His nightmare. She didn't need to—

"It matters to me." She turned in his arms. Her fingers went to the first scar. Lightly traced it. "I'm sorry that you were in pain."

He swallowed, wondering where the hell that weird lump in his throat had come from.

She slid down and pressed a kiss to one of his scars.

"Haley, you don't have to—"

She rose, sitting beside him and letting the covers fall. "I don't want you to have another scar because you decided to jump between me and a bullet."

He tensed.

"I don't want you doing that. Please promise me that you won't."

That was a promise he wasn't going to make. If she was in danger, hell, yes, he'd do anything necessary to protect her.

"And do *not* dare tell me that you're the sheriff and it's your job."

His lips curved. "It *is* kind of my job." Did she realize that her fingers were still lightly caressing one of the old scars? Such a gentle touch.

"Your job isn't to get hurt for me." She stopped touching him. Pulled back. Turned away as if she'd climb from the bed. "Maybe I should leave. I swear, I don't want to put you or anyone else in this town at risk and I—*Spence!*"

He'd grabbed her—being careful with her wrist—and tumbled her back into the bed. He caged her beneath his body. "No," he said simply although there was nothing simple about the way he suddenly felt. The idea of her skipping town, of her being out there alone while some bastard was trying to shoot at her... "*Hell, no.*"

She was stiff and wary beneath him.

"You don't have to face everything alone." *Not anymore. Not ever again.* "Running isn't the answer. Running makes you more of a target. You stay here, and you have protection. You have strength."

"And I can't have you getting killed because of me—"

He kissed her. A long, deep kiss. He would never, ever get enough of her mouth. "Baby, don't you get it? I'm not going to be killed or hurt. I'll be the one doing the hurting." His head raised. "I was shot three times on a mission that went straight to hell. I was ambushed by four men who were supposed to be there to provide aid to me and my team. I made it out of that desert. My attackers didn't." He smiled down at her. "But I've got to say, I love it that you're worried about me. That shit is sexy."

A startled laugh escaped her. He loved her laugh. It was warm and light, and it wrapped around him, and he just had to lower his head and kiss her mouth once more. Or a few times more.

Then he had to nuzzle her neck.

She gasped beneath his mouth and arched up toward him. Her hands closed around his shoulders and pulled him closer.

But then...

She pushed against him. "If anything happens to you, I am going to be severely pissed off."

"It's because you like me," he tried to tease her.

"I do like you." Her voice was serious. "And you won't be hurt."

"Hell, no, baby, like I said, I'll do the hurting..." He brought his mouth close to hers once more. "No one will touch you. You don't have a single thing to fear." He kissed her.

I'll be here for you, and I will stop any threat that comes your way.

***

He was in a freaking Podunk jail, and he was about to be railroaded for shit he hadn't done.

Francis glowered at the bars. The cot was a lumpy nightmare, so there was no way he'd get any sleep. He'd tossed and he'd turned, and he'd yelled for the deputies to help him.

They'd brought him a late-night snack. They'd given him his phone call—and, hell, yeah, he'd tried to call Andrew Bradley. That guy was his most powerful client, and he wanted Drew to get his ass out of that jail.

But Drew hadn't answered. In fact, the call had gone to a disconnected number. What was up with that shit?

So Francis stayed in his cell. He sat and he raged and he realized that he might very well be screwed. Mostly because...shit, he *had* broken into Haley Quick's little rental place on the bay. He'd gone inside to check the scene. To make sure he'd found the right woman. And *maybe* he'd been looking to score some cash and jewelry, but that dream had died a swift death when he'd only found clothes and some toiletries at her place.

When Drew had come to Francis, demanding that he track Haley, the guy had said, "She took something important from me. She doesn't get to do that. I want to know exactly where she is."

Francis had thought that "something important" had to refer to a big haul. Maybe Haley had stolen jewelry or cash and Drew was pissed about her theft. So *maybe* Francis had thought he could steal whatever she'd taken and sneak out of town...

Only nothing of real value had been in her place.

Andrew had lied to him, obviously. Now Francis was worried that maybe the small-town sheriff was right. Perhaps the big boss was setting him up to take the fall. It infuriated Francis that he'd helped to make the set-up happen.

I might have left evidence in the rental place. I tried to be careful, I wore gloves, but what if I left something behind?

Fuck, fuck, fuck!

The door to holding opened. Every time the door opened, the hinges groaned like an old man.

Francis stiffened and surged to his feet. "I want another phone call!" Okay, technically, he'd already had two.

The first had gone to Drew. A waste.

Then he'd called his ex-wife. Marsha hadn't answered him, either. And that was weird because the woman always answered the phone. She was pretty much fanatical about answering a ringing phone. He'd seen her actually get twitchy when he'd once told her to ignore a telemarketer.

Footsteps shuffled closer.

"Listen, I want out of this cell. Go get the sheriff. I'll...I'll tell him what I know, but it's not a lot, man, I swear, I was honest earlier with him—"

"Were you?"

Francis blinked. He wasn't looking at the young deputy who'd brought him a granola bar when Francis had been moaning about hunger.

The man before him wore a black ski mask. *Oh, shit.* "How'd you get back here?" He edged away from the bars.

A shrug.

His heart was jerking hard in his chest.

The fellow yanked off the ski mask. "Just how 'honest' were you, Francis?"

Fucking hell. He swiped his hand over his brow. "Look, I didn't know you were down here. Haley Quick is involved with the sheriff, and this whole scene is about to get *bad.*"

A nod. "You're right." He headed toward the cell. He had *keys* in his hand. How had he gotten keys?

He unlocked the cell. Motioned for Francis to come out.

Francis didn't move. "If I'm not here when they come back to check on me, every cop or deputy in the area will be hunting for me."

Another nod. "Absolutely. So you'd better hurry."

Francis choked on a rough, nervous laugh. "I'm not gonna be a wanted man. I mean, sure, I've done some...slightly shady things but I'm not—" He broke off when he saw the gun. The gun that was pointed straight at him.

"We have five minutes. Get your ass out of that cell and get moving." A smile. "Or I will shoot you right here."

Francis got his ass out of the cell.

CHAPTER THIRTEEN

"We have a problem."

That wasn't what a woman liked to hear first thing in the morning. Only...it wasn't morning. It was still night. She could see the darkness beyond her window.

Spencer was already dressed in his uniform, and he stood at the foot of her bed. She frowned because she hadn't even heard him get out of bed, much less put on his clothes. And, yes, he looked sexy hot in his uniform with the stubble on his hard jaw and his glittering eyes all focused on her, but...

His words sank in. "Problem?" Haley sat up, pulling the sheet with her. He was dressed. She was naked.

His gaze dipped. Heated.

She held the sheet a bit tighter to her breasts. "What kind of problem?"

"Cody was attacked at the station."

"What?"

"There was another deputy on duty with him, but the guy had stepped out for a minute. Cody was hit hard from behind, and he woke up to find that Francis's cell was open." A pause. "Francis was gone."

She could feel her skin icing. "Is your deputy going to be all right?"

"He's at the hospital now. Docs say he has a concussion." His lips tightened. "Titus is with him—he's the one who called me and told me what the hell was happening. Cody didn't get a look at his attacker. Didn't see Francis get out. Didn't see a damn thing."

"Wh-what about the other deputy?"

"Geno didn't see anything, either. When he came back to the station, he found Cody on the floor." Anger roughened his words. "I've got an APB out for Francis now. He has a lead on us, but we're going to find him."

There was more. She could feel it. "What aren't you telling me?"

"Francis had help on his escape. We have security cameras at the station. The 'help' who broke in...when he entered, he was wearing a ski mask. So we didn't get a clear image of him. We can't ID the bastard."

"You...you had thought that Andrew was here."

"Yes."

"No." She shook her head. "I mean, Drew wouldn't take a risk like this. He wouldn't *walk* into a sheriff's station and assault a deputy. He's not going to get his hands dirty like that."

"The guy has been getting away with shit for years. Maybe he thinks he's a freaking god. Arrogance can bring down anyone." He rolled back his shoulders. "We've got other security cameras in the area—especially out on the streets. They're being reviewed so we can find out where the hell those two went. Until then..."

She felt far too vulnerable as she stared at him.

"Until then, I think you need a guard on you."

Her mouth was dry. "Your deputies can hardly give me twenty-four seven protection."

He glanced away.

Uh, oh... "Spencer?" She slid from the bed. Wrapped the sheet around her and headed for him. "What have you done?"

A wince. "Okay, in my defense..."

"Nothing that begins that way is ever good."

"I just want you safe."

She waited.

"So, I forgot to mention that Eric Wilde sent two of his agents down here to help keep an eye on things."

"You didn't forget anything."

"Remember at the tree lighting when I told you I had folks undercover?"

A cautious nod.

"Andrew Bradley is a high-level crime lord who needs to be stopped."

And I dated him and now my life has gone to hell.

"I wanted extra eyes in town. I needed skilled agents that I could trust. My deputies are good. Hell, Titus is far more than a deputy. He's the man I want at my side in *any* firefight. We served together overseas, and every day I'm grateful that he's working to keep this town safe." A pause. "But the others are young, a bit too green, and they aren't necessarily up to the level I'd like when dealing with someone like your ex. It pays to have additional help, and the Wilde agents have been thoroughly trained and vetted. I wanted undercover eyes in the area, so I kept their presence secret."

"Okay."

"I know I should have told you, but I was trying to make sure they kept a low profile and—" His gaze sharpened on her. "You just said okay?"

"Yes. Okay. Okay as in…I get it." She did. "A deputy was assaulted. I was shot at. Now we're talking a jail escape. We need extra manpower, and I'm glad they are here." She huffed out a breath. "Tell me what I can do. I want to be able to help and not just hide."

His expression warmed. "I have to go down to the station. I need to be leading the manhunt. The Wilde agents are going to stay close and keep an eye on you. You will be safe."

That was awesome. Seriously. Awesome. But had he missed the part about… "I don't want to just hide."

"It's the middle of the night. You can't do much right now. And, hell, maybe by dawn, we'll have Francis in custody again."

Francis...and the man who'd helped him escape.

Spencer leaned down and pressed a quick kiss to her lips. "I need you safe."

Yes, she definitely wanted to be safe. That was a wonderful way to live. But... "You stay safe, too."

He gave her his slow smile. "Always."

It was the second time he'd said that to her when she asked him to be safe. Hearing the word again caused a little pang in her heart. A few moments later, he was gone, and she was alone in the cottage.

She'd never been more aware of the how heavy silence could be until that moment. Heavy and suffocating.

She didn't go back to sleep.

***

There was a quick knock on the cottage door.

Haley frowned and took a few quick steps toward the door. It was nearing nine o'clock, and she hadn't heard back from Spencer yet. She was pretty much going stir crazy as she waited to see what would happen.

Nothing has happened so far. Just me hiding.

She peeked through the window near the door and saw—wait, was that Blair? Yes, it was definitely the brunette that she'd met the night before, and Blair's fiancé stood a few feet behind her.

Blair caught her peeking out and waved happily at her.

Haley stepped back.

The knock came again.

How the hell had Blair found out where she was staying? Haley grabbed her phone and called Spencer. She'd programmed him into her phone the night before, and he answered her on the second ring.

"Okay, the couple I met last night at the park—they are at my door right now." She spoke quickly. Probably too quickly. "This is making me nervous as hell because how did they know where I was? What if they're working for Drew? What if—"

"They're working for me," he revealed quietly. "They're Wilde. You can let them in. It's okay."

She didn't move to let them in.

In the background, she heard some sort of announcement—kind of like a doctor being paged. Was he at the hospital?

"I told them to show you their identification. I should have called you first. I'm sorry."

"Yes, a call would have been good. It would have prevented a heart attack." She put a hand to her chest where her heart frantically raced. "I'm guessing you haven't found Francis yet?"

"No, but I'm heading in to talk with Cody right now. I want to make sure there is no detail he's overlooked about the attack."

Yes, great plan.

"I'll be back with you soon," he promised her.

She put down her phone and unlocked the door.

Blair beamed at her. "Haley!" She threw her arms around Haley and pulled her in for a big hug. "We're Wilde agents, and we're here to keep you safe," she whispered. "I have my ID in my pocket, and I can show it to you—"

Haley pulled back and kept a smile on her face. "I just spoke to Spencer." Her gaze darted to Blair's fiancé. She couldn't remember his name. Had she even been told his name? Everything was so jumbled. "He told me you'd be stopping by." She waved them in. "Come inside."

They slowly headed inside.

She bolted the door behind them. Then spun around. "What in the hell is happening?"

They'd both lost their smiles.

"You never know when someone's watching," Blair's fiancé told her. "Always good to keep an act in place."

"Who are you?" Haley demanded.

Blair blinked. "I'm Blair. This is my partner, Linc. I gave you my real name last night. I try to be as real as possible with people." She took a step away from Linc. "We're just definitely, definitely not engaged."

"You should be so lucky." Linc winked at Blair. Then he sobered when he focused back on Haley. "You're in good hands. You don't have a single thing to worry about."

She nodded. Waited a bit. Nothing else was said. So she had to ask, "Are you crazy?"

Linc's brow furrowed.

"My ex is a crime boss with connections to plenty of dirty cops. I was *shot* at recently. The guy who tailed me from New York—and the man possibly behind the shooting—escaped from a jail cell."

Linc nodded. "Yes, all true."

She fought the insane urge to scream. "I know it's true, and I know that means I have *lots* of things to worry about."

Now he winced. "I was trying to be comforting."

"I told you," Blair muttered, "you don't do that well. You're supposed to leave the comforting parts to me."

His mouth hardened.

Haley stalked past them. "I have to do something."

"Staying alive is something," Linc immediately assured her. "Staying alive is something very, very important. And with a guy like Bradley after you, staying alive can be tricky."

She spun and gaped at him.

"Again..." A sigh from Blair. "Another of your less-than-strong areas. Tact. *Tact.*"

"I am the most tactful person I know," Linc boasted as his hand lifted. He pointed at Haley. "You stay alive, then the bad guy loses. That is the most important thing here, don't you get that? If you die, then the sheriff will probably flip the hell out and your crime boss ex will get killed."

What? Her gaze darted to Blair. She'd rather deal with Blair than Linc.

Blair gave her a hesitant smile. "Hi. Can we start over?"

"My head is hurting."

"Totally understandable given the circumstances, but you have nothing to worry about. Like, literally, zero worries. Linc and I are very good at our jobs."

"I've protected a crown prince," Linc revealed in a stage whisper. "Half the country hated him. I made sure he kept breathing."

"Fabulous." Haley didn't look away from Blair. "What am I supposed to do? Just stay locked up in this cottage?"

Linc and Blair shared a long look. "Well, as to that..." Blair cleared her throat. "Linc has a plan he wanted to run by you."

"Okay. Good. Now that's something." She squared her shoulders. "What's the plan?"

"I think you need to go to a remote, deserted spot," Linc announced.

Blair pressed her lips together.

"And wait for the bad guy to come and get you," he concluded.

Silence. All thick and heavy and suffocating.

Linc rocked forward onto the balls of his feet. "What do you think of that?"

"I think I'd like to see proof that you're Wilde agents." She motioned toward them. "IDs, badges, whatever you've got."

"We don't have badges." He looked offended. "We're not cops. We're part of the best security firm on the East Coast." He handed her his ID.

So did Blair.

She scanned them. "The best security on the East Coast wants me to go to a deserted, secluded area...and wait for the bad guy to come and kill me?" Haley looked up. "Am I following along correctly? Getting all the details in order?"

"Oh, no, no, no." Linc took his ID back from her. Tucked it into the back pocket of his jeans. When he moved his arm, his jacket parted, and she saw his shoulder holster and gun. "You're not going to die. We don't get paid if you die."

Blair squeezed her eyes closed. "That crap is not funny. Tact, Linc, tact."

He sniffed. "A deserted area means that no civilians will get drawn into the crossfire. Seclusion means we can set up a controlled environment so that we're ready when the bad guy approaches."

Wait... "You're talking about setting a trap?"

He flashed a killer grin. "That is exactly what I'm talking about." He nodded approvingly. "See, I know you're brave enough to do this. You turned the guy in back when you were living in New York, didn't you? Ran right to the cops with your evidence. That takes balls. Big ones."

She frowned at him.

"So I figure you'll be up for this challenge. You'll want to stop the bad guy before any of the innocent locals get drawn into the crossfire. We take you to a secluded spot—by the way, I already have it picked out, there's a Christmas tree farm about ten miles from here that is shut down and will be *perfect*—and we wait for the bad guy to make our holiday by stepping straight into our trap."

Haley glanced over at Blair. "Is he serious?"

"He is, but there is no way—no way in the world—that Spence will go for this plan." She tossed a glower at Linc. "As I have told him three times already. Spence isn't just going to let his girlfriend waltz into the sights of the shooter. He wants her locked down and safe. He doesn't want her to be target practice for the bad guy." A wince. "And since Spence is paying the bills…"

"Wait!" Haley held up her hand. "Spencer is paying you to protect me?"

"Well, sure." Linc strolled around the den and started poking at various things. "Not like Wilde Securities is free. I mean, you want the best, you pay for the best."

Her temples throbbed. "You'll send the bill to me."

He stopped poking and glanced at her. "It's a really high bill, and your boyfriend has the cash to handle it. No big deal."

The throbbing got worse.

"I mean, dude is rolling in the dough. Old family money and shit. Seriously, don't worry about it." Linc waved away her concerns.

She wasn't waving away anything. "You're sending me the bill. I'll pay it. I can do it on installments or something." She didn't have old family money, but she had pride. She was paying her own bills.

"Of course…" Linc's voice was way too casual. "If we set our trap, you won't need protection any longer because we'll catch the bad guy and you'll be safe."

"You think I don't see you trying to manipulate me?"

He blinked, all innocence. There was nothing innocent about him. He was like six-foot-two and one hundred eighty pounds of manipulation.

"Look, buddy." She marched toward him and jabbed him in the chest with her index finger. "I don't buy the smile and the scruffy good looks. I don't go for that type."

He looked down at her finger. "What is your type?" His gaze lifted. "Let me guess...it's tall, dark and dangerous? A SEAL who gets off on adrenaline even while he craves a stable home and family 'cause he never really had that growing up?"

Her eyes narrowed.

"Linc," Blair cut in. "Watch your ass. Shit that I tell you in confidence isn't to be shared."

"Um. Sorry." But he didn't sound it. "Blair knows him, you see. He was almost her partner before she got saddled with me. I got her to spill the deets to me over coffee. Your guy is all about the danger. He hides it, though, with a slow drawling voice and that friendly sheriff veneer. Look past it, and you'll see you've got a very dangerous new lover." He considered that. "Though I suppose your last lover was dangerous, too. Hmmm. You know what? I *do* think you have a type."

"And I think you're trying to push me. It's almost cute."

His lips started to curve—

"Almost," she snapped. "But I don't like being manipulated. I had far more than enough manipulation when I was with Drew. You want my cooperation? Then you talk straight with me. You don't try to play games." Her hand dropped. She focused on Blair. "You think a trap will work?"

After a moment, Blair nodded. "It's obvious that you're the guy's target. I mean, he did try to shoot you."

"And if I'm in the open, you and your partner can keep me safe?"

Another nod. "It's our job. As I said, we're very good at our jobs. Even if one of us…" Her gaze cut to Linc before she added, "Can be a little hard to manage."

Haley still wasn't on board. "How do we know the bad guy will come for me? I mean, I could just go to the tree farm and stand there for hours."

"You could," Blair agreed. "And in that case, you've wasted an afternoon. Nothing more. But Linc and I think you're being watched. We think the attacker is waiting for a moment of weakness in order to strike, so if we give him that moment of weakness…"

"He'll come in." Her mind clicked through the possibilities. Options. There actually weren't many. "How does it work? I mean, what's the exact plan?"

Blair and Linc shared another long look. They seemed to do that a lot. A whole silent communication thing. Then Blair said, "You and I will head to the tree farm. They aren't selling trees so no one will be there, but you and I can act like we're tourists taking some pics. I've already put down that cover story in town. Linc will tail behind us. He'll make sure he's not seen but that he's in position. I know, I know, he can be a *lot* to handle, but the man is good at his job."

"I appreciate that," Linc responded. "You're a lot, too, but I love you."

Blair's eyes widened. "He…doesn't mean that." Her cheeks flushed a bit. "We're not…not involved. You can trust us. Linc will stay out of sight until we need him. We'll get the attacker, and—"

"You can be back to watching your sheriff singing karaoke at the local bar by nightfall." Linc appeared expectant as he waited on her.

If only things could really work out that easily. But...

What did she have to lose?

Um, my life. If she got shot. If the bad guy fired at her again. If—

"Oh, did I mention we came bearing a present?" Linc tapped his chin. "It's still in the car. My bad. I'll be right back." He hurried out.

Blair sighed. "I promise, he's not as bad as he seems. He kind of grows on you, if you give him a chance."

Haley crossed her arms over her chest. "If this was your life, would you be trying to trap the bad guy?" Before Blair could answer, Haley gave a rough laugh. "Wait, of course, you would. You trap bad guys for a living, don't you?"

"Normally, I'm more about protection. But the best way to protect someone is to eliminate a threat. And Linc, well, he used to be an Atlanta Detective, so he's always wanting to take the offensive in cases." A pause. "I would take this option, by the way. Because the guy opened fire when you were on the beach. That tells me he's desperate. If the shooter really is your ex, if Drew Bradley is getting his hands dirty because he wants to take you out personally, then this is your chance to send him straight to hell. Or, you know, jail. Which I think would be the same thing for a pampered jerk like him."

Linc came rushing back toward her. He had a big package in his arms. It was wrapped in green and gold paper and tied with a bright, red bow.

"A Christmas gift?" Haley was confused. Again. She reached for the package. Slowly opened it.

She blinked at the gift inside.

"You want to know the real gift that keeps on giving?" Linc asked her. "It's a bulletproof vest. You're welcome."

Another sigh slipped from Blair. "We wrapped it—"

"*I* wrapped it," Linc cut in. "And you told me I was doing a shit job."

"You were." She cleared her throat. "We wrapped the vest because a gift fit the cover. No one saw us bring it inside, and now you can put it under a coat and be safe."

"While we spring our trap." Linc appeared pleased as hell with himself.

Haley touched the bulletproof vest. The gift that keeps on giving, huh?

Her spine stiffened. "Let's do it."

CHAPTER FOURTEEN

And that was how Haley found herself walking through a sprawling Christmas tree farm, a bulletproof vest hidden beneath her sweater and coat, and the scent of rich pine filling her nose.

Blair was at her side, talking casually, but Haley sensed the tenseness in the other woman's body. She knew that Blair was completely focused on her surroundings. Haley was, too. She might not have Blair's training, but she was hyper aware.

Haley was also pretty much scared as hell. She supposed that was normal, though, when she was trying to lure a killer to her.

"Because of all the trees, he won't have an easy shot at you." Blair's voice was low. She smiled as she pointed to a nearby tree and took a picture. "He'll have to come in close. That's one of the reasons why Linc wanted to use this place."

The trees swayed gently as the breeze seemed to increase. Haley glanced up. The sky was darkening. Storm clouds were heading her way.

Such a bad sign.

They'd been out there for about forty minutes already, and there hadn't been so much as a hint of anyone else. The place had been dead quiet and—

A twig snapped.

***

"We've got us a situation."

When Titus spoke, Spencer glanced up from the computer monitors. He'd been reviewing every bit of security footage that he could find. He'd even used Eric's tech team to tap into some of the camera feeds when the official channels had been too slow for him.

He was pretty sure that he'd caught sight of Francis Callaway and the accomplice who'd helped the guy escape the jail cell. Only, in that one, faint shot he'd gotten—a shot from behind the sheriff's station—it had almost looked like the accomplice was holding a gun.

Threatening Francis?

"Do you know where your favorite New Yorker is right now?"

"What the fuck?" Spencer's spine snapped straight. "She's under the protection of two Wilde agents." She'd *better* be under their protection. He'd sent them to the cottage to keep an eye on her. Titus knew all about the Wilde agents.

Spencer trusted him completely, so he'd updated him right after they'd arrived in town.

"Uh, yes, she's under their protection, but do you know *where* they are?" Titus winced. "Judging by your expression...no. And that's why I said we have a situation."

Spencer strode toward him. "Tell me. Now."

"They were spotted out near the old Christmas tree farm. I am seriously doubting that they all wanted to go for a stroll, so when a patrolling deputy caught sight of Blair Kincaid's rental car out there and notified me, I thought you'd want to know."

Fury hardened Spencer's body. "Why the hell would they take her out there?" But he had a suspicion, one that had better be wrong.

Titus's tense features said he had the same suspicion. "It's a deserted spot, and if I were looking to lure in the bad guy—"

Spencer surged past him. "They're fucking using her as *bait*."

***

Blair pulled her gun, but she kept it down low, hidden behind her body. She also moved so that she was in front of Haley.

And Drew Bradley just stepped out from behind a tall cypress tree. *Just waltzed out.* He was dressed casually, in jeans and a long-sleeved button-down, one that stretched across his shoulders. His dark hair had been swept back, and he smiled at her, revealing his perfect teeth.

"*Get your hands up!*" Blair blasted at him.

Drew frowned at her. But he lifted his hands.

Haley could only shake her head. He'd walked out of the trees. Like it was nothing.

"I don't have a weapon on me."

His voice was charming and easy, but then, he was charming. If a snake was charming. He took a step forward.

"Don't," Blair bit out. Her body was tense, and her gun was aimed straight at him. "Don't move. You stay right there."

He blinked.

Did that count as a movement? Haley thought it did.

His gaze slid to her. Softened a little. "I've been following you. I'm sorry."

Wait, he was confessing? And apologizing?

"I followed you when you left your cottage today with this...uh, friend?"

Blair was slowly approaching him. "I'm going to pat you down."

"Feel free. I told you, I'm not armed." His gaze remained on Haley. "It's my fault, and I'm sorry."

She could barely breathe. He was just *there*. After everything that had happened, he was *there*.

"I hired someone to follow you after you left New York. I have a lot of enemies, Haley. More enemies than you know, and they realize you're my weakness. I was worried one of them would attack you, so I sent a PI to make sure you were okay." His breath heaved out. "But the bastard...he called me. There was something about the call. Something about him that felt off. I told him to stand down because I was coming here. I was planning to talk to you."

"No weapons." Blair stepped back. "But you keep those hands *up*."

His hands didn't lower. "By the time I got here, I learned that you'd been shot at and that Francis Callaway was in jail. I knew one of my enemies had paid him. Those bastards are everywhere. I'm sorry. I hate that you were brought into this mess."

Okay, she was in the Twilight Zone.

"Linc will be the calling the authorities right now." Blair still hadn't lowered her gun—something Haley was happy to see. "We're all just going to stand here and wait for them to arrive. You're going to keep your hands up, understand?"

Drew finally focused on her. "Are you a cop? I thought...thought you were some friend of Haley's."

"And I thought you were supposed to be Prince Charming, but we all know how those seemingly perfect guys turn out, don't we?" Blair fired right back.

"I'm not...look, it's not what you think." His stare cut to Haley again. "It's not what anyone thinks. I'm not trying to hurt you, Haley. I want to keep you safe. That's why I'm here—"

"Uh, huh." Blair's doubt was obvious. "While everyone is thinking you're out in Los Angeles, you snuck down here because you want her *safe*. Sure. Totally buy that."

"I didn't want my enemies to find her! That's the truth! I snuck down here so they wouldn't know how much she matters to me." His stare seemed to burn as he focused on Haley. "You got to me. I can't let you get hurt."

She finally found her voice. "I was shot at the other day."

"Not by me. Not by anyone under my orders. The PI was only supposed to find you. You vanished from New York, and I was worried someone had taken you. I had to make sure you were safe."

"Back in New York, your goon came and *threatened* me outside of the subway! Don't stand there and lie to me—"

"He wasn't working for me. I found out what had happened *after* you left town. And that guy? Hayden Phelps? He's vanished. I worried he was after you. They're all trying to hurt you because hurting you hurts me." He glanced around, his stare nervous. "Do we really have to stay here? I'm worried about her being out in the open."

He was worried...about her. *I don't buy it.* "You smuggle drugs. Weapons. You're a criminal."

"Things are not always what they seem. Let's go somewhere safe so we can talk." He took a step forward.

"I told you to *freeze*!" Blair snarled. "What part of that is hard for you to—"

"Francis is close, all right?" Drew glanced around, as if he expected Francis to pop out of the trees at any moment.

The same way Drew had popped out.

"I know the sonofabitch is here. I was watching Haley, and I'm betting he had to be, too. He's got someone powerful helping him out, and Haley needs to get the hell out of this place. He's got—"

"You're the only threat I see." Linc had appeared behind Drew. "But, yeah, let's take this little talk somewhere else. The sheriff is on his way here, should be pulling up any moment, and let's see what he has to say about you being in his town."

Drew didn't take his eyes off Haley. "Francis is here." His voice shook. "I know he has to be. The guy won't stop until he takes you from me. Don't you see? This isn't about *you*. It's about hurting me."

Haley shook her head. She wasn't buying his act. He'd fooled her once. Never again. "You don't give a shit about me. You lied to me from day one. Hurting me won't do anything—"

"I love you. I was going to marry you." He surged toward her.

Linc grabbed him and swung him around. "I believe the lovely lady told you to freeze, multiple times." He drove his fist into Drew's jaw. Drew stumbled back and fell onto the ground. "Next time, maybe you should listen." His gaze swept over Haley and Blair. "You both good?"

But Blair had turned away. "I don't like this..." She moved her body closer to Haley's. "Stay close."

A siren screamed in the distance.

"That's the sheriff coming to save the day." Linc had his gun pointed at Drew. "And coming to throw your ass in jail."

Drew spat out blood. "I haven't broken any laws. Haven't done *anything* but cooperate while you assaulted me."

Linc grunted. "Try your lies somewhere else, asshole. I know you for what you are. I've seen the bodies you left behind."

Wait...what?

Haley's gaze snapped to Linc's face. Suddenly, he didn't look so easy going.

"Does the name Shanna Sinclair ring a bell for you? Because it should. She's the dancer who went missing from Shade a year ago. A dancer who came from Atlanta because she thought she was getting her big break in New York. Only she wound up dead. *After* you screwed her."

"*Linc.*" Blair's voice shook.

"She was my fucking sister, asshole. And you will *pay.*" It looked like he was about to pull the trigger.

"*Linc, stand the hell down!*" Blair yelled.

Spencer and Titus ran from the trees. Spencer's face was locked into tight lines of fury. And Titus appeared ice cold.

Haley wasn't sure what was happening. But...Linc's sister? He thought Drew had killed his sister?

"This asshole just assaulted me." Drew was still on the ground. "I want him arrested!"

A muscle pulsed in Linc's jaw. "And I want you in a jail cell. Wonder which of us will get our wish first?"

"*Stand. Down.*" Spencer's voice thundered out.

Linc took a grudging step back. He lowered his weapon.

Haley sucked in a breath—and ran straight to Spencer.

He caught her with one arm and pulled her against him. "What the fuck is going on?" he rasped into her ear. "God, baby, I couldn't get here fast enough."

He smelled good. Clean. Crisp. He felt strong and warm against her.

"They were supposed to keep you safe." Tension thickened his words. "Not bring you to him."

She looked up at Spencer. His face was hard and brutal, his eyes blazing. But she knew it wasn't rage spilling from him. It was fear. He'd been worried about her. "I'm okay," she told him softly.

Haley eased back. Her head turned. And she caught Drew's gaze on her.

Her heart stopped.

For just a moment, she did see rage—the rage that hadn't been in Spencer's eyes. She'd caught a flash of hateful fury in Drew's gaze right before he'd blinked, and his mask slid back in place.

But that was what he didn't get...she'd bought the mask once. Never again. It didn't matter what lies he spouted because now she saw him for exactly what he was.

"I'm here to help Haley," Drew said, voice all slow and careful as he rose to his feet. "She's in danger."

"Yeah, from you." Spencer kept his hold on Haley. "Cuff him, would you, Titus?"

"My pleasure." Titus advanced.

"But I haven't done anything!" Drew's eyes were huge, and his lip was still bleeding from Linc's punch. "I was assaulted by that bastard."

He cocked his head toward Linc. "You can't arrest me! There's no crime here!"

"We're bringing you in for questioning because you're a person of interest in our investigation." Spencer's voice was flat. "You can come willingly, and in that case, Titus will put you in the back of his patrol car and bring you to the station. Or you can come unwillingly, and Titus will *still* put your ass in the back of his patrol car and bring you to the station."

Titus nodded. "That I will."

"I'll come *willingly*," Drew seethed. His nostrils flared. "But you've got me all wrong! I just want to save Haley, that's all. That PI has gone off the rails, and we have to stop him!"

Titus put his hand on Drew's shoulder. "Walk."

Drew started walking. Then stopped. "I want charges pressed against the man who assaulted me." His glittering gaze locked on Linc. "Throw him in a cell, or I will have a mountain of lawyers falling on your little town."

Linc sighed and didn't look even a little concerned. "Whatever. I'm not afraid of you, jerkoff. Never have been. Never will be." He nodded to Spencer. "Lock me up."

Haley could only shake her head. More deputies had arrived at the scene. It seemed like freaking chaos as they made their way to the vehicles.

Their trap had worked, kind of. But the prey they'd wanted was singing his innocence, and the Wilde agent was about to be locked up.

Titus paused near the back of his patrol car. He yanked open the door. "Get in."

Drew's head turned. He stared straight at Haley. "You'll see that I didn't try to hurt you. That wasn't me."

Titus pushed him inside. Slammed the door shut.

Drew's gaze stayed on Haley—

Until Spencer stepped in front of her. "Don't look at the bastard."

She blinked.

"It's what he wants. He is playing a game, yanking us all around, and I don't fucking like it."

She wet her lips. "I can't say I'm overly wild about anything that happened here."

He caught her hand in his. Held tight. "Why did you come to this place? What the hell were you doing?"

She stiffened. "Trying to catch the bad guy."

"Baby..." His other hand lifted and curled under her jaw. "That's my job."

"And it's my life. I wasn't going to stand by while other people were put at risk. We caught him, Spencer. He's going to your station."

His mouth was tight. "We don't have anything to hold him on. Nothing substantial to tie him to the shooting. Plus, we've got to lock up that Linc asshat until I can figure things out." He put his forehead against hers. "I just need you to be safe."

"I am."

His head lifted. "I want you to stay with me. I thought I could trust the Wilde agents—I can't. Not with Linc working his own agenda. Shit. Please, baby, stay with me."

Stay with him? "There's nowhere else I'd rather be." Strange...how very true that statement was. Her gaze darted to the left. To Titus's patrol car. To Drew.

He was still staring straight at her.

Even with Spencer so close to her, a shiver slid over Haley's body.

***

"What in the actual hell?" Blair put her hands on her hips and glared at Linc. "You held back on me. I'm your partner, and you held back." He'd also royally screwed the case.

Linc lifted his chin. His eyes normally gleamed with humor as he constantly seemed to tease her. In that moment, though, there was no humor in his eyes. "This was my chance to nail the bastard."

"You did it the *wrong* way. We haven't nailed him! He's got you for assault." Didn't Linc get it? "You're nailed!"

"His DNA is on me. Couldn't get a warrant for his DNA before. Couldn't get access. Tried and tried...I've got it now."

OhmyGod.

She realized her partner was being very, very careful with his hand.

"The killer's DNA was beneath Shanna's nails. She clawed him. I can finally get the evidence I need to send his cocky ass to jail. Merry Christmas to me."

Merry Christmas...*if* the DNA was a match. It would take time to test it. And Linc would still be locked up. "Did Eric know about this?" Was she the only one who'd been kept in the dark?

The flicker of his long lashes was her answer.

And it hurt. *Hurt.* Because Linc was her partner. Your partner was supposed to trust you. Partners weren't supposed to be keeping secrets. But Blair had the feeling that maybe Linc had been keeping secrets from her for a very long time.

Maybe...maybe she didn't know him nearly as well as she'd thought.

CHAPTER FIFTEEN

"You put her at risk because you were working your own agenda." Spencer glared through the bars at Linc as the other man sat in the jail cell. "You knew I wanted her safe, but you took her out to that tree farm and paraded her around." His hands grabbed for the bars. "You sonofabitch."

Linc winced. "Okay, I get it. You're pissed."

Pissed? Pissed didn't even come close to describing the fury pouring through him. "I'm calling Eric. I don't buy that he was in on your little plan. Sure, he might have known about your sister, but I'm guessing Eric thought you were professional enough not to jeopardize the woman you'd been hired to protect."

"She wasn't jeopardized." Linc's eyes narrowed to slits. "Look, your girl was protected the whole time, all right? I was there. Blair was there." He motioned to Blair. "Tell him. We weren't risking anything. We had the situation under control."

Spencer swung his gaze to a silent Blair. "Did you have the situation under control?"

Her shoulders squared. "No." Her voice was soft. She met his gaze without flinching. "We didn't because I was not fully aware of all the elements involved. For example, I had no clue about my partner's personal agenda. I didn't know what he wanted, and since I didn't know, I was walking in the dark. The dark is dangerous for anyone."

Spencer sucked in a deep breath. Then another. The breaths didn't do a single thing to calm his ass down. He still wanted to slam his fist into Linc.

"Blair..." Linc rose from the cot. "You're... angry? Look, I keep my private life separate, you know that, and you know—"

Her furious gaze swung to him. "I know partners don't lie."

"I *didn't* lie. I just didn't tell you—"

"Do not feed me a load of bull. Not telling me is the same thing as lying. And I'm not here for that. You disrespected me. You put our client at risk. I don't even know who the hell you are anymore." She exhaled. "I'm sorry, Spencer. I thought we were helping."

"We *are* helping," Linc snapped. "I got DNA from him! I got—"

"There are other ways," Spencer snarled through gritted teeth. "Ways that don't involve Haley being jeopardized." He backed away from the bars. "I have to try and fix the mess you made."

Blair headed for the door with him.

"Blair?" Linc's voice wasn't as confident. It was stilted. "I...I'm sorry."

She didn't look back. "You should be." She yanked open the door.

As soon as they were clear of the holding area, she faced off with Spencer. "This isn't how we work." Faint shadows smudged her eyes. "You know that. Wilde is *better* than this. We don't work personal agendas. I had no idea...Spence, I didn't even know my partner had a sister! I thought he was an only child." Her lashes flickered. "I don't know him."

Yes, the situation was a clusterfuck, but they had to deal with one fire at a time. "Andrew Bradley is in my interrogation room, and he's going to walk if I can't find a way to hold him." The whole thing was wrong. Wrong, wrong, wrong. The guy had just strolled right up to Haley? In the middle of the day? Acting like he was keeping her safe? That he was worried about her? "Your partner can cool his heels in holding. I have to handle Andrew first."

Titus marched toward them. "Still no word on Francis. It's like the PI vanished into thin air."

"Doesn't happen." *Where the hell are you, Francis?* "We know he had help."

"Sure, but that help could have gotten him all the way to New Orleans by now. Man is in the wind, and he might not show up on anyone's radar again."

Francis had been their tie to Andrew. Without Francis...

We are so screwed.

"How long will the DNA comparison take?" Blair asked quietly.

"Oh, you mean the DNA that a good lawyer will probably get tossed out with his first breath?" Spencer shook his head. "It's the holidays. Half the offices down here are running on a skeleton staff. No telling when we'll have results." He raked a hand through his hair.

"I'll call Eric." She nodded. "He has his own team for things like this." She hurried away. Stopped. Blair glanced back at him. "I didn't know, Spence. I wouldn't put someone at risk that way. That's not who I am."

"No, but it's who your partner is." He still wanted to rip the man apart. Linc had used Haley to get what he wanted, and it infuriated Spencer.

Blair marched for the front of the station.

"Look, man, I get it, but take a breath," Titus urged him. "We need to go in there with that snake Bradley, and you have to be in control."

Spencer met his friend's worried gaze. "I'm in control."

Titus lifted his eyebrows. "You sure? Because it looks like you want to tear someone apart."

Titus wasn't wrong. Okay, fine, he needed to calm his ass down, and the number one thing that would calm him?

Haley.

"Give me ten minutes, all right?" Spencer muttered.

"Dude, take as long as you need. We both know perps start to sweat the longer they wait."

Spencer headed for his office. He'd left Haley in there moments before, mostly because he hadn't wanted her to watch him rip into Linc. But when he swung open the door to his office...

Haley wasn't there.

His heart gave a quick squeeze, but, shit, they were in the sheriff's station. It was a safe space.

Safe...right...except Francis busted out last night.

With help. With freaking help.

Spencer rushed through the station. He peered into the waiting area. No dice. She wasn't in the small break room, either. Where was she?

He almost ran into Titus.

Spencer grabbed Titus by the arm. "Haley isn't in my office."

"That's because I saw her go out front while you were in holding."

And you didn't mention that sooner?

"She wanted some air, so she strolled out with a deputy. And Blair just headed outside, too." He motioned toward the blinds that were open to reveal the street outside. "You can see Haley from here if you—"

Spencer let him go as he caught sight of her. He double-timed it toward the front of the station.

"Sure, you're welcome. Happy to help!" Titus called after him.

Tension filled Spencer's body. Something was nagging at him. Not just something. Everything.

Francis had escaped from the sheriff's station. With mystery help.

Then he'd vanished. The last time Francis had been seen on any security camera had been when he'd left the station. That brief moment out back. Why hadn't he been picked up on any other cameras? He couldn't have disappeared into thin air.

And then there was the whole deal with Andrew turning up at that tree farm. Acting like he was the good guy and simply strolling right up to Haley and the others as if...

As if he wanted to be caught. As if he wanted to be brought in to the station.

Spencer's hands slammed into the front door as he shoved it open. "Haley!"

She was talking with the deputy. Smiling. Blair stood near her, but the Wilde agent was on her phone.

At his shout, Haley glanced up at Spencer. Her eyes sparkled at him.

And someone moved behind her. A shadowy figure that shot out from the thin alley between the station and the nearby Italian restaurant. A restaurant that was closed for the holiday season because the owners had gone back to Italy in order to visit family.

The figure moved with a dangerous stealth. *No, no, no.* Spencer caught sight of Francis's face. The guy appeared pale and grim as he lifted his arm up and aimed a gun at—

Haley. Oh, God, at *Haley.*

That was why they hadn't seen the PI on any other video footage. He'd been right fucking there all along. He hadn't escaped from the little town.

Hadn't headed for New Orleans or another big city so he could vanish.

He'd been right there.

Deputies had been sent to search the restaurant. They'd missed him. *They'd missed him!*

Fucking hell. Francis had a gun in his hand. His hand was shaking as he stared at Haley.

"Sorry!" Francis called out. "So f-fucking s-sorry—"

Haley rolled toward Francis.

"*No!*" Spencer roared. He was too far away. He was racing, lunging for Haley, but he couldn't get to her in time.

Bam!

Bam!

The bullets exploded from Francis's gun. Haley's body jerked. Once. Twice. Then she was falling back, her brown coat swirling around her as she tumbled onto the sidewalk.

The deputy near her struggled to pull out his gun.

"I'm...sorry..." Francis staggered and lurched to the side.

Spencer fired. He had his weapon out, and he fucking fired. He hit Francis in the chest. Two shots in quick succession because that sonofabitch had just shot Haley twice.

He shot her. He shot my Haley.

Francis's eyes went wide. The gun slipped from his fingers, and he fell to the pavement.

"Secure him!" Spencer shouted.

Haley, Haley, Haley...

The deputy scrambled to get near Francis and grab his discarded gun. Blair followed right on his heels, while Spencer dropped to his knees beside Haley.

"Oh, God, baby." Rage and fear twisted through him. "It's going to be okay." His voice was hoarse. Ragged. "We're going to get help."

Shot. The bastard had shot her. *He shot my Haley.* The litany cycled through Spencer's mind over and over.

"Get an ambulance!" Spencer bellowed as he yanked open her coat. "Get an—"

Haley's eyes flew open. She sucked in a sharp breath. "OhmyGod."

"Baby, I'm here. It's going to be all right. I'm going to make—"

"It hurts...like a bitch."

"I know, baby, I know. It's okay. I've got you, I've—" He...didn't see blood on her. Two bullet holes in her top, yes, but no blood.

Her hand grabbed his. "Best...Christmas present...ever." Each word seemed to be a bit of struggle.

"Haley?"

She jerked his hand toward her stomach. Shoved it under her sweater. Only instead of touching her skin, his fingers felt—

"A bulletproof vest?" His lips curled as relief poured through every cell in his body. "You're wearing a bulletproof vest?"

"From...Linc. Said I had to be...careful." She stared up at him. A tear slid from her left eye. "I...didn't get chance...take...off..."

He hauled her into his arms.

She groaned.

"Shit, Haley, I'm sorry!" He knew she'd be sporting some serious bruising from the bullets, but only bruising. The vest had saved her. She was okay. He held her tighter as relief made him lightheaded.

She was going to be fine.

In that one moment, when the bullets had hit her and Spencer had thought he was watching her die in front of him...

I lost my mind.

Because he'd realized exactly how much Haley Quick mattered to him.

She mattered to him more than any fucking thing. Her raspberries and cream scent swept around him as he held her tight. He shuddered. *Too close. That was too fucking close.* He never, ever wanted to be that afraid again. For a while, he simply held her.

The rest of the world slowly penetrated the haze that had surrounded him. Spencer heard other voices. Shouts. Sirens.

His head turned. Titus was on the sidewalk. He was bending over Francis as he tried to save the shooter's life.

Blair was working feverishly on Francis, too.

A crowd was watching.

"What?" Titus put his head closer to Francis's mouth. "What the hell are you saying to me?"

Spencer had no idea what Francis said. If he said anything.

Titus swore and whipped his head up. "Where's the damn ambulance?"

It was coming. Coming...the scream of the siren was getting louder.

Would the ambulance get there soon enough?

"Go," Haley whispered. "Go to him."

Spencer motioned for his deputies. "Put up a fucking wall around her," he ordered them. "Don't let *anyone* else close to her. Only the EMTs when they arrive." He kissed Haley. Hard and fast. "I will not lose you."

But he wanted her off the street. Because Francis still had a partner.

A partner...

Fuck.

While the deputies surrounded Haley, Spencer rushed to Francis. "You failed, bastard. Haley is okay."

Blood trickled from Francis's mouth. "S-sorry..."

"You will be sorry. If you survive, you'll go to jail for attempted murder. No getting out of it, we all saw you pull the trigger this time."

Francis's lips trembled. "S-saved...her..."

"I don't know what the hell he's rambling about," Titus muttered. His fingers were covered in Francis's blood. "I swear, he mentioned some other woman a minute ago. Marsha? Said he was protecting Marsha."

The name clicked for Spencer. It was a name that Wilde had produced when the agency sent over a file on Francis. "That's his ex-wife." But...protecting her?

Spencer glanced around the street. An ambulance was racing toward them with its lights flashing.

Francis had already nearly bled out on the street. Spencer was a damn good shot, and he'd been aiming for Francis's heart. But the guy had lurched just as Spencer fired the first bullet.

That lurch might have saved the PI's life.

Or he could die before the ambulance got him to the hospital.

The scene was chaos as the EMTs arrived and frantically loaded Francis into the vehicle.

"I want a deputy with him every moment. Even when he's in the OR, I want eyes on him," Spencer told Titus.

Titus responded with a grim nod before he turned and gave an order to one of the deputies. A female deputy immediately jumped into the vehicle. The sirens were screaming as it raced away. The people on the streets were whispering. Watching. Wreaths swayed drunkenly in the breeze, and blood stained the pavement.

He knew what the townspeople were thinking. What they were feeling. The fear was plain to see on their faces. Things like this weren't supposed to happen so close to home. They were supposed to be safe. They counted on him to keep them safe.

He'd been elected sheriff because these people trusted him. They depended on him.

They were supposed to be safe.

Unfortunately, that wasn't how life always worked. Danger could be anywhere. Safety could be shattered. And in the blink of an eye, you could lose the thing that mattered most.

His gaze went back to Haley.

A second group of EMTs had loaded her into another ambulance. They were checking her out and he bounded toward them.

"This is becoming a terrible habit," she muttered when he climbed inside. "I don't like ambulances." Her gaze flickered to the nearby EMT. "No offense."

"None taken." It was his old high school buddy again. And Dodge had cut away part of Haley's shirt so he could remove the bulletproof vest. Dodge turned his head and looked over at Spencer. "She's okay. Going to be sore for a few days, but the vest saved her hide." He hesitated. "I can take her to the hospital—"

"Spencer, no." She struggled to sit up and pushed away Dodge's hand when he tried to press her down. "I just want to go home." Her eyes were so big and deep. "Can we please go home?"

He wanted to take her home. He wanted to scoop her into his arms and take her a million miles away from any danger that might ever come toward her. And he would take her home. But... "I have to take care of one thing first."

Her lower lip trembled.

"Baby, I'll be right back. And I'll take you home, I swear, and I'll make sure you're safe all night long." Because he would be holding her in his arms all night.

If he could, he'd hold her forever.

***

Spencer threw open the door to the interrogation room. Two deputies had been ordered to watch Andrew, and one had run out at the sound of gunfire to check the situation on the street. He'd immediately been sent back in to guard the prisoner, but Andrew hadn't tried to flee during the chaos.

Because Spencer knew that fleeing wasn't part of his plan.

Andrew sat at the table, his hands folded on his lap, and a furrow between his brows. "I heard there was a shooting outside." He blinked his eyes. Looked extra worried. So unbelievable. "The deputies told me that someone might have been killed."

The deputies needed to stop telling that guy jackshit. That was the problem with a young, green crew. *Too trusting*. Too untrained. Too unprepared when real evil was right in front of them.

Spencer marched toward Andrew. He leaned in close. Got right in Andrew's face. "You know what I hate?"

"I could hazard a guess that you're not a big fan of—"

"Bastards like you who think they can control the world. Newsflash, asshole. This is *my* town."

Andrew's eyes gleamed. "You seem upset." He sucked in a sharp breath as his eyes widened. "Someone *was* hurt out there, oh, God, was it—"

"Haley is fine. She's guarded, and soon she'll be going back home with me." Because he was watching the jerk so closely, Spencer saw the stiffening of Andrew's jaw.

"Haley?" Andrew swallowed. "I-I didn't even realize she was outside."

Seriously? He could only shake his head. "You must have been dealing with some real dumbasses before. I see through your shit. You arranged it all. You didn't put up a fight about coming back to the station because this is where you wanted us all to be. You had Francis staked out nearby, and you ordered him to wait. You directed him to keep waiting and as soon as he saw Haley, you told the guy to shoot." *It fit. Every piece of the puzzle.*

Andrew licked his lower lip. "So...Francis tried to hurt Haley?" He shook his head and appeared distraught. "I told you that man was unhinged. He's working for my enemies, and they will do anything to hurt me...even targeting an innocent woman. It's such a good thing that I got here to help Haley."

"Oh, yeah, because you're a real fucking hero."

Andrew didn't speak. He sniffed.

"Francis shot Haley. He didn't know she was wearing a bulletproof vest, so the bullets bruised her, but they didn't do anything else."

Andrew's breath came a little faster. "Bulletproof vest, huh? That's good. That's so good that you were protecting *my* girl like that."

Rage boiled inside of Spencer. "She's not a girl. She's a woman. And she's fucking not yours."

Andrew smiled at him. *Smiled.* "Because you think she belongs to you? That's so cute. You're a hick sheriff in a nothing town. You don't know a thing about Haley. Not the real Haley. She will never be satisfied with a guy like you or in a place like this. She's using you for a hiding spot. A safe shelter because she was running from Francis. Give her the choice, and she'd choose me over you in a heartbeat. I'm everything that she ever wanted. I'm the man she was going to marry. I am—"

"You're a monster." Haley's voice was flat.

Spencer stiffened.

He glanced over his shoulder. Haley stood in the doorway, with Titus right behind her.

Titus shrugged. "Sorry, boss." He didn't sound sorry. "She wanted to know what was happening. We were watching through the one-way mirror." He pointed to the left. "But then the guy called you a hick—"

"And it pissed me off," Haley finished.

Spencer shoved away from the table and headed for her. "Baby, you shouldn't be in here."

Her cheeks were flushed. Her furious gaze locked on Andrew.

"I'm so glad you're okay." Andrew rose to his feet. "When the sheriff told me that the PI had tried to hurt you, I was terrified."

"I have a choice," Haley threw at him. "I always have a choice. And I don't choose you. I won't choose you. You're a liar. You're a criminal."

Andrew put his hand to his chest. "You don't understand what's been happening. That persona was a cover, nothing more. You have to listen to me. I've been working with the Feds. I can call them right now, and they'll back up everything I say. That's how the charges were dropped against me in New York. They weren't dismissed because I'm some mob boss with connections. The charges—the whole case—it all went away because

I'm undercover." His voice broke with emotion. "But I'm getting out of that life. I don't want it anymore. I want you." He lifted his hand toward her. "I realized how much I need you when you left me. No one has left me before. Other women wanted the money and the power I possessed. They didn't care about anything else."

Spencer positioned his body protectively near Haley.

"If that's the case, then you chose the wrong women," Haley told him flatly. "Your mistake."

Andrew took a quick step toward her. "Haley—"

"You'll want to stand the hell down," Spencer warned him grimly. "Now."

"*My* mistake was ever falling for you in the first place." She shook her head. "I have a choice," she said again. "I choose Spencer. Not because I'm looking for a place to hide. But because I like the way I feel when I'm with him."

"Haley." Andrew's breath shuddered out. "Didn't you hear what I told you? I have FBI agents who can back me up. I was working with them in New York. I was doing the right thing. I couldn't tell you the truth back then. I'm being painted as the bad guy, but I'm not."

Haley's fingers curled around Spencer's arm. "I know a bad guy when I see one."

Andrew's jaw hardened. "You don't know shit. You think the sheriff is some kind of super hero? He's not. I did my digging on him. The guy is a lethal bastard. He's *killed* people, don't you get that? He was a gun for hire back in the day."

Well, well...so Andrew had been digging into his life, huh? *Way to confess, dumbass.* Andrew had obviously been studying the town and the people there. He'd been making his plan of attack. *Now it's my turn.* "I think we're done here for now." Spencer turned toward Haley. "You need to rest." She had to be sore as hell. "Let's go home."

Haley nodded.

"You aren't leaving with him!" Andrew shouted. "You aren't ditching me for some asshole sheriff who you don't even really know—"

"I know him far better than I know you." Her chin notched up as her gaze darted over Andrew. "And I trust him." Her lips pressed together. "Just so you know, I don't think I ever really trusted you, not the whole time we were together. Something always felt off."

"Because I had to lie! I was working undercover! I had to—" He stopped. His gaze flew to Spencer. "It's your fault. You've been fucking *my* fiancée, and you've turned her against me. You will pay." He lunged forward with his fist swinging toward Spencer's face.

Spencer shoved Haley back because the last thing he wanted was for her to get caught in the crossfire. Andrew's fist pounded into his jaw, and the guy had a solid hook. Spencer would give him that much.

But Andrew's reflexes were shit.

The fool smiled in grim satisfaction when his fist thudded into Spencer's jaw. Maybe he thought that punch was going to take Spencer down. He should have thought again.

Spencer smiled back at him. "That's assaulting an officer. You're gonna be arrested for that shit."

Andrew's eyes widened.

"This'll be fun," Titus muttered.

Andrew tried to swing again.

Haley was safely out of range, so Spencer dodged the blow. Then he had his chance to attack. He drove his right hand into Andrew's stomach. Heard the *ooof* as Andrew's breath expelled. Spencer's left hand slammed hard into the SOB's jaw. A fast hit that had Andrew staggering back. He bumped the table's sharp edge. He blinked. Narrowed his eyes. Shot forward.

Really, you're coming again?

And it was like the bastard ran straight into Spencer's fist. So easy.

This time, Spencer used *his* right hook on Andrew. His hit was one hell of a lot more powerful that Andrew's. Andrew fell down, sagging like some deflated balloon. He shook his head, tried to shove back to his feet, but Spencer had his gun out and pointed at the fellow in an instant. "You're going to stay down," Spencer told him. "Game's over."

Andrew's breath heaved in and out. His gaze blazed with fury.

"Congratulations, asshole." Spencer gave him a cold grin. "You're under arrest."

CHAPTER SIXTEEN

"What in the fuck is going on?" Linc yelled as soon as Spencer entered the holding area. Linc stood at the bars, his face pale, and his eyes wild. "I heard gunshots."

"That's because there was an attack on the street." Spencer's voice was still too rough. He was too rough. About to lose it. *Breathe. Hold on.* Adrenaline poured through him. He wanted to grab Andrew again and pound the ever-loving-hell out of the guy. He wanted to *destroy.*

That BS about being undercover? Working for the Feds? He'd check out the story, but every instinct Spencer possessed said it was a con.

Andrew Bradley was trouble, and he needed to be locked away. Put far away from Haley.

Linc glanced over Spencer's shoulder. "Where's Blair?"

Blair? Where was she? Spencer squinted as he thought. "Out in the ambulance."

Linc took a step back. "No." He shook his head and paled. "Fuck, no, she's not—"

"She's not hurt." The dude needed to calm the hell down. "She wasn't the target. Haley was."

Linc's eyes widened.

"But she was wearing a bulletproof vest you gave her, so she's still alive right now." He strode toward the cell. Shoved the key in the lock and opened it. "You and I are coming to an understanding."

Linc glanced down at the door. "Are you letting me go? *Can* you even do that shit? I mean, I heard stories about small towns being all crazy and stuff but—"

"Close your damn mouth and listen." He didn't have time for this jackass.

Linc snapped his mouth closed.

"You're getting a roomie for tonight. Consider it your Christmas present."

"What? What the hell are you—"

The holding room door opened with a groan.

"You can't do this shit to me!" Andrew yelled.

Titus just pushed him forward, right toward the open cell.

Linc smiled.

"I want to talk to my lawyer! I want to talk to my FBI contacts! You can't—"

"I can do anything." Spencer grabbed him and shoved him inside the cell. The clank of the cell door closing seemed wonderfully loud and satisfying. "I'm the hick sheriff of this town. My town, my rules."

Andrew spun toward him. "You're doing this because you want *her*! You're turning Haley against me! You're—"

"You didn't ask what happened to the shooter." Spencer crossed his arms and slanted a glance at Titus. "Did you notice that, too?"

"I did. Wondered about that."

Spencer turned his attention back on Andrew. "I mean, I told you Francis shot Haley. But you never asked what happened to him after he fired those shots."

Andrew swiped his hand over his lip. Aw, poor baby. Was his lip bleeding from the punch? Or maybe from when he'd hit the floor?

"I-I figured...he's dead." Andrew's hand dropped. His head jerked toward Spencer. "You killed him. Told you, I did some digging on you after I got in town. My FBI buddies..."

The guy sure did like to talk a lot about them. These wonderful FBI friends of his...

"They told me what you did. How you left the bodies in your wake when you were a SEAL."

Spencer didn't let his expression alter.

"Someone shoots at Haley, with you right there, I figure you only had one response." His breath sighed out. "And I'm glad. I fucking hate you, but I'm glad you killed Francis. He deserved to die. Now Haley can be safe."

"Oh, Haley will definitely be safe." Spencer rolled back his shoulders. "But Francis isn't dead."

Andrew stiffened.

"Nope," Titus said quietly. "Not dead. Was still breathing when that ambulance rolled away. Bloody, but breathing."

Linc was in the cell, just a few steps away from Andrew. Linc's hands were fisted at his sides. His angry stare was locked and loaded on Andrew.

"Still breathing?" Andrew blinked. "But...he was shot. I-I heard multiple shots."

"Four shots were fired," Linc said flatly.

"Two were at Haley." Titus locked his eyes on Andrew. "Two were at Francis. He's still alive, and maybe—just maybe—he'll even be able to pull through. If he does, I'm betting he will have a very interesting story to tell us."

"I like stories." Spencer let his stare drift from Andrew and to a furious Linc. "Like I'm pretty interested in this guy's story. Linc swears you killed his sister."

Andrew seemed to *just* notice who his new roommate was. "Get me out of this freaking cage!"

"Can't do that. We're a small facility. And our other cell...well, someone broke out of it the other night. It's closed off for now while we finish investigation procedures. So you two—you two will be roomies for the night."

"No." Andrew's face reddened. "No! I want my lawyer! I want my—"

"FBI buddies?" Spencer inserted. "I would like to talk with them. I want to ask them about another story I know. You see, before Francis was taken away, he was telling Titus over there about his ex-wife."

"He was gasping out her name," Titus offered helpfully. "Saying that he'd saved her."

If possible, Andrew's cheeks flushed even more.

"Do you know her?" Titus asked. "I believe her name is Marsha."

"No, I don't know her. Why would I?"

"Just did a little checking while you and the sheriff were having your...talk in interrogation. Seems she's gone missing back in New York. Very suspicious timing if you ask me."

"I don't know a thing about her!" Spittle flew from Andrew's mouth. "Get me out of this cage!"

Spencer smiled at him and leaned closer to the bars. "If you didn't want to be in a cage, you shouldn't have taken a swing at the sheriff."

Andrew's nostrils flared. "You did that. You pushed me and pushed me until I attacked."

He shrugged. "Not my fault you've got a short fuse."

"You wanted me locked up. You wanted me away from Haley!"

Spencer nodded. "If I have my way, you'll never be around her again." And he'd just been given the time he needed. Andrew would stay locked up at least until dawn. Possibly longer. By then, maybe Francis would be able to tell them more about his missing ex-wife. Or about the mystery guy who'd helped to break him out of his cell.

It's no mystery. I'm staring at the asshole who helped him.

Wilde agents were already hunting for Francis's ex in New York. Titus had talked to Eric and gotten his team involved. And the DNA that Linc had acquired from Andrew was being tested.

Money could get things moving so fast. Money and the right connections. Wilde had both.

And, lucky for Spencer, Wilde was on his side.

"You want her for yourself," Andrew accused. It sounded like the guy might be choking on fury. "You saw her, you wanted her, and you're trying to take her from me."

"You're such a prick." Spencer turned away from him. "She doesn't want you. She left your ass." He stilled. Glanced back. "And that's why you're here, isn't it? Because she's the first person you couldn't control. You couldn't keep her. She left you. She turned on you, and you hunted her down."

"I'm here to protect her!"

"You just tried to get your PI to kill her. You think if she won't be with you, then you'll see her dead?" He stepped back to the bars. Glared at Andrew. "Let's be very clear here. You will not kill her. You will not hurt her. You will not get within fifty feet of Haley again."

"Oh, really?" Andrew smirked at him. "What you gonna do? Not much, because you got that badge on. So you can talk a big game, but we both know you can't cross—"

Spencer took off the badge. "You think I won't end you?" His fingers closed around the badge. The edges of the star pressed into his palm. "The badge is off, bastard. You're the one bragging about digging into my past. About knowing who I really am." He held the other man's gaze. "You think for a second that I won't kill you if you come after Haley again?"

Andrew backed up a step. "You're threatening me." He motioned toward Titus. "You heard him." He looked over at Linc. Blanched. "You did, too."

"I didn't hear jackshit," Linc snapped.

"I don't care who hears me." And he didn't. "I wasn't threatening. I was promising. You've been warned." His control was splintering with every moment. He needed to get out of there. Needed to get back to Haley. She was the one person who could calm him down.

She was the person he wanted most.

He turned and headed for the door.

Titus immediately fell into step with him.

"Don't leave me with him!" Andrew yelled. "This guy is a freaking psycho! Don't leave me here!"

Spencer glanced at Titus. "You hear something?"

"I didn't hear jackshit," Titus replied, using Linc's response.

With a grunt, Spencer yanked open the door. Spencer waited until he and Titus were clear of the holding area before he turned toward his friend.

Titus held up one hand. "You don't have to say anything, man. We've been friends for a long time. I *know* you."

Spencer's brows pulled together.

"You were trying to rattle him. The badge matters to you. You won't cross the line."

Spencer glanced down. He opened his palm. Stared at the star. At the marks that had been left on his hand when he'd gripped it too tightly. "If he hurts her, there is no line. Not for me."

A low whistle escaped Titus. "You're that far gone?"

That far? "Hell, I've been gone since the first moment I met her." He pushed the star against Titus's shirtfront. "Take this. I'm not the sheriff tonight."

"That's some bullshit. I'm not taking the damn star. It's yours."

Haley was his. No, he wanted her to be. And he would do anything to keep her safe. Crossing lines? He'd do it over and over again. "I lost a piece of myself when we were fighting in the desert." His voice was low, carrying only to Titus. "I came back here, and I was empty inside."

Titus watched him with a steady, unblinking gaze. If anyone would understand, it would be him.

"For the first time...the *first* time, I could feel again...I could feel when I pulled her into my arms." She'd been right in the middle of the street. Surrounded by lights. Soft music playing in the air. He'd looked up, seen her, and seen everything that he'd ever wanted. "I can't lose her."

"You won't."

He stepped back. Titus didn't take the star. It fell to the floor. Spencer raked a hand through his hair. "She was shot in front of me." His hand was shaking. The adrenaline was crashing through him. He was barely holding his shit together. "Shot. I didn't know she had on a vest. I thought those bullets tore into her. I saw her fall, and my world *ended.* I was afraid she was dead. I fired back at Francis, and the only reason that bastard is alive right now—hell, *barely* alive—is because he lurched to the side right before my first bullet hit him. He lurched, because otherwise, that bullet would have been in his heart."

"Spence, we got this. I have your back. You got your lady. It's going to be okay."

The door to Spencer's office opened. Haley stood there. Looking pale and fragile. Beautiful and heart-breaking. Looking like every dream he'd ever had. The dreams that he'd almost given up when he'd seen blood and death all around him.

"I can't lose her," he rasped. "I won't." He walked away from Titus and left the star on the floor.

Haley's lips lifted in a faint and so very tentative smile as he approached her. "Everything...okay?"

No. No, things were not okay. But they would be. He bent and brushed his lips over hers. "Baby, let's go home."

He thought he saw tears in her eyes, but she blinked them away.

He kissed her again. Softly. Tenderly. His fingers laced with hers.

As they passed by Titus, he gave his friend a slow nod.

But Titus stepped into his path. "What's the plan for the two prisoners? You really gonna leave them in there all night?"

The plan... "No. I suspect that in about five minutes, Andrew will remember that the only reason Linc is in there...it's because Andrew said he was pressing charges against the guy. Andrew will drop those charges in order to get away from Linc."

A half smile flashed from Titus. "Clever. Trying to free the Wilde agent, huh?"

All part of the plan he was crafting. "We might need him later. And I'm not letting him get sent to jail by a guy like Andrew Bradley." If Bradley had killed Linc's sister, the fellow deserved justice. Not a jail cell. "Give them five minutes. But I'm betting it won't even take that long."

Andrew was the kind of jerk who liked to dish out pain. The man couldn't take it, though. He'd be screaming for a deputy soon enough.

***

"This is freaking bullshit!" Andrew pressed his back to the cell bars as his wide eyes swept over Linc. "I'm not staying in here with you."

Linc shrugged. Every muscle in his body was tight with fury. "Then I'm guessing maybe you shouldn't have insisted the sheriff lock me up. I'm only in here because of you."

Andrew blinked.

"Let's call that shit...a happy coincidence." Linc's hands were tight fists at his sides. "Do you even remember her?"

"Who?" A bead of sweat trickled down Andrew's temple.

"My sister."

"Look, buddy, I meet a lot of women. Women like me because I'm rich and handsome, and they are always throwing themselves at me and I—Why the hell are you laughing?"

"Because you're a freaking dipshit. You're rich because you have dirty money. You stole and you lied your way to the top, and I'm betting you buried a ton of bodies in your time, too, didn't you? Bodies like Shanna's. Shanna Sinclair. She was my step-sister. She went to New York to be a dancer. She was young and beautiful and she had dreams, and then she wound up in your club, and you fucking got obsessed with her. The same way you're obsessed with Haley. If you can't have a woman, you don't let her go. You play that old school stalker bullshit. You take and take until nothing is left." One menacing step forward. "You destroy and you leave death." Another step. "But there's no running for you right now. There's no way out. You're done. Because it's me and it's you, and there is no one here to save your sorry ass." Linc smiled. "I'm going to tear you apart."

"Cops don't—"

"I'm not a cop, dumbass. I'm a prisoner, thanks to you." Another step. "And I'm going to enjoy this."

"No, no! Deputy! *Deputy!* I want him out of here! I want him out! *Deputy!*"

***

Blair rubbed bleary eyes as she walked back into the station. Francis Callaway was in surgery. It was going to take one hell of a while, *if* he made it out okay. She'd come back to the station to check in on Linc, then she was going back to the hospital. Spencer had made sure one of his deputies stayed there, but she wanted to be present, too. Just in case.

The station was eerily silent. Titus was sitting on the edge of a desk and staring down at his hand.

"Uh, Titus?" She cleared her throat. "May I see Linc for a moment? He tends to be a worrier." Understatement of the century. She'd noticed that tendency with him on their first case. If he thought she was hurt, the guy flipped out. "After the gunshots, I think he'd probably rest better if he saw for himself that I was okay."

Titus shook his head. "Can't let you go in there right now." His hand fisted. "Been five minutes. Spencer was wrong. Let's give them a little longer."

"What?" She was running on fumes and would very much appreciate a nice collapse somewhere.

He looked up at her. "What's the story with you and your partner?"

"Story?"

"Um...Is it one of those business-only deals? Or more like partners-with-benefits?"

She stopped. "You're trying to distract me."

He gave her a charming grin. One that made the faint lines near his eyes crinkle. "Am I?"

Her stare darted toward the holding area. "You're distracting me to keep me away from Linc."

"Visiting hours are over. You should come back to see him in the morning."

Her gut clenched. "What's wrong? Is he hurt?"

"See...*that's* why I asked what the story was between you two. I've noticed that tendency you both have to get a little antsy when you think something might have happened to your partner."

Okay, forget this. She headed for holding.

He blocked her path. The man could move *fast*. "I think we should give them longer."

"Them?"

"He's not alone in holding. He's got company back there. Want to guess who?"

She did not.

"*Deputy!*"

She jumped at the shout.

Titus didn't move.

"You heard that," Blair whispered. "I know you did."

"*Deputy!*"

"Does he sound desperate?" Titus tilted his head. "Maybe he does. Maybe—"

She ran around him.

His sigh followed her.

Blair threw open the door to the holding area. "Linc!"

He was right in front of Andrew Bradley. Andrew was pinned between Linc and the bars.

"Get him out of here!" Andrew screamed. "Now! And I want my lawyer! I deserve my freaking phone call!"

"Hmmm...well, you're the one who put Linc in jail..." Titus ambled in behind her. "So if you want him out—"

"I'm dropping the charges. Is that what you want to hear? I'm not pressing charges, just get this psycho out of my cell!"

Blair's breath left her in a hurried rush.

"That's what I wanted to hear, yes." Titus unlocked the cell. Motioned toward Linc. "Come on."

He made no move to exit. "I want to stay."

"No, what you want is to pound the shit out of the guy, but I can't actually let you do that. He dropped the charges. You're a free man. Worked just like Spence said it would." Titus rolled his hand. "Come on. I don't have all night."

Linc shot a fuming glare at Andrew. "We aren't done."

He marched from the cell. Blair stiffened because Linc headed straight for her. She'd never seen his eyes look quite so intense before. His hand lifted and his fingers curled around her jaw. His touch sent heat racing through her.

Linc stared at her as if she was the only thing around him. "You weren't hit by the bullets."

"No."

"You're okay."

"Yes."

Some of the tension slid from him. His hand dropped. "Then let's get the hell out of here."

The sooner, the better.

They strode for the door.

"Oh, I do remember her now..." Andrew's voice was mocking. Cocky all of a sudden, when he'd been afraid before.

Blair turned slowly and stared at him through the bars. Titus had already closed the cell door.

"Shanna. Bleached blonde. Too thin. Thought she was going to be a prima ballerina. Girl had no talent. Told her so." He smirked. "She couldn't handle the truth. Last time I saw her, she was running away, crying."

Linc surged forward.

Blair caught his arm. "Stop. You got what you wanted. You have his DNA."

Andrew smiled. "Shanna probably met a bad end. That's what happens sometimes to girls like her."

Linc's body vibrated against Blair. She pushed him back and narrowed her eyes on the man in the cell. The man who'd been screaming for a deputy moments before but now seemed arrogant as hell. "*You'll* be meeting a bad end."

"Promises, promises..." His gaze drifted over her. "Well, aren't you something new and shiny?"

Linc locked his arm around her shoulders. "*Don't fucking even think it.*"

"You two—get out," Titus ordered at the same time. "I'll clear the paperwork out front. *Go.*"

Blair turned with Linc. He kept his arm around her shoulders. She could feel his fury. It was like a living, breathing beast filling the air around them. He didn't speak until they were out of the holding area, and as soon as that door closed behind them—

Linc cornered her. He turned his body and slapped his hands against the wall behind her. He was in front of her, the stone wall behind her, and she couldn't look away from his eyes.

"You weren't hurt." His voice was low and growling. This wasn't the Linc she knew. The Linc who always had a funny one-liner. Who was mocking and easy going and kept a ready smile.

This wasn't him.

But...

Maybe she didn't know Linc so well. She hadn't known about a sister. Hadn't known he was working his own agenda, and as she stared into his eyes, she actually thought...

I don't know him at all.

"Blair."

She swallowed. "I already told you, I'm okay."

He didn't back away.

Her hand lifted and pushed against his chest. A spark of electricity seemed to burn through her fingers. Her breath caught, and she saw his eyes flare. He'd felt it, too.

No, no, absolutely *not*. They were not doing this.

His hands fell down as he backed away from her.

"You can't lie to me, Linc." Her voice was low, carrying only to him. "Not if we're going to be partners. That's a deal breaker for me. I have to be able to trust my partner completely, and if I can't trust you..." No, she hadn't been the one holding back. That had been him. "If *you* can't trust me, then we're done."

"That an ultimatum, B? I tell you all my secrets or you find a new partner?"

She held his stare.

A faint smile curved his lips. It never reached his eyes. "I'm not the only one with secrets."

"I haven't held anything back from you."

"You sure about that? You're sure that you're being completely honest with me...about everything?"

Her breath came too fast. "I don't know what game you're playing." She brushed past him. "I can't stay here all night. I need to get back to the hospital and see how Francis is doing."

He grabbed her arm. Not in a tight grip. He never did that. Never hurt her.

But then, she would have said that he never lied to her, too. She'd been wrong about that.

"Blair..."

Her face angled toward him. "Do your paperwork with Titus. Try to *not* get arrested again, if you can help it. I'll update you about Francis's condition when I learn more."

He didn't let her go. "Watch your back. Andrew Bradley isn't going to give up and sit in a cell like some model prisoner. He'll have a backup plan in place."

Her head inclined.

His hand slowly slid down her arm. A caress that sent a shiver over her body. What was happening? They were partners. *Partners.* Nothing more. Nothing less.

Her steps were quick as she hurried away from him. No, she wasn't hurrying.

She was fleeing.

CHAPTER SEVENTEEN

"I know you're sore. Do you need some help taking off your clothes?"

They were in Spencer's house—the main house, not the cottage—and standing at the foot of his stairs. The Christmas tree waited nearby, and the house smelled of fresh pine.

He'd been careful with her since they'd left the station. His jaw had been clenched tightly, his movements brisk and a little rough, but he'd spoken gently to her. Touched her with only the lightest of caresses.

As if he thought she'd break.

She wasn't the breaking type. He should know that.

Her gaze slid around the room. Toward the tree. They still hadn't decorated the tree. They'd planned to do that before...

Before the world had gone crazy.

Her gaze darted past the tree and slid to the comfy couch. The area was tidy and warm, and it felt like home.

Or maybe *he* felt like home.

"Baby?"

Her gaze returned to him. "I need help."

"Okay." He released a breath. His hands were at his sides. "Let's go upstairs. I'll help you get the clothes off and then you can slide into bed and rest."

"No."

Spencer blinked. "No?"

"No, I don't want to go upstairs. I want to stay right here. I want you to take my clothes off right here."

Silence. Thick.

A low growl came from him.

She saw the flare of desire in his eyes.

But then...

"I don't think you understand the situation," Spencer rumbled. His voice sent a roll of heat through her body. It was so dark and deep and sexy. "I'm trying to keep my control right now. I'm fucking on edge. You nearly died. That SOB set you up. If you hadn't been wearing the vest—"

Her hand lifted and touched his stubble-covered jaw. "I was wearing the vest. I'm all right."

He shuddered at her touch. "That's a...bad idea."

"What is?" Her fingers slid down his throat. Moved to his chest. "Touching you?"

He caught her hand. "You need care."

Haley laughed. "What I need is you."

"You're hurt. I'm not sure I can keep my control. Not sure I can be gentle."

He was precious. "Because I asked for gentle?"

His pupils flared. "You have bruises from the fucking bullets."

He was trying to look out for her. And it was sweet and it made her heart ache, but what she really wanted right then...was him. "I was scared, too."

His jaw hardened.

"The bullets blasted, and I felt them hit, and when I was falling, do you know what I thought about?"

A hard shake of his head. His hold on her hand was so tight.

"I thought about you." She pushed up on her toes and her lips brushed over his neck. "I want you, Spencer." Her tongue slid out and licked him. "I don't care about gentle or rough. I don't care about control. I just need you."

He yanked her against him. Her head tipped back and his mouth crashed down on hers. *Yes.* The kiss was exactly what she craved. So much passion and stark need. Fierce desire. She kissed him back with a wild desperation. Her hands curled around his shoulders and held on for dear life.

His tongue thrust into her mouth. She moaned and took more. Adrenaline, fear, lust— everything swirled like a tornado in her. In the storm, he was her center.

Her nails raked him. His shirt was in her way. She wanted skin to skin. She pushed her hands between them and yanked at the shirt. Haley was pretty sure she heard a button pop, but she didn't care. She shoved the shirt open and touched warm skin. Muscled strength. She pulled her mouth from his and kissed his chest. Licked. Bit. Loved every single moment.

"Baby...*I'm trying to hold on...*"

Screw control. She licked his nipple.

Haley could have sworn she heard his control shatter.

He grabbed her shirt. Had it flying across the room a moment later. His hands went to her breasts. He yanked the bra out of the way. Took her breasts into his warm, strong hands. She arched toward him. He plucked her nipples with his fingers, then took one nipple into his mouth, sucking hard and deep, and her knees went weak.

He caught her. Lifted her up and held her easily as he stalked toward the couch. He put her down and jerked off her shoes. Her jeans. Took her underwear with them so that she was naked before him and spread out on those soft cushions.

He still had on his pants and boots. Still had—

He knelt near the couch. Hauled her toward him. Spread her legs and put his mouth on her. She cried out because his lips and tongue felt so good. She was going crazy. Haley surged her hips toward him even as she grabbed for the cushions and clenched them in her hands. Her body was bow tight. He was licking and sucking. Working her clit with his fingers. There was no way she could hold back, and Haley came with a fast, sharp scream.

Her hips bucked against him. He kept working her with his mouth. Licking her over and over again. Like he was starving. Desperate.

"*Spencer!*"

She came a second time. Or maybe she was still coming from the first release. The pleasure pounded at her. Her eyes were squeezed shut, and her breath heaved out as her whole body trembled.

He pulled back. Her sex quivered—

She let go of the cushions and reached for him. Greedy for more. Everything.

He pressed a kiss to her side.

She quivered.

He'd...he'd just kissed one of the bruises from the bullets. His mouth moved up, and he kissed the second one, too. The one so close to her heart.

His head lifted. Her eyes had opened at his tender kiss, and she stared at him. Lust stamped his features. He looked wild and savage.

He stripped and grabbed a condom from his wallet. Shoved it on. He kissed the mark near her heart once more, and then he drove his cock into her. He filled every single inch of her. Her legs locked around his hips.

Spencer's hands came down, pushing on the cushions near her as he kept the weight of his body off hers. His gaze pinned her. Slowly, he withdrew.

She wanted him *back*.

Spencer plunged into her and filled her completely once again. Her body was so sensitive. Every glide and thrust had her panting and jerking. Spencer wasn't restrained. Wasn't holding back. He let go and surged into her over and over. He was thick and full, and he was driving her insane.

Another orgasm was building. She could feel it coming. He was kissing her neck. Slamming into her, and her body was just his. *His*. There was no stopping. There was no slowing down. She came for him again, screaming his name this time because it felt that good.

He caught her legs. Lifted them higher. Opened her even wider for him.

He drove into her. Withdrew. Thrust.

His face was locked into primitive, dangerous lines. His eyes gleamed.

He stared at her as if she was his. As if he needed her more than anything else in the world.

As she fought to catch her breath, she realized she did want him more than anything or anyone else. She'd never felt this way for another man. *Never*.

He erupted in her. Bellowed her name.

And she whispered, "I love you."

***

Her eyes flew open. Haley's breath shuddered out as awareness came back to her in a fast, desperate rush. She'd had sex with Spencer. Awesome, amazing sex. At the end, she'd...

Oh, God...had she said that she loved him?

Her hands flew out and grabbed the soft cover that was over her. How had the cover gotten there? Where was Spencer?

And, jeez, had he heard her confession?

"I didn't want to wake you up." His voice came from the right.

Her head whipped toward him. He was sitting on the nearby chair, wearing a pair of loose jogging pants, and that gorgeous chest of his was wonderfully bare.

"I figured you'd had one nightmare of a day, so you needed your rest." He gave her a half smile. "You're cute when you sleep. Sometimes, you smile."

She smiled in her dreams?

Only when I'm dreaming of him. And she had been. They'd been walking through town, with all of those gleaming Christmas lights around them, and she'd felt safe. Happy.

The way she seemed to always feel with him.

"Actually, you're not cute." He leaned forward. "You're fucking beautiful."

She sat up, pulling the cover with her because, yep, she was naked. Super naked. "You were watching me sleep?"

"I was watching over you. I..." He glanced away. "After today, I can't shake this tightness in my gut. Like danger is still coming."

Coming for me.

"When I was a SEAL, my instincts never steered me wrong. This isn't over, not yet. The bastard has another plan in place, I know it."

She pulled the cover even closer. "You didn't buy that bit about him being undercover and working with the FBI."

His gaze returned to her. "Did you?"

No. "He's really good at lying. I learned that when we were together."

His jaw hardened. "For the record, I hate hearing about when you were with him."

She blinked at him.

He rose. Towered over her with his muscles tight. "See, here's the thing. I think I'd hate hearing about you and *anyone* else. Because I'm a jealous bastard."

Haley swallowed. "If it makes you feel better, I don't want to hear about you and anyone else, either."

His head cocked. "That why you kissed me under the mistletoe back at Maureen's?"

Their first kiss. A kiss that had changed everything for her. "There was no way that Keri was kissing you."

He laughed. God, she loved that sound. So warm and rich.

But as he stared at her, Spencer's laughter faded. "If that SOB comes for you, I will do anything necessary to stop him. I'm not going to lose you."

She didn't want to think about losing Spencer, either. Not when she'd just found him.

"You didn't answer my question. Did you buy his undercover story?"

"No." Her head tilted back as she gazed up at him. "Because his mouth was moving. I've learned that when Drew is talking, he's lying."

"I think he's the one who helped Francis escape. I think he has Francis's ex-wife. I think he forced Francis to shoot you."

"How is Francis?"

"In recovery. Got an update a little while ago. He's not conscious, not yet. But I have a deputy with him, and we'll know as soon as the guy wakes up and can talk."

Good. She nodded.

Spencer didn't move.

She couldn't look away from him. Didn't want to look away.

"Did I hurt you, before?"

"You've never hurt me."

His hand caressed her cheek. "I want to destroy anyone who does. I'm not controlled, hell, I'm barely even civilized when it comes to you. Your safety matters more to me than anything else."

Her head turned. Her lips pressed to his palm.

"Baby..."

She looked back at him. Realized that Spencer was in the absolute perfect position. Her hands reached out. Her fingers were shaking, just a little, as she pushed down his jogging pants.

"Haley..."

His cock sprang toward her. Thick and full. Already erect.

"Yeah, that happens when I'm near you." His voice was rougher. Even deeper. "I look at you, and I want."

She glanced up at him. "What a coincidence. Same thing happens to me." She leaned forward and put her mouth on him.

Spencer hissed out a breath. His hands curled around her shoulders.

She licked him. Sucked him. Took him in and savored him.

"Fuck, yes."

Her lips skimmed over the head of his cock. Her tongue licked him again, a series of fast, short licks. Then long, teasing ones.

"You are making me *crazy*."

Good. She took him inside her mouth again. Sucked him and licked that thick length and then—

"No." He pushed her back. "I'm about to fucking *explode*."

He said it like that was a bad thing.

His eyes glinted down at her. His cock bobbed toward her. She wanted another lick. But he'd backed away so...

She rose. Let the cover slip to the floor with a rustle of sound. He drank her in. His expression hardened as his gaze slowly drifted over her body. She waited for his gaze to rise. Waited for him to look into her eyes once more. When he did, she smiled at him.

"I think it's time we went to bed." Haley turned away. Made sure to walk all nice and slow toward the stairs. After all, she was trying to give him a show. When her hand touched the bannister, her fingers were still trembling. Sure, she was trying to act confident, but she was nervous as hell inside. Haley risked a quick peek at him. Spencer hadn't moved. "Don't you want to join me?"

"Hell, yes."

"Don't you want me to...finish what I started?"

"Hell the fuck yes." He bounded toward her.

Before she could climb the stairs, he'd scooped her into his arms. The man was so strong.

Sexy and strong and he held her easily. He carried her up the stairs in no time, and when they got to his bedroom, he was kissing her. Kissing her like he couldn't survive without her mouth.

She loved the way he seduced her with his tongue and lips. Loved the way he kissed her neck and made her moan. Her nails raked over him when he put her on the bed. She wanted him in her, deep and hard.

But he pulled back to grab a condom from the nightstand.

She watched as he put it on, her greedy gaze taking in every moment. He ditched the jogging pants. Flipped on a light. He was so sexy to her.

"On your knees, baby," he growled.

A shiver skated over her.

"Turn toward the headboard. Hold it tight."

That sounded like fun to her. She rose and moved toward the headboard. Her hands clutched the wood. "Like this?"

He kissed her shoulder as he moved behind her. "Exactly like this." His hand slid around her side, moved down her stomach, down between her legs. "Because now I can touch you...like this."

One hand pressed to her clit. The other hand guided his cock to her sex. Her hips surged back against him and took him in all the way...and his fingers rubbed fast and hard against her aching clit.

His thrusts had the bed shoving against the wall. Every time he filled her, she arched back against him with the same fierce passion. His fingers kept working her. He touched her just the way she needed. Over and over again, and when she climaxed, her body arched like a bow. She clawed at the headboard as the orgasm pounded through her.

He grabbed her hips, sealed her tightly to him, and roared her name.

Her heartbeat thundered in her ears. Haley opened her eyes and saw her hands gripping the headboard. As she fought to steady her heart, his hands rose and covered hers. His mouth pressed to her shoulder. He covered her. Surrounded her.

His voice was low as he told her, "I'll make sure the bastard never hurts you again...but, baby, when you leave me, it's gonna rip me apart."

She turned her head. Met his gaze. "Why?"

"You know why."

She didn't. She only knew how she felt. She didn't know what they were to him. Yes, he wanted to keep her safe, but he was the sheriff. Safety was his thing and—

His lips brushed over hers. "You know why," he said again. He pulled out of her.

She didn't move for a moment. He padded toward the bathroom. Shut the door. Turned on the sink and she could hear the surge of water.

She—

Jumped out of the bed. Marched toward the bathroom and yanked the door open. "You heard me."

He turned toward her.

Yum. No, no, *focus.* "You heard me downstairs. You heard what I said to you."

His expression didn't alter.

"You told me that you didn't like lies." She was naked. She should have grabbed a sheet.

They'd just had mind-blowing sex, and *now* she was nervous about being naked with him?

She was because...he suddenly seemed so intense. A dark aura surrounded him.

"I don't like them. I won't lie to you. I'm not *him*."

Okay, good. Wonderful. "I never thought you were."

He stepped toward her.

They needed clothes. But first—"You heard me downstairs."

"Maybe I didn't. Maybe you need to say the words again."

Her gaze searched his.

"Or maybe..." Spencer growled. "Maybe you didn't mean the words. It's easy to say things in the heat of the moment that you want to take back later. You just met me. The sex is great."

All right, fine. They had just met. The sex *was* great.

"You don't have to say anything else to me. You don't have to make me any promises, Haley." His jaw was hard. His eyes were burning hot. "I'll stand between you and any threat, any day of the week, and you don't have to promise me a thing."

It wasn't about promises.

He brushed by her. Gave her a killer view of his fine ass. He grabbed his gray jogging pants and yanked them on.

She stumbled after him. Haley spied one of his t-shirts on a nearby chair, and she jerked it over her head. It was soft against her skin, and it carried his crisp scent. "I'm not promising."

He turned toward her. A frown pulled at his eyebrows.

"I never told Andrew that I loved him."

He stiffened. "Why not?"

"Because I didn't."

"You were going to fucking marry the sonofabitch. You didn't mention *that* to me before." He took a hard step toward her.

"He said he wanted to marry me. But there was never a proposal. Just him talking. I liked him. He was charming and—"

Spencer growled.

"I didn't feel the spark. I didn't feel the connection. It was never there. It had *never* been there before, not with him or anyone else. Do you get what I'm telling you?"

He stared back at her.

"I thought maybe it wasn't real—this big, earth-shattering emotion that people are supposed to feel. I never felt it. Look...I lost my parents the summer after I turned eighteen."

Sympathy flashed on his face. "I'm sorry."

"It ripped me open. It was a car crash. One minute, I had them. I was loved. I was happy. The next minute, I was alone." And terrified. She wet her lower lip. "I didn't get close to people after that. I put up a wall. I didn't want to hurt again, not like that. Time passed and I realized the wall was keeping me away from everyone. It was stopping me from living. From falling in love. So I tried to let down the wall with Andrew. I tried, and then I found out that I'd made a terrible mistake."

Spencer stalked closer to her. "He never deserved you."

Her stomach twisted in knots. "I didn't have a chance to put the wall up with you." Did he get what she was saying? "You barreled into my life."

"You barreled into mine." A pause. "I lost my parents when I was ten years old. I know what it's like to have your world ripped away."

"Oh, God, Spencer…" Sorrow pierced her heart.

"My grandfather raised me, but he passed when I was seventeen. I would have been alone after that but…I had this town."

She didn't understand.

"The town took care of me. The people here surrounded me and protected me. That's why I came back here when I needed to step back from the life I led as a SEAL. The people here needed me, and I needed them." A pause. "The place can heal you, if you give it a chance. It can change you. Hell, for a while, this town was the only thing that kept me going."

It wasn't the town that was healing her. But she was changing. "I'm so sorry about your family."

"And I'm fucking sorry about yours, baby."

He understood her, in so many ways. He…"You were past my guard before I even realized it," Haley confessed, understanding as she slowly spoke. "Everything that I *thought* I should feel for Andrew, I felt it with you. Without even trying, it was there." The instant connection. The desire, yes, but more. So much more.

Determined now, she said, "I meant what I said downstairs."

A phone rang somewhere in the house. *Jingle Bells.*

No. Dammit, no.

She'd been afraid when she woke on the couch, terrified that he'd heard her confession. But why bother with fear? Why not tell him exactly how she felt? Life was too short for hiding. Nothing was guaranteed. *Nothing.* "I love you."

"You don't have to say—"

She grabbed his arms. "I love you. I know how I feel. This isn't about sex or adrenaline or anything else. It's about me falling in love with you before I could stop myself. It happened fast and hard. It *happened.* I love you."

The phone was still ringing.

And he hadn't said a word. But then, she hadn't told him how she felt to force any kind of confession out of him. She'd done it because she was afraid there wouldn't be another time for her to say the words. She'd been shot hours before. Been cold on the ground and realized how easily her life could be over.

She'd made the confession for herself. Not for him.

The phone on the nightstand gave a loud peal of sound. It startled her and she jumped. She hadn't even noticed the old landline.

Spencer swore and grabbed the phone.

Haley put a hand to her chest.

"What?" Spencer barked into the phone. Talk about sounding pissed off. His face darkened as he added, "No, I don't give a shit who he is.

Andrew is not getting out of that station until I arrive. Yeah, yeah, I'll be there soon. You can count on it."

He hung up.

Haley's hands twisted in front of her.

"The FBI finally showed up. Not the locals from across the bay in the Mobile, Alabama, office. Some strangers that Titus has never seen before. They've got paperwork demanding Andrew's release." His hand pressed to the top of the phone. "Titus won't let the bastard walk. He'll stay there until I arrive. I'll get this straightened out."

She glanced toward the window. It was still dark outside. How long had she slept?

Had Spencer slept at all?

Or had he been watching over her all that time?

"I want you to come with me." He was staring down at the phone. "I want you at my side. I need to know that you're safe."

She nodded but realized he couldn't see the move. "Okay. I'll get dressed." Going with him meant returning to the station and facing off against Andrew. Chill bumps rose on her arms as she turned away and stumbled a bit toward the bathroom.

Haley heard the creak of a drawer behind her and, a moment later, Spencer's fingers curled around her arm.

"Stop."

Immediately, she stilled. His fingers were warm and strong. Would she ever get used to the way his touch made her feel?

His fingers slid down her arm. Caught her hand. Opened it. And pressed a gun to her palm.

Holy shit. She almost dropped the gun. But he curled her fingers around the gun's base. Held tight.

"If some sonofabitch is coming to hurt you, you fire and you keep firing until you stop him."

A lump rose in her throat.

"If I'm not there, if anything should separate us, then you're going to have this gun for protection. You're going to shoot, and you will stop anyone who comes at you."

Her head turned so that she was staring into his eyes.

"Because if you die, I will go fucking insane."

"Can't have that," she whispered.

He didn't smile at her. If anything, his expression became even grimmer. "I don't trust the Feds. I don't trust Andrew. Something is going down, and we have to be prepared."

The gun felt heavy in her grip.

"Shoot, baby. Don't hesitate."

Don't hesitate to kill. Could she do that?

In order to survive...yes.

She nodded.

"Good." He kissed her temple. "I'll get fresh clothes for you."

Clothes. Crap. She'd forgotten all about them. All of her stuff was still down in the guest cottage.

"I'll set the alarm and lock the door. You go ahead and get showered. I'll be right back." He eased away from her. Strode toward the door.

She stared down at the gun in her hand. Her world had changed so much since New York. Since the parties. The gallery shows.

All of that felt like another world. So far away. So distant.

Another life.

One that she wasn't so sure she wanted anymore.

*****

"He left the house," he muttered into the phone. "Move, now. You have to be fast. He'll be back in moments. Yes, man, I got eyes on him." He could see the big bruiser right then.

The sheriff was rushing toward the cottage. Moving far too fast. Hell, at this rate, the guy would be back before his partner even had a chance to get past the security system at Spencer Lane's home and inside to Haley Quick.

So...

He had to fucking improvise.

He slid from the shadows. Took the knife from his boot. He'd been at the property for a while as he waited and watched, so he knew exactly where all the cameras were positioned. He could avoid them.

Easy.

Spencer had entered the cottage. How long would he be inside? Long enough for Haley Quick to die?

I can't let him get back to her. My job is to stop the sheriff.

But Spencer was already heading back out of the cottage's front door. Looked like he was carrying something. Spencer turned to secure the lock.

He rushed up behind Spencer and lifted the knife toward the sheriff's back.

CHAPTER EIGHTEEN

She took a shower in record time. Fear helped to make her even faster. Haley jumped out of the shower, wrapped a towel around her body, and left her hair dripping over her shoulders as she hurried toward the bedroom. The gun was on the nightstand. The bedroom door still open.

No sign of Spencer.

Rocking forward onto the balls of her feet, she let her gaze dart around the room. Heavy furniture. A few framed photos. She inched closer to one of the photos and felt a smile curl her lips. She was staring at Spencer, obviously, but it was a teen Spencer. Thin, gangly, with a wide grin. A man with white hair had an arm around Spencer's shoulders, and they were both smiling proudly as they held up a fish. She recognized the dock that they were on—it was the one down below, on the beach.

Spencer and his grandfather. The resemblance was there in the strong features and hard jaws and—

The door opened downstairs.

There was silence. That was...odd. Spencer had said that he'd reset the alarm. Shouldn't she have heard it beep when the door opened?

Her head cocked as she strained to listen. Haley expected Spencer to come rushing up the stairs. Instead, the silence stretched.

Unease slithered through her.

She crept toward the bedroom door. The heavy carpet swallowed the pad of her steps. She eased out of the room and peeked down below.

A flash of shaggy, blond hair caught her eye. *Not Spencer.*

Her lungs hurt because she sucked in a breath so fast. She rushed back toward the bedroom. Headed straight for the nightstand—

Footsteps thudded up the stairs.

She grabbed the gun.

She didn't hear the steps any longer. Was it because the blond was already upstairs? The carpet now muffling his steps?

"Hello, sweetheart."

That *wasn't* Spencer.

Her back was to the intruder. His slightly nasally voice was familiar to her. Just as the cut of that blond hair had been familiar.

"I think I warned you once before, you need to stay the fuck away from cops."

Yes, that voice had scared the hell out of her before. It was the voice that belonged to the man who'd attacked her in New York. The jerk who'd grabbed her outside of the subway station and told her that if she ever betrayed Andrew again, it would be the last thing that she did.

Her breath came slowly even as her heart thundered in her chest. "I'm not alone. I—"

"Your boyfriend isn't coming back to save you. Hell, I don't think he'll *ever* be back."

No. Her breath stopped being slow. She didn't breathe at all. And her heart wasn't thundering. It had frozen.

He laughed. "I am going to enjoy driving this knife into—"

She spun around. Pointed the gun at him.

Surprise flashed on his face, but then he lunged forward.

She fired.

*****

Spencer whirled at the blast of gunfire, and he saw the bastard who was rushing toward him with a knife. He dropped Haley's clothes, caught the attacker's hand, shoved it back, and twisted.

The perp—wearing a black ski mask—screamed as he dropped the knife.

Spencer drove his fist into the guy's face. A hard hit that he knew broke bones, and he didn't fucking care.

The blast of the gunfire echoed in his ears. A shot that had come from the main house.

Haley.

Spencer's attacker staggered back, but the fool rallied and lunged forward again.

Spencer yanked out his weapon. Pointed it at the fellow. "Try me," he dared. "Do it. Keep coming. See if I don't bury a bullet in you."

The masked attacker stopped. His hands were near his sides.

"Get them up!" Spencer barked. "Now. I want them *up!*"

The guy lifted his hands into the air.

Spencer looked toward the house. The light was on in the bedroom upstairs, but he couldn't see any movement up there.

"She's dead."

Spencer's head whipped back toward the piece of shit who'd just spoken.

"You'll run back to that house, and she'll be dead. And when you step inside, my partner will kill you, too." A grating laugh. "There is no way you make it out alive tonight. Your mistake was fucking her in the first place. Never should have touched her."

He wanted to pull that trigger. So badly.

"Big, bad sheriff. Can't do anything, can you? You want to rip me apart. You want to rush off and save her. Too late. My partner doesn't miss. He gave her a warning before. She should have listened back in New York. Now it's all over for her. It's—"

Spencer hauled the bastard forward. "If she's dead, so are you."

The masked attacker pounded his fist into Spencer's stomach.

He barely felt the blow. He shoved the fool back, and the man scrambled for the fallen knife.

He picked it up, laughing, and surged toward Spencer.

Bam.

For the second time that night, the knife dropped. This time, so did the attacker. He fell to the ground, body shuddering, as blood soaked him.

Spencer raced past him. He had to get to the house. Had to get to Haley. He ran as fast as he could. The front door was locked. *He'd* locked it when he left. Locked it and set the alarm so that Haley would be safe.

I promised to keep her safe.

He didn't bother yanking out the key. He just kicked in the door. It flew back and bounced into the wall. But the alarm never made a sound.

They cut the alarm. Fuck, Fuck! "Haley!" He raced up the stairs. Fear and rage were all he knew. Absolute terror and fury. If Haley had been hurt, if that bastard had hurt her—

What if he killed her? What if he—

Spencer stopped dead in the open bedroom doorway. He could see a man's body slumped on the floor. The guy wasn't moving. Blood had already soaked the carpet around him.

Spencer's gaze whipped up.

Haley stood near the nightstand. Her hand still gripped the gun. She had it aimed at the figure on the floor.

"Y-you said to keep shooting...but I shot once, and he fell..." Her voice was soft and lost.

Shock.

He knew the signs. "It's okay, baby. You're perfect. You did the right thing." He stepped over the body. Bent to check for a pulse.

There wasn't one.

Spencer looked up at Haley.

"I killed him," she said in that same lost voice. "I could see it. The life—when the bullet hit him, I was staring in his eyes, and everything just went away."

Fuck. Her first kill. It was never easy to take a life. He hurried to her. Took the gun from her and hauled her into his arms. She was soft and warm, and her delicate body shuddered against him.

"You said to shoot. You said—"

He eased back. Stared into her eyes. "He was going to kill you. You did the right thing. The only thing you could do."

A tear leaked from her eye. "He was the man from New York. The guy who attacked me near the subway. Andrew sent him after me then. He sent him after me now." She shook her head. "It's never going to stop."

"Yes, baby, it is."

Another tear. "He won't let me go."

Then I will just send his ass to hell. "He fucking will. I promise."

***

Spencer didn't go to the station. He put in a call and had Titus stay the hell on top of the FBI agents. Then he called in backup from the area and got authorities to swarm his house. Two dead bodies had to be explained, and the scene had to be contained.

He wanted those attackers traced back to Andrew Bradley. The blond who'd broken into his house and gone after Haley—Spencer knew they could link that guy to Andrew.

He'd attacked Haley in New York.

He'd come to kill her.

We can find proof of his link to Andrew and nail the SOB.

"What can we do?" Linc and Blair stood in the middle of the chaos at Spencer's home. They'd arrived in record time to the scene.

Spencer glanced to the right. Haley was three steps away from him. He wanted her even closer. "You can cut through the bullshit," he told them bluntly. "I need Francis Callaway's ex-wife. Get in touch with the Wilde agents in New York. I don't care if they have to tear that town apart, but they need to find her."

"What if she's already dead?" Blair asked quietly.

Not quietly enough. Haley flinched.

"If she's dead," Spencer responded, "then I need her body. Because Francis isn't going to play ball unless she's safe or she's dead. She's the reason he went after Haley. I know it. When he wakes up, I want him ready to nail Andrew. And he'll only do that if we have the ex."

If she was dead, Francis would want revenge.

If she was alive and in Wilde custody, then Andrew wouldn't be able to manipulate Francis any longer.

Blair nodded as she listened to him, but then her phone rang. She pulled it out and glanced down at the screen. "Hold on," she told them. "Maybe we have news now." Putting the phone to her ear, she stepped back.

Spencer glanced at Haley. Shadows lined her eyes, and he hated that. He wanted the threats gone to her. Every last one of them.

"What?" Blair's voice rose, jerking his attention back to her. "Was that sanctioned? Yes, yes, I've heard of him. Just didn't realize he was part of the team." Her long lashes flickered. "I see. He *isn't*." A small line grew between her brows. "Right. Yes. I'll tell them now." Her hand tightened on the phone as she lowered it to her side. "Well..." Her throat cleared. "The ex-wife has been found."

Linc eased closer to her. "Wilde agents brought her in?"

"No, a...freelance operator tracked her down."

That was surprising. "Since when does Eric use freelancers?" Spencer asked.

"Since Ghost." Her lips twisted. "Apparently, the guy makes his own rules."

"Ah, excuse me." Haley stepped forward as she squared her shoulders. "Who—or what—is Ghost?"

"He's an asshole," Linc muttered. "And he's very much *not* Wilde."

"He wants to be." Blair cut him a glance. "You know the man is more than qualified for the job."

Spencer's temples were throbbing. "I do not have time for this shit."

"Right." Blair nodded. "Ghost is—um, he's just that. A ghost. For years, he was whispered about—"

"Talked about like a freaking legend—" Linc cut in with a roll of his eyes.

"—but we recently found out that he is very much a flesh and blood man."

Linc's mouth tightened. "He's seriously not all that. The guy is a *douche*."

"Get to the point," Spencer gritted out.

"Ghost found the ex-wife. Used some of his highly shady connections and got to her. She was being held in some old warehouse in Brooklyn. He pulled her out, and she's safe, but Eric said the woman was blindfolded the whole time, so she has no idea who took her."

Yeah, but would Andrew know that? Andrew had been locked up, out of communication with his crew. He wouldn't know what had happened with the ex-wife. *We can use what Andrew doesn't know against him.* Spencer caught Haley's hand, lifted it to his lips, and pressed a kiss to her knuckles. "Will you trust me?"

"Of course."

Just that simple. That fucking simple.

He looked at her hand and wondered if she realized that she held his heart in her delicate palm. Soon, he'd tell her how he felt. First, though, he wanted her safe. He wanted her to be free.

"Ahem." Linc cleared his throat—twice.

Spencer glowered at the guy.

"What can we do?" Linc wanted to know.

Spencer smiled. "You can disappear."

CHAPTER NINETEEN

"See this?" The FBI agent's thin hair had been shoved back on his high forehead. His suit was wrinkled, and his eyes were hard with determination as he lifted a paper toward Spencer and waved it in the air like a flag. "This is an official document from my boss saying that Andrew Bradley is to be released into my custody, immediately."

Spencer blinked. "Do I look like I give a shit what your boss wants?"

Titus snickered. "Told you." He lounged with his hip propped on a nearby desk and his arms crossed over his chest. "Agent Morris, didn't I tell you that he wouldn't give a shit? I think those were my exact words."

The agent slammed the paper down on the desk. "The FBI trumps some backwoods sheriff's office any day of the week."

Haley stood beside Spencer. Her hand was gripped in his. He gave her a reassuring squeeze right before he said, "Not this day." His gaze flickered to Titus. "Who are these assholes?"

"Asshole Number One..." Titus pointed to the red-faced agent. "That is Special Agent Troy Morris. The fellow beside him is Asshole Number Two, his partner, Ken Doggett."

Ken had close-cropped, pale blond hair and bright green eyes. His eyes were locked on Haley.

Spencer waved a hand in front of her. "Hey, agent, over here."

Doggett's gaze snapped toward him.

Spencer smiled and knew it wouldn't be a pretty sight. "There a reason you're staring so hard at my companion?"

"I know who she is."

"Good for you."

"I know *she* shouldn't be here." A sniff. "She's the one who almost blew Andrew's cover to hell and back in New York. She needs to get out of this station. You need to send her away."

"That's a hard no. But thanks." Spencer let his stare drift around the station. Just after dawn and only a skeleton crew was there. His deputies were stretched thin because of every damn thing that was happening, but he had reinforcements coming in from Mobile. And, of course, there were the Wilde agents.

Some of the authorities were still at his house. Dealing with the bodies. The others, well...

Sometimes, help is closer than you think.

"You need to let Andrew go, now," Agent Morris snapped. "You have no right to hold him."

"He assaulted me. I think that gives me lots of rights."

Doggett pointed to Haley. "It's because of her. Trouble follows her. Now she has two lovers fighting over her and that has led to a fucking mess for the FBI."

"You jerk!" Haley fired back at him as she surged forward. "I'm not trouble. I'm not the criminal! I—"

"I heard on the police radio that you shot a man earlier." His angry stare raked her. "You going to tell me that's not trouble?" He focused on her and Spencer's joined hands. "And I'm guessing the fact that you're screwing the sheriff has nothing to do with the reason *you* weren't locked up for that crime?"

Spencer moved in front of her. "You want her?" He wasn't smiling. Wasn't pretending. "You go the fuck through me."

Her hands pressed to his back. "Spencer..."

Doggett retreated a step.

"Her shooting was self-defense, and it was also tied to that so-called upstanding citizen you're trying to vouch for, Andrew Bradley."

"Andrew's been locked up," Morris reminded him quickly. "Not like he could do anything."

"Really? I'm supposed to believe he can't pull strings?" Spencer inclined his head toward the Feds. "He got you two here, didn't he?"

They looked at each other.

"You've verified their IDs, Titus?" Spencer asked.

"Verified us?" Morris puffed out his chest. "How *dare*—"

"Wouldn't be the first time we had a prick in here pretending to be someone else." He shrugged.

Titus still had his hip pushed up against the desk. "They checked out. They're stationed up in New York. Came a long way for their 'friend' on this trip."

Yes, they had.

Spencer glanced back at Haley and sent her a reassuring smile. "It's okay."

She shook her head. "Nothing about this is okay." She was aware of his plan. They'd talked about it on the ride over. He knew she didn't like it. "Spencer..."

"Trust." A soft whisper. She'd given him her trust, and he would not let her down.

Haley nodded.

"Titus." Spencer turned toward his friend. "I need to see our prisoner. I'm going back to—"

"You're not getting near him without us there," Doggett barked. "We told you, it's time for you to release him."

"Not yet, it isn't. I have some questions for him first. I'm not even close to letting him go." His muscles were tight as adrenaline poured through him. "But how about this? I'll be generous. Hospitable, even. You two can come in the interrogation room with me while I question the prisoner. That work for you?"

The two agents exchanged a fast glance.

Spencer slid his gaze to Titus. "And you can watch from the observation room."

A slow nod.

"*I'll* be in observation, too," Doggett said quickly. "Morris, you can stay with Andrew."

Spencer stiffened. Then, as he held Titus's stare, he lifted his right hand and rubbed his index finger under his eye.

Titus gave a barely perceptible nod. On the way over, Spencer had called and spoken with Titus already, wanting to warn him of possible danger. But the old hand gesture—a sign they'd used back in their SEAL days—was still a message to stay on alert. *Keep your eyes open. Expect betrayal.*

They'd seen plenty of that back in the day.

Betrayal was always waiting to spring. That was why you had to be ready for it.

"Before we go in to the interrogation room..." Spencer curled his lips in his most genial smile. "All weapons have to be secured. I'm sure you understand the drill. Can't have weapons where any prisoners can get a hold of them." A pause. "So if you're going in to interrogation, Agent Morris, I'll need you to surrender all weapons to my friend Titus. Now."

***

Her palms were sweating. Her stomach was churning. And Haley was trying very, very hard not to be sick. This whole keeping-it-cool-in-the-face-of-danger thing? So not her style.

She had *killed* someone. Shot and taken a life, and goosebumps still covered her skin. She would never forget the look in that man's eyes.

The door to the interrogation room opened. She stiffened in her chair. She'd been waiting in the room with Spencer and Agent Morris. A young deputy—she remembered his name, it was Cody—brought Andrew into the room. Andrew's hands were cuffed in front of him and a bruise lined his jaw. His eyes went immediately to her.

And narrowed.

Yes, jerk. I'm still alive. How about that? Suddenly, she didn't feel quite so cold as anger churned inside of her.

Then Andrew blinked and his expression filled with soft concern. The charming lie was in place on his face. "Haley!" He smiled at her. "I knew you would come to your senses. I knew you would—"

"*I want those cuffs off him,*" Morris ordered. "Now."

Spencer motioned to Cody. "You can go. I've got this." He marched around the table. Shoved Andrew into a chair. Kept his hand planted on Andrew's shoulder.

Agent Morris stood near the one-way observation mirror. His back was to the mirror, and his narrowed gaze was on Spencer.

Her hand slid inside her coat. A big, encompassing coat that sheltered her completely.

The door closed behind Cody. The soft click seemed so final.

"The cuffs," Morris said once more.

"Yeah, they aren't coming off." Spencer's grip on Andrew's shoulder tightened. "By the way, your team failed. As you can see."

Andrew's head turned so that he was staring at Spencer. "I have no idea what you're talking about."

"The two jackasses you sent to my place? They didn't take me out. They didn't kill Haley. Since they failed, I'm sure you have someone else already in place. Someone that you think will finish the job."

Morris surged forward. "This man is an FBI asset, he has nothing to do with—"

"This man is a cold-blooded criminal. In order to get what he wants, he threatens people around him. Like say...the PI who shot Haley right outside of this station." Spencer let Andrew go and took a step away from him. "Andrew had his goons kidnap Francis Callaway's ex-wife. If Francis didn't do exactly what he wanted, then Andrew said he'd have the woman killed."

Andrew stared at him...and laughed.

God, I hate his laughter. "This isn't funny," Haley snapped.

Immediately, his stare whipped to her. "No." He stopped smiling. "It's not. Come on, Haley." His cuffed hands rose and stretched across the table, as if he'd reach out and touch her. "You know me. You loved me. I would never do something like that."

She could feel Spencer's eyes on her. Haley shook her head. "I never knew you. Not the real you."

A muscle flexed in his jaw.

"And I didn't love you."

His eyes flashed with fury, a crack in his perfect mask.

"We have the ex-wife," Spencer announced. "She's been taken into custody."

"What?" Morris shook his head. "No, no, I have not been informed of anything—"

"I just informed you," Spencer told him. "You're welcome."

The FBI agent's face was truly an unnatural blend of purple and red.

As cool as you please, Spencer continued, "She's in custody, and she's going to testify that it was *your* men who abducted her, Andrew."

Andrew just shrugged. "If that's what they say, they're lying. They don't work for me." His stare never left Haley. "How could I be behind something like that? I'm here in Point Hope. Obviously, it's just my enemies, trying to make me look guilty. I'm an innocent man."

The man was such a lying snake. "You've never been innocent a day in your life."

"This is *over*," Morris announced. He rushed toward the table and hauled Andrew to his feet. "No more questions, no more farce, no more—"

The lights went out. Darkness filled the interrogation room, and for a moment, Haley didn't breathe.

There was a sharp grunt. A thud and then—

The lights came back on.

The FBI agent was against the wall, and Spencer had his forearm shoved under the fellow's throat. A knife was on the floor, just a few feet away.

"I am sure," Spencer growled, "that I said we couldn't bring weapons into the interrogation room. Did I stutter, Agent Morris?"

"Get the fuck off me!"

"Sure thing. Right after I cuff your ass." He flipped the guy around and yanked out cuffs as the agent struggled against him. But Spencer just slammed the agent's head into the wall and grabbed Morris's right wrist—

"*Sonofabitch!*" Andrew surged from the table and rushed toward the knife.

Haley lifted her legs and kicked at the small table as hard as she could, and it slammed into Andrew's side. He stumbled and whirled to glare at her.

"You're next, bitch, you're—"

Spencer shoved the FBI agent into the wall again. The fellow fell down, not moving.

Haley leapt to her feet. Andrew grabbed the knife. He held it in his cuffed hands as his gaze darted from Spencer to Haley.

"Haley, come here," Spencer said flatly.

"*Haley,*" Andrew snapped. "Don't fucking move. Not an inch, you understand?"

Her gaze shot to the one-way mirror.

Andrew started to laugh. "You think you're going to get help from that end?" More laughter. "Not happening. When the lights went out, that was our signal, you see. The FBI agents—they came in and talked with me while you bozos had me in that cell. We worked everything out." He was so damn proud. Smirking. "Those two guys who came after you at the sheriff's house? They were a diversion. I mean, hey, if they'd gotten lucky and taken you out, win."

Spencer took a slow step toward Haley.

"But you're pretty good, Sheriff Lane." Andrew pointed the knife at him. "So I figured you'd probably get the drop on them. And the way you get all territorial about *her,* I knew you'd be shooting to kill. I mean, look what you did to Francis. No hesitation, huh? *Bam. Bam.*"

Spencer eased closer to her.

"Morris was the one who told me you'd pull most of your deputies over there after an attack. So we just had to wait until this station was nearly cleared out. Then it was all about dividing and conquering. Morris came in here with us, while Doggett got to take care of that Titus bastard."

Once more, Haley's gaze darted to the one-way mirror. She swallowed to ease the desert dryness in her throat, and her stare slid back to Andrew. "I guess you're done claiming to be an innocent man who's working for the FBI?"

"*The FBI fucking works for me*! See those two agents who rushed down to my side? They work for me. They been working for me for a very long time." He smiled. "This is how it's all gonna go down. It's gonna look like the sheriff freaked the hell out. He got crazy because of you, Haley. You do that, you know." His gaze flickered over her. "You make a man crazy."

"You were crazy before you met me."

His lips thinned. "The FBI story will be that the agents had to take out the sheriff and his crooked deputy. They had to shoot and kill them. They had to—"

"Problem with this story," Spencer cut in. "Big problem. In case you haven't noticed, one of your agents is unconscious on the floor. He's not going to be shooting anyone."

"The other agent isn't." Andrew's chin jerked up. "He's right behind that mirror, watching everything. Your deputy Titus? He's already dead. The signal was the lights shutting off. I told you, that's what we were waiting for. When the lights went off, it meant that things were under control. It was time for Morris to act."

Spencer turned his head to look at the unconscious agent. "He did a bang-up job." He glanced over at Andrew. "You understand that we record what happens in this room, don't you? So some fake story about the agents having to stop me would never have worked—"

"There is no recording. Why do you think the agents were here all night? They got access to your system. Disabled that shit. Just like they helped to remotely disable the alarm at your house. There will be no way to prove what really happened here tonight." His hand was tight around the knife. "You'll be dead. I'll be a free man. And as for you, Haley..."

She stiffened when he focused on her.

"I fucking loved you." Spittle flew from his mouth. "I would've given you the world, but you betrayed me. Now, I am going to cut you into pieces."

Her hands were clenched at her sides. "I don't think that you will."

He smirked. "'Cause you think that the new boyfriend is gonna save you? You think that?"

Spencer lunged forward and ripped the knife from Andrew's hand. Did it so fast that Haley didn't even have time to blink. One minute, Andrew had the knife. And in the next, Andrew had been thrown back against the nearest wall.

"Dumbass." Spencer curled his fingers around the knife. "I was a SEAL. You think you can beat me at hand-to-hand? You think I'm scared of a cuffed man, waving a knife at me?"

Andrew straightened. "Agent Doggett!" Andrew screamed. "Shoot this bastard! Get in here and shoot him now—"

The door opened.

Agent Doggett stood there, face grim.

He took a step inside.

And Titus came in right behind him. Titus had his gun pointed against Doggett's back. "Yeah..." Titus drawled. "I don't think he'll be shooting anyone today."

Andrew's mouth dropped. "What? How—"

"Fucking SEAL, you idiot. The day some stiff in a suit takes me is the day that will *never* happen." Titus rolled one shoulder. "Didn't even need the backup that I had ready and waiting." He shoved Doggett forward. "Move."

Andrew flattened his back against the wall. "Wh-what backup?"

Linc and Blair strolled into the room. Linc gave a friendly wave. "Hi, asshole! Remember me?"

"Fuck."

Spencer used the knife to tap on the one-way mirror. "They were in there, watching. And, by the way..." He flickered a glance at Linc. "I'm assuming you got my equipment to *start* recording again?"

A nod. "Child's play."

Andrew was sweating bullets, and it was Haley's turn to smile. Spencer's plan had worked. He'd been sure the agents were dirty. Sure that they could trick Andrew into giving a confession as long as they set the scene right, and they had.

"Got him making his full confession." Linc whistled. "I mean, seriously, dude, you are a straight-up idiot. You really thought you were holding off Spencer with a knife? He could have ripped that thing from your hand at any moment."

A nod from Spencer. "True. I was just waiting for him to talk and brag long enough so that we had enough evidence to send him away for the rest of his life."

"No!" Andrew's frantic gaze swept the room.

Morris groaned.

"Oh, look," Titus murmured. "Someone is waking up to join the party. About time. Hey, Agent Morris, how do you think the other inmates will react when they find out a Fed is going to be in prison with them? Good times are coming your way..." He slapped his left hand on Doggett's shoulder. "You and your partner are going to have such fun."

Doggett drove his elbow back at Titus. The gun Titus held fired.

Chaos.

Morris lunged up. Haley realized he'd been awake for longer than she'd thought. He was lunging up at Spencer and—

"You bitch!"

Andrew rushed toward her. His cuffed hands were outstretched, and he was staring at her with wild fury in his eyes.

But he didn't touch her.

Spencer grabbed him. Swung Andrew around. Andrew attacked him and the two men slammed together. They hit hard. Andrew's hands clawed at Spencer and then...

He just fell.

Andrew fell to the floor, and Haley saw the knife sticking out of his chest.

Her gaze flew around the room. She'd been so focused on Andrew that she hadn't seen what happened to the others—

Titus had a bleeding Agent Doggett pinned on the floor. Literally pinned beneath his boot as he aimed his gun at the agent's forehead. "Give me a reason," Titus said, voice guttural. "Give it."

And as for the other agent...Blair had him against the wall. She'd drawn her weapon and had it locked on him. Morris had put his hands up in the air and his eyes were wide.

"Son-of-a-fucking-bitch!" Linc dropped to his knees beside Andrew. Andrew was clawing at the knife as blood soaked his shirt. "I wanted him to suffer. He deserved to suffer!"

He was dying. Haley could see it. *So much blood.*

Spencer ran to her. Caught her chin his hand. "Baby?"

She nodded. "I'm fine."

He yanked her against him. Held her tight. She felt a shudder run through his body.

As he held her, Haley's head turned. She stared down at Andrew. At the man who'd wrecked her life. Who'd sent people to kill her.

He was the nightmare who'd haunted her.

And he was...

"Get an ambulance," Spencer ordered flatly.

Cody had just hurried into the room. He caught Spencer's order, bobbed his head, and ran right back out.

An ambulance wasn't going to help.

Because her nightmare...it was finally over.

***

Andrew Bradley was pronounced dead at the scene. The two FBI agents were arrested. The backup that Spencer had called in from Mobile swarmed, and the crooked agents were taken away.

The town of Point Hope slept through most of the excitement. By the time the streets started to fill, the bad guys were all gone.

And Haley didn't have to hide any longer. She was free.

Free to do whatever she wanted.

Haley stood on the steps of the sheriff's station and watched the town come alive. Spencer was at her side, as he'd been the whole time. Since she'd first come to town. God, that seemed like a lifetime ago.

But it had really only been a few days.

Sometimes, you can live a whole life in a few days.

"I didn't intend to kill him."

Her head turned.

Spencer's gaze was hooded. "You think I did, don't you?"

"Spencer..."

A throat cleared. Titus had approached so silently. As Haley watched, Titus extended his hand to Spencer. "Think you should take this back."

What was he giving to Spencer?

Spencer glanced down at Titus's palm.

"Figured you'd be needing it again."

It was the sheriff's star. Why, no, *when* had Spencer given it to Titus?

"The town needs you, man." Titus kept his hand extended. "You know that. They want you here. We all do. You're the sheriff. Take the damn badge."

He'd given up his badge?

Spencer's gaze slowly lifted. Locked on hers.

And she knew that he'd done it for her.

I didn't intend to kill him.

But he had killed. He'd killed for her because he'd been trying to protect her. Just as he'd given up the badge because he'd been willing to do anything necessary to keep her safe.

To do all that...to do so much...

A tear rolled down her cheek.

"There's a mountain of paperwork to fill out," Titus mumbled. "And about a million people you need to talk with. The sheriff has a job to do."

"Take the badge," Haley told Spencer. "*Take it.*"

"Haley—"

She swiped at her cheek. This was all wrong. "I never wanted you to give up anything for me." But now, she could see that he had. She'd been falling in love with him, but not realizing what she was *costing* him. "I'm sorry."

His eyes widened. "Baby, no—"

"I'm sorry, Spencer. I'm so sorry." She had to get away. Just for a few minutes. It was too much.

The man she'd killed that night. Andrew. The crooked Feds. And most of all...

What did I do to Spencer? What had she made him become?

He'd killed for her, twice. *Twice.*

And he'd given up his badge. The town mattered to him. Hadn't he told her it was the only thing that had once kept him going?

She would not let him give it up.

"Haley—"

"I have to go." She backed away. Couldn't look in his eyes. "I just...I have to go right now." She would not break down in the street.

She loved Spencer. Loved him more than anything, and right then, she was running from him.

***

"I fucked that up, didn't I?" Titus muttered. "Sorry, man."

Spencer glanced at the star.

"Take the freaking thing. Go after the woman. Do your thing."

She ran from me. She was crying. "She doesn't want me to follow."

Haley was safe now. The threats were all gone. She didn't have to hide. Didn't have to stay in some small town that was a dot on the map. Haley could go back to her real life.

"She loves you."

His head snapped up.

Titus rolled his eyes. "Seriously, you know she does. You can see it in the woman's eyes when she looks at you."

I love you. Her sweet voice drifted through his mind.

"And you love her."

Spencer swallowed. His eyes were on Haley as she hurried down the street.

"So, Sheriff Lane, if the woman you love is leaving you with tears in her eyes, what in the hell are you going to do about that situation?"

Her tears hurt him. No, her pain gutted him.

Spencer released a slow breath. "I'm going to fucking fix it."

CHAPTER TWENTY

The parade was scheduled to start in ten minutes. Spencer paced as he checked the line-up one more time. He was supposed to be the Santa, and his red sleigh was all set to ride. The floats would go first. Then the elves on their bikes. Then the snow—all right, fine, the bubbles—would shoot out from the custom machines on his sleigh. He'd wave and be jolly and the whole town would celebrate.

Where in the hell is Haley?

He'd been tied up with Feds and cops and crime scene investigators all day long. The whole scene in interrogation had been caught on video, but there had still been questions to answer. More red-tape to clear up.

Francis was conscious. He'd talked and talked his ass off. He'd been beyond relieved that this ex-wife was alive. Turned out, while they were divorced and he enjoyed complaining about her, he actually still loved the woman. So when Andrew had threatened her, Francis had been forced to act.

He'd apologized a million times for shooting Haley, and he could damn well apologize a million more. Spencer wasn't exactly going to ever forget that act.

Francis had revealed that Andrew had been the one to break him out of the cell. He'd taken him out at gun point and hidden Francis nearby. When the deputies had searched the Italian restaurant, they hadn't found Francis because he'd been locked inside an empty wine barrel. Hayden Phelps had monitored Francis and sent him out like an attack dog when Haley had gone outside of the station. Hayden had apparently loved doing dirty work for Andrew. He'd been Andrew's go-to-guy.

Correction, he *had* been the go-to-guy.

Andrew was gone, his empire was imploding, and the two dirty Feds were willing to sell out everyone they could to try and make a deal. Plenty of bad cops and agents were going to fall in New York.

And as for Linc, the DNA results had come back, thanks to some mighty fast work by Wilde Securities. Linc's step-sister's killer had been confirmed.

Andrew Bradley.

May the sonofabitch rot in hell.

"Yo, Santa!" Titus grabbed his arm. "You're supposed to be on the sleigh, not pushing through the crowd." He wiggled his brows. "Now go up there and make merry."

"Have you seen Haley?"

"Since she walked off and your fool self didn't drop to his knees and shout his undying love to stop her?" Titus tapped his chin. "Nope, haven't seen her since then."

He'd been supposed to say he loved her? Right then? "She *left*. That's usually a sign that a woman is pissed."

"Yeah, it's also a sign that a woman is freaking out. You killed a guy in front of her. She'd had one hell of a night and morning already. Then she found out that you'd tried to ditch your sheriff job—guessing she didn't know about that—"

"No," he muttered. "She didn't." Because he'd been willing to cross every line—and break any law—for her. He hadn't wanted her to know that. He'd...

I was trying to protect her. From the darkest parts of himself.

He truly hadn't intended to kill Andrew in that interrogation room. He'd had a plan in place. But...

When Andrew had gone for her, when he'd tried to grab Haley that final time...

I stopped him.

He'd twisted the guy's wrist when their bodies collided, and Spencer had buried that knife in Andrew's chest without a second thought.

"She needed space." His gaze raked the crowd again. *She hasn't left town yet. She couldn't have left.* "I was just trying to give her what she needed."

"Uh, huh. I think we both know what she needs."

His attention shot back to Titus. "Seriously, when the fuck did you become some kind of romance god?"

"Since *always*?" A shrug. "Ask the local ladies, they'll tell you. God of romance. That's me."

The elves glanced over at Spencer. Frowned. One tapped his wrist—no, his watch.

Spencer waved to him. "Right, Frank. I get it. Thanks." Spencer looked back at Titus. "So what do you think she needs?"

"It's Christmas. Try a grand gesture."

"Uh, in case you missed it, I *killed* the bastard after her." And that was the problem. "And I think I scared the hell out of her. The last thing she wants is to trade one killer for another." He blew out a breath. "Since being with me, Haley has been nothing but terrified. How does she even know what she feels for me is real? Huh? How does she know? She said she loves me—"

"She *told* you? Damn, you didn't mention—"

"But what if it's just circumstances? Fear? Adrenaline? What if—when things are back to normal—she wants her old life? She wants New York? She wants action? She doesn't want me. I'm boring and—"

His friend's laughter cut him off.

Spencer glared. "It's not funny."

"I'm betting she doesn't find you boring, Santa." Titus slapped a hand on Spencer's bulging, red belly. "But here's the thing. You won't know what she *really* wants until you ask her."

"*Ahem.*" Frank the Elf tapped his watch again. His green, pointed hat bobbed.

Spencer's eyes narrowed. "Don't push me, Frank."

"You have time," Titus assured him.

"Not according to Frank." The *annoying* elf.

Titus pushed Spencer toward the sleigh. "No, I mean you have time with Haley. The danger is clear, and now you two can, you know, just be normal again. You can date her. Romance her. Show her how you feel." He stopped pushing. "Have you *told* her how you feel?"

"I—" Shit.

"Dude. She said she loved you and what did you do?"

I killed for her. And would do it again in a heartbeat.

"You are so lucky you have me in your life." Now Titus shoved him again. "Play Santa. Then find your lady. *Tell* her you love her. Give her a gesture. Make it a big fucking deal. Then she'll never think you're boring."

Spencer climbed onto the sleigh. Settled against the red seat. "I loved her from the first moment I saw her."

"That is some sweet shit." Titus tossed him the fake reins. There were no reindeer. Maybe the elves were supposed to be pulling the sleigh? Yeah, it looked that way from this angle.

Titus cleared his throat. "Spencer?"

He stopped staring at the elves and focused on Titus.

"Don't tell that sweet shit to me. Tell it to her."

His hold tightened on the reins. *I will. I absolutely will.* Because that last memory he had of her? With tears in her eyes as she turned away from him?

He had to banish that memory. He could not stand her pain. He wanted to give her a lifetime of happiness.

And, if she'd give him the chance, he would.

Bells began to ring. Loud and strong. Up ahead, he saw the first floats take flight. The streets were lined with men and women, kids and teens, people of every age, as the parade began. Music filled the air. Everyone was happy. Safe.

His town.

His people.

When his grandfather had passed, when he'd had no family left, these people had stepped up. The librarian had made sure Spencer always did his homework. She'd had a desk cleared out for him in her office. He hadn't been sent to foster care because the former sheriff—gone for the last year—had taken over temporary custody of him. Cane had been a gruff guy, a grizzly on the outside, and a teddy bear on the inside. He hadn't had any kids of his own, no wife, and Spencer had become his family.

Spencer had been at Cane's bedside when he passed.

Then the people of this town had voted to make him sheriff. He'd taken the job at first because...this was home.

He'd kept doing the job because...

Home.

The elves were biking ahead of him. Some were weaving a bit. Music was blasting. His fake snow was shooting out of the sleigh, and the whole scene seemed perfect. Except...

It wasn't.

One thing was missing. One very important thing.

She was missing.

His gaze scanned the crowd. He was waving as the sleigh headed forward. So many people were there. The kids jumped up and down. Everyone was celebrating.

Everyone except for the blonde woman who was walking with her head down. The blonde in the flowing, brown coat. The blonde in the tight jeans who was hauling a suitcase behind her.

A suitcase?

The fuck, no.

Spencer dropped the reins. "Haley!"

She didn't turn. Didn't glance up. It was a parade, for shit's sake. The woman should be glancing up. She wasn't.

She was heading away from the crowd and dragging her suitcase with her. And if she was dragging her suitcase, then *...she's leaving.*

She was leaving him? No. No.

Titus had been right, dammit. He should have said something sooner. Should have done more than just let her walk away with tears in her eyes.

He bounded off the sleigh. "Haley!"

One kid asked his mom, "Is Santa supposed to do that?"

Spencer darted through the crowd. Or tried to dart. It was hard with the costume and belly padding, but he rushed as best he could while fighting to keep her in sight. "*Haley!*"

She spun around. Blinked at him.

Shit. He had on the hat. The fake beard. The giant belly.

He ripped off the hat and beard. "Where the hell are you going?"

The folks around them went quiet.

Her eyes widened. "Spencer?"

Okay...*Where the hell are you going?* That had probably not been the most romantic thing ever to say to a woman, but his heart was about to burst out of his chest and he wasn't exactly thinking clearly. "What are you doing? Where are you going?"

She looked at him, then over his shoulder. "Shouldn't you be on the sleigh?"

No. He stepped forward. Caught her hand in his. "I'm exactly where I'm supposed to be." With her. Where he *wanted* to be. Because yes, the town had been a haven. But...shit, *she* was his home. When he was with her, he felt whole and happy. Living, not just going through the motions. "Don't leave me."

Her lips parted.

"Wait, that's not right." He had to make a gesture. Had to do this the *right* way. He dropped to his knees in front of everyone. "I love you." There. Much better. The right words.

"You're telling me now?"

"I should have told you the first moment we met." He shrugged one shoulder. "But I was worried that might freak you out."

"What?"

"Love at first sight isn't supposed to be real. But, I swear, I took one look at you, and I thought, there she is." He still thought that. *There she is.* "I saw you and realized...*I've been looking for her my whole life, and there she is.*"

Haley shook her head. "You, you—"

"The more I'm with you, the more I love you. I wanted to wait until you were safe, until you weren't afraid anymore before I told you. But, God, when you looked at me today with tears in your eyes..." It had ripped him apart.

She moved toward him. "You were giving up your job for me. You didn't tell me about that!"

"I would give up everything for you." Do anything. Go anywhere. She wanted New York? Fine, he'd get used to the real snow. She wanted the North Pole? He already had his Santa coat. He would do—

"I don't want you giving up anything." Haley gazed at him with her incredible eyes.

"What do you want?" He was still on bended knee. Still...He let his breath out. "What would it take for you to want to marry me?"

The people around them were dead silent.

So was Haley.

Hell, he'd moved too fast. He should have held back. He should have—

"You love me?"

Spencer nodded.

"You want to marry me?"

Once more, he nodded.

She pulled on the suitcase behind her. The damn suitcase. His gut clenched. "You were going to leave. Going to head out without telling me good-bye?" His head lowered.

"No, Spence. I wasn't."

His head snapped back up.

"I was taking the luggage to the resale store." She pointed to the store behind her. "Sally told me that she'd give me two hundred dollars for the case. I wanted to use the money to buy you a Christmas present."

What?

"I wanted to give you something special." She licked her lips. "And I didn't have a lot of cash left on me, so I thought I could sell the luggage—because I didn't need it, I wanted to stay here, with you. I could sell the luggage and get you something nice that you wanted—"

"*You* are the only thing I want." He rose. Stood in front of her. Wanted to pull her into his arms and never, ever let go. "Just you."

"Because...you love me?"

"Because I would fucking die for you in an instant." Love seemed far too tame for the way he felt about her. "You want to get me something for Christmas? I want *you*."

Her arms lifted and curled around his neck. "Yes."

His brows came together. "Yes?"

"You asked me to marry you, didn't you, Sheriff Lane?"

Fuck, yes!

His head lowered toward hers.

"You're the only thing I want for Christmas, too," she whispered. "Always...you."

He kissed her. Open-mouthed, demanding, wild, possessive. He kissed her and craved her and didn't care who saw them or what the hell was happening around them.

He had Haley.

He had his Christmas wish.

He had everything.

EPILOGUE

One Year Later...

She was standing under the mistletoe. A deliberate choice. Part of her careful plan. Haley stood in the middle of her gallery—she'd opened the gallery in Point Hope right before Halloween, just one week after she and Spencer had gotten married—and she absolutely loved the place. Turned out, Point Hope had been filled with artists and those artists needed a keen eye to help them sell their work.

The windows of her gallery were decorated with lights and tinsel, and she had Christmas music playing on her speakers. Beyond those windows, she saw the wreaths on the street lamps and the occasional elves who weaved by on their bikes.

The holiday parade had finished about an hour ago. Haley glanced at her watch. Her Santa should be making an appearance any moment, and she couldn't wait to give him his present—

The door opened with a jingle. "Damn elves." Spencer's grumble. He headed inside, still wearing his red Santa coat. "I told them once, I told them a thousand times, don't—"

He stopped. Saw her. His gaze drifted up. Landed on the mistletoe. "Oh, I like this." He stalked forward. Wrapped her into his arms and lifted her up for a kiss. The kiss made her toes curl and her heart melt.

No, he did that. Not just his kiss. *Spencer*.

"I have a surprise for you," she murmured against his mouth. "An early present."

He kissed her again. Then nuzzled his way down her neck. "You're the only present I need."

That was sweet. But... "Maybe it's not really an early present. I mean, the present won't technically be here until the summer so I guess that makes it a *late* present."

His head pulled back. Very carefully, he lowered her until her feet touched the floor once more. "Haley?"

Her fingers slid down to her stomach. "Merry Christmas."

A wide grin curled his mouth as his eyes gleamed. "You're serious?"

Haley nodded.

He kissed her again. And again. And he slowly twirled her around the gallery, and she laughed and she was happy. Happy because she'd found her safe haven, but it wasn't the town that was her shelter.

It was the man. He was everything she wanted, and their life together? It was everything she needed.

And if I have a little girl...we are totally naming her Noelle. "Merry Christmas, Spence," Haley whispered.

THE END

A NOTE FROM THE AUTHOR

Thank you so much for reading ONE HOT HOLIDAY! And happy holidays to you!!! If you enjoyed this story, be sure to check out the books in my Wilde Ways series. All of the books are stand-alone romances with guaranteed happy endings. I have a brand-new romance coming out in early 2020...GHOST OF A CHANCE will be here in January! Ghost was whispered about in ONE HOT HOLIDAY, but it will soon be time for him to star in his own book.

If you'd like to stay updated on my releases and sales, please join my newsletter list.

http://www.cynthiaeden.com/newsletter/

Again, thank you for reading ONE HOT HOLIDAY.

Best,
Cynthia Eden
www.cynthiaeden.com

ABOUT THE AUTHOR

Cynthia Eden is a *New York Times, USA Today, Digital Book World,* and *IndieReader* best-seller. Cynthia writes sexy tales of contemporary romance, romantic suspense, and paranormal romance. Since she began writing full-time in 2005, Cynthia has written over one hundred novels and novellas.

For More Information

- *cynthiaeden.com*
- *facebook.com/cynthiaedenfanpage*

HER OTHER WORKS

Wilde Ways

- Protecting Piper (Book 1)
- Guarding Gwen (Book 2)
- Before Ben (Book 3)
- The Heart You Break (Book 4)
- Fighting For Her (Book 5)
- Ghost Of A Chance (Book 6)
- Crossing The Line (Book 7)
- Counting On Cole (Book 8)
- Chase After Me (Book 9)
- Say I Do (Book 10)

Dark Sins

- Don't Trust A Killer (Book 1)
- Don't Love A Liar (Book 2)

Lazarus Rising

- Never Let Go (Book One)
- Keep Me Close (Book Two)
- Stay With Me (Book Three)
- Run To Me (Book Four)
- Lie Close To Me (Book Five)
- Hold On Tight (Book Six)
- Lazarus Rising Volume One (Books 1 to 3)

- Lazarus Rising Volume Two (Books 4 to 6)

Dark Obsession Series

- Watch Me (Book 1)
- Want Me (Book 2)
- Need Me (Book 3)
- Beware Of Me (Book 4)
- Only For Me (Books 1 to 4)

Mine Series

- Mine To Take (Book 1)
- Mine To Keep (Book 2)
- Mine To Hold (Book 3)
- Mine To Crave (Book 4)
- Mine To Have (Book 5)
- Mine To Protect (Book 6)
- Mine Box Set Volume 1 (Books 1-3)
- Mine Box Set Volume 2 (Books 4-6)

Bad Things

- The Devil In Disguise (Book 1)
- On The Prowl (Book 2)
- Undead Or Alive (Book 3)
- Broken Angel (Book 4)
- Heart Of Stone (Book 5)
- Tempted By Fate (Book 6)
- Wicked And Wild (Book 7)
- Saint Or Sinner (Book 8)
- Bad Things Volume One (Books 1 to 3)
- Bad Things Volume Two (Books 4 to 6)
- Bad Things Deluxe Box Set (Books 1 to 6)

Bite Series

- Forbidden Bite (Bite Book 1)
- Mating Bite (Bite Book 2)

Blood and Moonlight Series

- Bite The Dust (Book 1)
- Better Off Undead (Book 2)
- Bitter Blood (Book 3)
- Blood and Moonlight (The Complete Series)

Purgatory Series

- The Wolf Within (Book 1)
- Marked By The Vampire (Book 2)
- Charming The Beast (Book 3)
- Deal with the Devil (Book 4)
- The Beasts Inside (Books 1 to 4)

Bound Series

- Bound By Blood (Book 1)
- Bound In Darkness (Book 2)
- Bound In Sin (Book 3)
- Bound By The Night (Book 4)
- Bound in Death (Book 5)
- Forever Bound (Books 1 to 4)

Other Romantic Suspense

- Never Gonna Happen
- One Hot Holiday
- Secret Admirer
- First Taste of Darkness
- Sinful Secrets
- Until Death
- Christmas With A Spy